the
New
Couple

BOOKS BY ALISON JAMES

The School Friend

The Man She Married

Her Sister's Child

The Guilty Wife

THE DETECTIVE RACHEL PRINCE SERIES

1. *Lola is Missing*

2. *Now She's Gone*

3. *Perfect Girls*

the
New
Couple

ALISON JAMES

bookouture

Published by Bookouture in 2022

An imprint of Storyfire Ltd.
Carmelite House
50 Victoria Embankment
London EC4Y 0DZ

www.bookouture.com

ISBN: 978-1-80314-783-3
eBook ISBN: 978-1-80314-782-6

PROLOGUE

So this is it, she thinks. *This is how I'm going to die.*

The truck lurches around a sharp left-hand bend, and then rumbles to an abrupt halt.

The door opens and he drags her out of the truck, depositing her awkwardly on her feet. The smell of petrol and hot plastic gives way to fresh, salty air. She staggers, tries to speak, but her lips are numb, her mouth so dry that her tongue sticks to the roof of her mouth. A whirlwind of emotions tears through her. There's raging fury and paralysing fear, of course, and also a strange, misplaced swell of irritation. She shouldn't be here, doing this – whatever this is. This shouldn't be happening. But, above all, she experiences a profound sense of betrayal at being put in this situation when all she was trying to do was to help. To do the right thing.

She half walks, half stumbles as he propels her from behind. Eventually, the shape of a low, squat building looms out of the darkness. It's damp and echoey and smells of decay and marsh water. A door opens onto a flight of steps. 'No!' she gasps, finding her voice at last. 'No, please you've got to let me go! You can't do this.'

'Don't worry,' he says with a strange little laugh. 'You're not going to be down there long.'

Unable to see where she's placing her feet, she's pushed down steps and onto the floor with her back against a cold surface. Chains are looped around her ankles. He stands over her for a few seconds as though trying to decide something, and she fears the worst. Then he turns abruptly and his footsteps retreat. Apart from the faint call of birds, there's silence. He's deliberately chosen the most remote, isolated place he could find. Has he left her here to die? She surely will, unless she can free herself somehow.

She pulls and struggles at the chains, but it's hopeless: they're secured to the wall. Eventually, her eyes become sufficiently accustomed to the dark for her to take in her surroundings. The building seems to be derelict, abandoned. Well, of course it is, she chastises herself. He's hardly going to put her anywhere that's in use. Ventilation shafts above her somewhere are open to the elements and letting in a breeze, but it fails to mask a terrible stench that makes her gag. In the half-light, she sees something on the ground about ten feet away, something lumpy and human-shaped. A dead body.

Then she hears it. A faint croak, only just audible. Not quite a word, more of a moan or a whimper, but recognisably human.

So that body is not dead after all. She's not alone. There's another person here.

PART ONE

JANE

ONE

APRIL

It's always soothing, Jane Headley thinks, to turn from the busy, traffic-filled London arterial road into the serene oval of pretty mid-Victorian architecture that is Sycamore Gardens. The houses, some detached, some in semi-detached pairs, curve in a crescent around a communal garden enclosed by wrought-iron railings. Her own house, home to her family for nearly two decades, is a late Victorian semi-detached towards the top end of the cul-de-sac.

On this occasion, her next-door neighbour Danielle Salter waylays her, stepping into her path as she's turning into the cul-de-sac. Jane doesn't have much time for Danielle. In fact, she privately thinks Danielle is a pain in the backside.

But then Danielle demands, 'Have you heard the latest about number twelve?' and Jane experiences a distinct flutter of interest. Especially since the other woman's face – usually a vivid amber from all the fake tan she uses – is flushed pink with excitement.

'No, what?' Jane asks her. 'What have you heard?'

'Come round to mine for a coffee, and I'll tell you all about it!' Danielle's tone is triumphant. 'I've got another hour or so before I have to go and pick up the boys.' Her two loud, ill-disciplined sons are only seven and nine; yet another reason she and Jane have little in common.

Jane glances at her watch. She works a half day on a Wednesday, and she planned to make the most of her free afternoon with a soak in a scented bath, followed by long-overdue phone calls to her mother and sister. She works as a classroom assistant at the local primary school and since her own children are now nineteen and twenty-one, in her free time she's no longer tied by the demands of school drop-offs and pickups and regular mealtimes. In her mind, she's come up with a plan that she and her husband will order in from their favourite takeaway, open a bottle of wine and watch a movie she's been keen to see for a while. She'll light some candles, dress in something other than her usual sweats, and maybe one thing will lead to another.

But, in reality, Fergus will probably be back late, wanting only to shovel down some food and collapse into bed, his back turned to her. That has been par for the course in her marriage lately, although she tries to convince herself that after twenty-five years together, it's probably normal. And Jane is quite keen to hear what information Danielle has gleaned about number 12, Sycamore Gardens, a house on their quiet close that has stood empty for a while. It used to belong to an elderly couple called Glenys and Lionel Beamish, but at the street's annual barbecue the previous summer, they announced that they were retiring and moving to the south coast. Then – with some coyness – they revealed that they had been approached by Prodomus, a charity that sells lottery entries with a prestige property as the prize. Number 12, Sycamore Gardens, a detached mid-Victorian house in what estate agents like to describe as one of South West London's premier addresses, is perfect for their business model. A huge number of people would be willing to purchase the tickets in the hope of bagging themselves a house worth close to three million pounds. Sure enough, a few months later, the Beamishes have moved out, and builders and decorators have started working on the house, turning it from a slightly dilapidated late-Victorian villa into a show home with a freshly-painted crimson front door. Even so, for the last couple of months, it has remained empty. An empty house on their street with no prospect of a move-in date made Jane unsettled.

She follows Danielle to number 6, a smart detached villa next door to number 5 where she and Fergus live. Danielle's husband, Robert, is a successful architect, and on the off chance that she fails to mention this fact, it quickly becomes apparent from the cantilevered steel staircase, clever skylights and state-of-the-art bifold doors that open the entire back of the house to the garden. Jane's own house is scruffy and a bit dowdy in comparison, not having been redecorated for at least a decade. But then she and Fergus pride themselves on having lived on the street the longest, after buying the house for a song when the children were tiny and this corner of South London still ungentrified. There is no way they could afford a house on Sycamore Gardens now, not on an academic's salary, but they have recently paid off what twenty years ago seemed a terrifyingly huge mortgage.

'Coffee?' Danielle enquires brightly, flicking on the sleek espresso machine without waiting for a reply. She dumps her shopping bags unceremoniously on the huge, gleaming marble island at the centre of the kitchen. She doesn't have a job, and when she isn't trying and failing to keep her feral children under control, she seems to spend a huge amount of time shopping. As far as Jane can tell, that's all she does. That and going to the gym.

'Just a quick one,' she says with a forced smile, unwilling to spend longer at number 6 than she has to. 'So what have you heard?' Jane asks. 'What's the latest?'

'So...' Danielle reaches into her designer bag for a pot of

crimson gloss which she slicks onto her lips, then makes a big show of smoothing her blonde hair behind her ears. It's vigorously bleached to a colour that reminds Jane of the clotted cream ice cream they had on the beach as children. 'You know that charity raffle company bought the place from the Beamishes?'

'Yes,' agrees Jane, a touch impatiently. 'I remember.'

'The draw's been held. Someone's won it!'

'Goodness! Do we know who?'

'It's on this news site – here.' Danielle picks up her phone (the latest model, naturally), scrolls to the page and holds it up, too close to Jane's face for her to actually be able to read. She has to take hold of the other woman's wrist and push the phone a little further away to make out the words.

Parents win dream home in fundraiser for children's cancer charity

Richard Hamlin (31) and his wife Stephanie (29) have won a multimillion-pound property in South London in the Prodomus fundraising draw for Young Cancer UK. The couple entered the draw, which has raised over half a million pounds for the charity, in February with the purchase of a £25 ticket. Stephanie, a part-time visual merchandiser, and Richard, a chartered accountant, are parents to nine-month-old baby Poppy.
'We're so happy that money was raised to help other children,' Stephanie says, while her husband adds, 'We've been saving up to buy a home of our own for years, so winning this amazing home is a dream come true.'

There is a small and not very distinct photo of the Hamlins. They're sitting on a sofa in what is presumably their current home. Stephanie is holding the baby and Richard has his arm around her shoulders. She's of mixed heritage, with long wavy black hair and olive skin, while he's averagely good-looking: average height and build, light brown hair and glasses.

'Well,' Jane says, handing the phone back to Danielle and picking up the espresso cup that's just been pushed across the island in her direction. 'They seem to be a nice young couple.'

Danielle purses her filler-enhanced lips. 'If you ask me, they look a bit boring, but then I don't know what I was expecting, really.'

When the residents of Sycamore Gardens heard that the house was to be raffled for charity, there were undertones of concern in the general reaction. After all, if the house was sold in the usual way, then the purchaser had to be a person of substance in order to afford a detached period property of that size. Someone professional, and therefore of good social standing. A solid citizen. But a legal owner who has won the place with the purchase of a lottery ticket... well, they could be anyone. Anyone at all. The people who live in the Gardens are a varied lot, yet they all belong to the same privileged tribe. And although they might not admit it, they are uneasy with the idea of someone from outside that tribe invading their comfortable way of life.

Jane finishes the espresso and paints on an upbeat smile. 'I'm sure they're going to be perfectly nice.'

She leaves number 6 and walks back to her own house. In the pretty railed communal garden at the centre of the cul-de-sac, the daffodils are now over, but the horse chestnut and magnolias will soon open, and the window boxes that adorn many of the mid-Victorian façades are bristling with red, yellow and purple tulips.

She and Fergus live in one of the half a dozen semi-detached houses on the Gardens, built in 1890. Although more modestly proportioned than the detached villas, it's still a handsome three-storey building, with the original sash windows and a flight of stone steps up to the front door, which they have painted a dark-blue grey. Fergus is a professor of economics at the LSE, and their home is lined with overflowing bookcases and carefully curated pieces of art, mostly modern line drawings. The comfortable kitchen, with its Rayburn and stripped oak floor is on the basement level. Jane goes down there now, switches on Radio 5 Live and starts preparing supper. She's already abandoned the idea of a romantic night in before even getting to the bath stage.

'Pasta, I think,' she says to Oreo, the black and white cat snoozing on an armchair, because there's no one else in the house to talk to. The cat merely sighs and tucks his tail more tightly around his paws.

When they moved here, their son, Joss, was a toddler and she was heavily pregnant with Evie. Joss recently graduated from Sussex University and is still living in Brighton, working as a barista while he tries to find something more substantial as a career, and nineteen-year-old Evie is in her first year at Glasgow School of Art. While she's happy that her children are doing well, she misses them badly. Especially since Fergus no longer seeks out her company. She and her husband may live under the same roof, but they couldn't be said to live *together*.

Jane sets about preparing a basic pesto, which she sets aside for later before going up to the top floor to run her bath. She wonders if having a glass of wine in the bath at three in the afternoon would be decadent and decides it would, but takes one with her anyway. She won't tell Fergus about it when he gets home, though. A running theme of their arguments lately has been that she's bored and underemployed now that the children aren't around and she's only working part-time. She doesn't want him thinking she's turning to drink to while away the empty time. As it happens, Jane has been thinking hard about changing jobs and taking steps towards a more substantial career of her own. She's aware she's not fulfilling her potential.

But that's her call to make, and the more Fergus carps, the less she feels like discussing it with him.

She does tell him about the house-draw winners, though, over supper when he finally returns home. From the kitchen, she hears the sound of him slamming the front door and the clatter of his keys being tossed onto the hall table. Once, he would have called out to her, or come straight down to the kitchen to give her a kiss, but instead he stamps up the stairs to change his clothes without greeting her.

When he does finally come down to the kitchen, he's mono-syllabic, which she allows, on the grounds that he's had a long day at work.

'Good,' is his brusque response when he tells her about number 12. 'Not a good idea having that place sitting empty, especially now it's all been done up.'

That's Fergus; practical and sensible in his approach at all times. He's tall and long-limbed, his dark wavy hair starting to grey at the temples now, but still a strikingly attractive man. He and Jane are both practical people: doers. Both outgoing and sociable, both interested in fine art and travel. 'Perfect for each other': that's what people said about them when they first met at university, and again when they married. So why do their inter-actions now feel so stale, so forced?

'I wonder when they'll actually move in,' Jane murmurs as she ladles the bright green swirls of spaghetti onto their plates. 'Might even be this weekend.'

Fergus frowns. 'I doubt that, given that it's Easter. I'd be surprised if they got a removal company to do it on Good Friday or Easter Saturday.'

Jane has forgotten all about Easter. The children won't be around, so there'll be no celebrations in the Headley household. 'Perhaps the week after then.'

'Probably,' Fergus says without enthusiasm. He uncorks a bottle of red and pours it with precision, taking care to get the exact same amount in each glass. 'From what you said, it doesn't sound like they have another place to sell first, so I doubt they'd want to delay.'

'I was thinking...' Jane lifts her glass and takes a slow sip, savouring it. 'When they do, we should have a dinner party to introduce them to some of the neighbours.'

He frowns. 'You said they were quite young, though. I doubt they'd want to do something so formal.'

'A drinks thing then, or a barbecue.'

'Hmmm.' Fergus is now talking round a mouthful of pasta. 'That would be more appropriate. Although do we really have time to manage the social lives of the neighbours?'

'I'll talk to some of the other women, see if we can organise something.' Jane smiles at him, trying to inject some cheer into the conversation.

'You said they were a professional couple?'

Jane nods. 'An accountant and a visual merchandiser, apparently. Whatever that means.'

'Sounds like they're the types who'll toe the line.' He lays down his fork and gives her a hard look. 'But it's not like they're going to be next door to us. What they do won't impinge on us, and vice versa. So just leave them to it, Jane, please.'

Fergus is probably right, Jane tells herself. But she can't quite suppress a frisson of curiosity about their new neighbours.

TWO

APRIL

When Jane first sees them, she assumes they're something to do with the flats.

There's a small post-war block of flats called Regency Court, positioned at the main road end of the Gardens and distinct from the rest of the nineteenth-century architecture. The flats are usually rented out, and have a shifting occupancy of students, single professionals and Eastern European workers. So on that Thursday evening in late April, about a week after her conversation with Danielle Salter, when Jane sees the dirty silver pickup truck on the road, she automatically thinks that someone new must be moving into one of the flats.

But then she goes upstairs to the first-floor window to get a better vantage point and sees that the truck is parked outside number 12. Two hulking figures in jogging bottoms and hoodies are hauling what appear to be black bags of rubbish from the flat bed of the trailer. Their hoods are half obscuring their faces to start with, but as they grow hot and strip off the sweaters, tossing them carelessly onto the privet hedge in front of the house, it's impossible to tell the men apart. They look almost identical. These must be the removal men who are helping the

Hamlins, Jane decides, although they don't exactly look like professionals.

The door of number 12 is open now, and they are stamping up the path, holding cans of lager in their left hands and hoisting the bin bags into the hallway of the house. Jane presses her face close to the glass to see more clearly. So these bags must contain the Hamlins belongings. That seems a little unorthodox, but perhaps they didn't have time to order proper packing materials.

A couple of carboard boxes overflowing with kitchen appliances follow, but apart from a huge flat-screen TV and a set of gym weights, she can't see any furniture. Then she remembers that the prize house was to include a 'luxury furnishing package'. Perhaps they have decided to sell or give away their old stuff and start afresh with the new. You can't blame them for that, Jane thinks, turning round and looking at the tired fabric headboard and chipped nightstands in her own bedroom.

Eventually, the unloading finishes, but the pickup truck stays, parked by the kerb outside number 15. Trish Oldenshaw won't appreciate its presence, that's for sure. There's an unwritten rule amongst the residents that you park outside your own house, and your own house only. The properties are sufficiently spaced to make this quite easy, and some have off-street parking. Those who own two cars park the second in the bottleneck where the Gardens joins the main A road, outside or opposite Regency Court.

A couple of hours later, just as the sun is setting, a small red hatchback pulls up outside number 12 and a young woman, who must be Stephanie Hamlin, gets out, tipping the passenger seat forward so that she can haul her daughter from the child seat in the rear. Jane is alerted to this by the sound of the child crying miserably. By this time, she's down in the basement kitchen preparing a casserole for a late supper – Fergus has yet another of his interminable academic meetings – and is forced to peer up the area steps to the street above.

'Poor things,' she sighs to Oreo. 'They must be worn out with it all.' She hunts around for a tin of flapjack she made earlier in the week and puts several slices into a Tupperware. Once the casserole is in the oven on a low heat, she picks some tulips from the back garden, wraps them in tissue paper and ties them with a jaunty raffia bow. Armed with these gifts, she walks to number 12 and rings the doorbell.

The door is opened by Stephanie Hamlin. Behind her, in the shiny new kitchen diner, resplendent with dark teal-coloured units, the removal men are sitting at a pristine table with their cans of lager. Propped awkwardly in a corner of one of the beige linen sofas is the baby. She has a rusk in her hand and is calmer now, but her chubby cheeks are still red and tear-stained.

'Hi, I'm Jane Headley,' she says, holding out the tulips and the flapjack. 'We live at number five: my husband Fergus and I. I just wanted to come and say welcome to Sycamore Gardens, and to give you these.'

'Thanks,' replies Stephanie flatly, putting the flowers and Tupperware down on the countertop without looking at them. She's wearing a pair of black leggings in fabric so cheap you can see through it, and a grey T-shirt with a sparkly logo of the kind found on market stalls.

'How are you managing?' Jane asks. She is aware that everyone in the room – even baby Poppy – is staring at her, and feels her cheeks turning pink. 'Moving's such a nightmare. I expect you'll be glad when your husband gets here to help you.'

One of the two removal men extends his left arm and prof-fers his hand, but without standing up from his chair so that Jane is forced to lean in at an awkward angle.

'Richard Hamlin,' he says in a nasal South London drawl.

'Nice to meet you.' He jerks his head in the direction of the other hoodie wearer. 'This is my brother... Elliott.'

'Oh, gosh, I'm sorry,' Jane stammers, feeling her cheeks flush further. Richard is much better looking in the flesh than in his photo, strikingly so. 'I thought...' She decides she may as well come clean. 'It's just that we saw your picture in the news and you were wearing glasses, so I...'

She tails off as Richard reaches into the pocket of his track-suit bottoms and pulls out a pair of steel-framed glasses. 'Lenses,' he says simply, pointing at his intensely blue eyes. 'Only wear the bins sometimes. You know, for work and that.'

'I see. Sorry,' Jane repeats.

Baby Poppy has slid down the sofa cushion so that she's slumped uncomfortably, and the rusk has fallen out of reach. She's grizzling again.

Jane looks around the brightly lit, unlived-in kitchen. 'You don't have a highchair,' she observes. 'That's awkward for you. I'm just trying to think which of the neighbours might have one you can borrow. The Perrys at number nineteen might: they've got a little one who's recently grown past that stage. I'm afraid my two are far too old for me still to have baby equipment.'

As she speaks, she wonders whether, in fact, Evie's old high-chair might be among the stuff stored in the attic.

''S okay,' Richard says easily. 'We've got one, we just haven't brought it over yet. There's more stuff we need to go back and fetch.'

Bringing workout equipment but nothing for the baby to sit on demonstrates a strange set of priorities, but then winning the house must have been so unexpected that perhaps the Hamlins haven't planned their move very well. Jane smiles, determined to give them the benefit of the doubt.

Stephanie, who has been standing there silently, goes over to the sofa and picks up the baby, resting her against her hip as if to demonstrate that she does know how to care for the child.

The lookalike brother, Elliott, reaches for the Tupperware and shoves one of the flapjacks in his mouth without looking in Jane's direction.

'Well, as I said, I'm at number five, and I'm sure I can ask around for baby stuff for you to borrow until your own gets here.' Jane thinks back to the items she watched being unloaded from the pickup truck. 'Do you have a cot?'

'She'll come in with us,' Stephanie says in that same flat voice. 'Just till the cot gets here, you know.'

'Fine,' Jane smiles brightly. 'I'll leave you to get on with it, shall I? I expect you've got loads to do.'

Nobody offers to show her out or even says goodbye, so she gives a brief, awkward wave and hurries back through the front door and onto the street.

'Sounds like you're embellishing a bit,' Fergus says when he's arrived home from his meeting and Jane has recounted her visit to number 12.

She looks at him quizzically. He often accuses her of exaggerating, or having an overly vivid imagination.

'I know it's a long time since we've had to endure a house move,' he continues easily, scooping mashed potato onto his fork, 'but it's no surprise that it always gets listed as the most stressful human experience after bereavement and divorce. As I recall, it's hell on earth. So many things to remember, so much bureaucracy, so many things that can go wrong.' He takes a gulp of wine, before giving his wife a sardonic smile. 'It's no wonder the poor wretches looked like rabbits in the headlights. They were probably dead on their feet.'

'I know, darling, all I was saying—'

He cuts across her. 'The way you were talking it's as if Reggie or Ronnie Kray was moving into Sycamore Gardens.'

Jane snorts, grabbing the wine bottle and filling her own glass. 'Now who's exaggerating?'

'I'm just saying no one's at their best during a house move, and for practical reasons they're going to be wearing their crappiest clothes. So give them a break.'

He's probably right, Jane reflects as she sets off to her job at Danepark Primary School the next morning. She's judged the Hamlins too quickly, given the unusual circumstances. Nevertheless, she plays the scene back in her head several times between 9 and 3.15. As she deals with a four-year-old who has thrown up their lunch, or a fight between seven-year-olds in the playground, or a box full of battered Key Stage 1 reading books that needs patching up with Sellotape and reordering on the shelves, her mind wanders. As it so often does at work.

Fergus thinks being a classroom assistant is beneath her. Before Evie was born, she worked as a paralegal in the City, but once they had two children, the commute and the long hours became impossible and she resigned from her job. Her plan was to find something part-time and local once Evie was old enough to be left at nursery. A teaching assistant post came up at Danepark Primary, where Joss was in Year One, and it seemed an obvious solution for the two of them to arrive at and leave Danepark together three days a week, dropping Evie off on the way and collecting her at the end of the school day.

The job isn't exactly rocket science, nor is it well paid, but she likes the other staff. Especially Zoe Clifford, who started out as a reception-class teacher and is now the school's head. She has become a good friend over the sixteen years of this transition, during which Jane's own children both left Danepark and went on first to secondary and now tertiary education. Zoe nagged Jane sporadically to take time out for training and become a full-time member of the teaching staff, but as Joss and Evie grew, so did their demands, and the time never felt right. And now Zoe herself is on maternity leave, having become a first-time mother at the age of thirty-nine. Her replacement is a thin, sour man called Damien Thwaite, who has changed the whole atmosphere of the place just by being there.

'Maybe this means it's time to start looking around for something else,' Fergus suggested, when she came home complaining about Damien. 'With the kids not at home, and now Zoe gone for the time being at least. Maybe something in the law again?' And Jane agreed that, yes, at forty-seven and with at least another decade of working life ahead of her, it was probably time to move on from Danepark Primary. Once they reach the end of the school year in a couple of months' time, she will make her final decision. Things at the school are changing, and it seems right that her own life should change too.

Walking home after work today, she's relieved to see more stuff being unloaded from the back of the Hamlins' pickup truck, and that these items include a highchair, a changing table and a cot. There's no sign of baby Poppy, but when the front door of number 12 is opened, Jane can hear the faint sound of her crying. There's a dog too, this time, some sort of terrier cross that lunges on its lead, growling as Jane walks past.

'Sorry,' says Richard Hamlin, not sounding it. He yanks the dog back and leads it into the house. Once the door is closed, baby Poppy is no longer audible, but the dog's barking carries loudly and menacingly over Sycamore Gardens.

THREE

APRIL

When she wakes up on Saturday morning and checks her phone, Jane finds a text from Trish Oldenshaw, who lives at number 15.

Trish is nearly a decade older than Jane, but probably her favourite among the female residents of Sycamore Gardens. She's enjoyed a high-flying career as an actuary, but has recently reduced her hours from five days to four each week. 'Actuaries have the reputation of being extremely dull people,' she confided with her attractive dimpled smile when the two women first met. 'Let me apologise in advance.' But although she has a logical and methodical mind, Trish is anything but dull. She's sparky and quick-witted, with a love of flamboyant clothes.

You around this morning? Tx

Jane replies with a thumbs-up emoji.

Thought I'd take advantage of it being a weekend and

get some of the others over, and we can talk party plan-
ning? Ages since we've had a Gardens do!

Trish has appointed herself chair of a completely informal events committee, which meets to plan the occasional barbecue or garden party and coordinate Christmas staples such as the tree-lighting ceremony and carol singing. The house she lives in with her partner, Tony, is a mirror image of the Headleys, only with a pared-down, Scandinavian-style interior. Trish has two bichon frises but no children, something she openly informs people was a deliberate choice. She's a chic, petite woman with steel-grey hair worn in a pixie cut.

'Come in, come in!' She greets Jane with a warm hug an hour later, leading her through to the open-plan first-floor living space. She's wearing a flowing orange kaftan and huge gold earrings. 'Danielle's here – you know each other, don't you?'

Danielle, resplendent in a sugar pink tracksuit, curls her fingers at Jane, then returns to sipping her coffee.

'... And Rani?'

Jane nods yes. Rani is a psychology PhD student who lives with her Spanish husband, Xavier, in one of the Regency Court flats. Fergus has spoken to her a few times, but Jane really only knows her by sight. She smiles at Rani and gives her a little wave. Rani is heavily pregnant, she notices, as the other woman half stands to reach for the sugar bowl. She and Xavier will probably be looking for somewhere bigger to move to soon.

Trish pours her coffee, then disappears into the hall to answer the doorbell. She returns followed by Irina Semenova, who lives at number 17, the biggest and most distinguished detached house on the Gardens. Her fiancé Michael is a hedge fund manager, and Irina herself a Siberian model. She has pale, slanting Slavic eyes, a tumbling mane of light chestnut hair and is breathtakingly beautiful. Her body is so svelte and toned it's difficult to imagine that she's had children, but she has two preschool-aged daughters. They're at home with the nanny, naturally.

'I cannot stay long,' she says in her thick, husky accent. 'I have an appointment.' She gives a little shrug that suggests she doesn't much care about being here anyway, her perfect features remaining blank as she perches on the edge of Trish's dove-grey linen armchair and accepts an espresso. Black, of course.

It can't be a hair appointment, Jane thinks idly, because Irina's stylist comes to the house at least four times a week to maintain that big, Hollywood hair, along with a beauty thera-pist who does spray tans in a portable nylon tent.

'I have waxing,' Irina states baldly, as if reading Jane's mind, and shrugs again.

'Ladies, I was thinking,' Trish begins, sitting down on one of her plush chartreuse green sofas and crossing her legs neatly, 'It's time we held another party in the garden. A barbecue, perhaps, when the weather's a little warmer? Or just an evening drink with some cold canapés? We could serve Pimm's: people always enjoy that when it's an outdoor thing.'

The oval garden at the centre of the cul-de-sac, bordered with black wrought-iron railings, is mostly taken up with mature trees: lime, horse chestnut, oak and a fine black walnut. The western end, nearest the main road, is land-scaped, however, with flower beds and areas laid to lawn and flanked with wooden park benches, and it's here that social events are held. All the residents are entitled to hold a key to the locked gate and can enjoy the space whenever they wish, year round.

Jane is relieved that Trish has come up with a similar plan to the one she suggested to Fergus. He can hardly object to her involvement if it was Trish's idea.

'Knowing our luck, it will probably rain, like it did last year,' Danielle says with satisfaction.

'We can organise some sort of shelter, though?' Rani suggests.

Danielle snorts. 'There's not really enough grass for a marquee. Anyway, they cost the earth and that would mean we'd have to do some sort of fundraiser.'

'I was thinking more one of those temporary canvas gazebos,' Rani adds quietly. 'They don't cost a lot.'

'Michael will pay, if I tell him,' Irina states baldly. 'Is not so much money.' She slaps her espresso cup down in its saucer and shrugs on her cashmere camel coat. 'And now I must go.'

She gives Trish perfunctory kisses on each cheek and struts out, her caramel locks swinging.

Once it has been agreed that they will throw a barbecue ('Burning meat gives the men something to do with their hands,' Trish observes drily), the talk turns to the arrival of the Hamlins.

'I'll tell you something,' Danielle says waspishly, 'They're going to have to do something about that bloody dog of theirs. 'Robert was all for going over there last night and complaining, but I said to leave it until they've been there a bit longer; see if it settles down.'

'I met them,' Jane says simply. 'I went round there with a welcome gift.'

The other women's heads all swivel in her direction.

'Were they nice?' Rani asks. She strokes her pregnancy bump self-consciously. 'I saw online they have a baby too?'

'They were...' Jane reaches for one of the chocolate biscuits Trish has left out as she considers the next word. '...I mean, they were fine. We didn't exactly have a proper chat, but, to be fair, they were in the middle of a house move.'

'I expect they were a bit overwhelmed,' Trish observes, echoing what Fergus told Jane. 'With their lives changing so drastically pretty much overnight.'

'Well, they've certainly gone up in the world, if that crappy old pickup of theirs is anything to go by,' Danielle points out with a disapproving curl of her filler-plumped lips.

'Perhaps the barbecue will be a nice ice-breaker,' Rani suggests. 'Give them a chance to get to know people.'

'If they show up.' Danielle sniffs.

Jane thinks about this later as she tackles a pile of ironing in front of the window in the first-floor sitting room. She doesn't want to be disparaging, but considers it unlikely the Hamlins will want to attend a Sycamore Gardens soirée. Some people want to keep a distance from their neighbours and that's fine, she reminds herself. This is London after all, not some cosy little village in the Yorkshire Dales. Most people in the city don't feel the need to live in one another's pockets.

As she looks out, Stephanie Hamlin walks along the pavement outside, pushing Poppy in the buggy and trailing the dog on its lead. Jane ducks her head so that it won't seem as though she's spying, only lifting it again once Stephanie has passed the window. She really is quite pretty, Jane reflects, but she looks so miserable, her head hung and shoulders hunched, not interacting with her daughter.

Twenty minutes later, Stephanie trudges past again, this time dangling a bag of groceries from the buggy handles. Poppy is crying and arching her back against the harness.

Jane waits a tactful few minutes to give the younger woman time to get the buggy inside and unpack her shopping, then tugs on a jacket and walks the hundred yards to number 12. There's a cool, spring wind buffeting the tulips and showers of blossom petals drift over her trainers as she walks.

'Hello again,' she says when the door finally opens on the third ring. 'I saw you going past just now, and...' Her voice trails off as she realises it sounds as though she's a stalker.

Stephanie stands in front of her, her arms crossed over her

body. It's not an aggressive gesture; more as if she's holding in some sort of pain or distress. Close up, she looks very young, much younger than in her photograph. She does not step back to allow Jane in, nor is there any invitation to do so. In fact, there's no verbal communication at all, just that impassive stare. The dog rushes to the open front door, yapping loudly, and Stephanie pushes it away.

'I wondered... I know it's a bit of a nightmare getting everything sorted out when you first move... is there any help you need?'

'No,' says Stephanie firmly, adding, 'thank you.' Out on the street, Richard Hamlin's pickup has just come to a halt and is reversing into a parking space. Stephanie gives a brief nod of acknowledgement and then, as Poppy lets out a shriek, says a quick, 'Got to go,' and closes the door firmly in Jane's face.

She won't go round there again, Jane decides. She's done her best to be neighbourly, but if her help isn't wanted, then so be it. She isn't going to pester them. Stephanie has made her position clear, even though she's not articulated it: she wants to be left alone.

It's a surprise, therefore, when, on Monday morning, Jane finds the girl on her doorstep as she's leaving for work.

'Hiya,' Stephanie gives a self-conscious little wave. She's wearing grey marl jogging bottoms and a tight white Lycra crop top that exposes a band of olive skin round her middle.

'Hello,' Jane replies warily. She holds up her tote bag. 'You'll have to excuse me, I'm just off to work.'

'What time do you get back?'

Jane frowns. 'Between 3.30 and 4 usually.'

'Only you know you said you would help? Well, I need someone to mind the baby for me. I have to go somewhere. Somewhere I can't – you know – take her. Because you said you'd had kids of your own and that...'

'Of course.' Jane forces a smile, hiding the fact that the girl's abrupt change of attitude has thrown her off. At first, she wants nothing to do with the neighbours, and now she's happy to hand over her own baby to one of them. This seems unusual to say the least. 'I don't see why not.'

'Thanks. See you here later, yeah?' Stephanie returns the smile, then turns to go.

Jane follows her down the path. 'Actually, wouldn't it be better if I came over to you? All Poppy's stuff's there... save you dragging it over here.'

A cloud passes over Stephanie's face. 'No,' she says flatly. 'He... Richard... my husband... he wouldn't like it. Having a stranger in the house.'

And yet it's fine for me to take charge of his daughter, Jane thinks.

'Okay, sure. Just make sure to bring what she needs. Nappies and so on.'

Stephanie appears at number 5 at four o'clock sharp, a few minutes after Jane has got back from Danepark Primary. She has Poppy in her arms, and a large changing bag slung over her shoulder. She wastes no time with pleasantries but simply shoves both baby and bag into Jane's arms and scurries off down the path before Jane has a chance to ask how long she'll be gone.

Poppy Hamlin is an attractive child, with wispy curls, chubby limbs and eight teeth, which Jane counts during her roar of displeasure at being handed over to a complete stranger. The article about the house win said she was nine months old, so Jane calculates she must be nearer ten months now. Fortunately, Oreo is in the sitting room, and the bawling turns to squeals of delight when Poppy sees the cat and crawls across the room to try and catch him.

Jane spreads a washable cotton throw over the Turkish rug and gives Poppy a battery of wooden spoons, bowls and other harmless kitchen gadgets to play with. Stephanie has said nothing about feeding her, but Poppy grasps eagerly at the carrot sticks, cubes of cheese and yoghurt that are offered. When she becomes fretful and grisly, Jane puts cartoons on the television while she heats the bottle from the changing bag, then sits with the baby on her lap, feeding her until her eyes grow heavy and close, her black lashes making crescent moons on her cheeks.

She's still sitting there when Fergus gets back from work at six forty-five, holding a finger to her lips as he does a double take. She texted him to say she was minding the Hamlins' baby but that Poppy would probably be gone by the time he returned.

'She still here?' he says in a stage whisper. 'Time she was going to bed, surely?'

He fetches Jane a glass of wine, then, when Poppy stirs again, holds her while Jane runs a bath. She bathes the baby and dresses her in a clean nappy and the spare Babygro she finds in the bag, then – at a loss as to what else she can do – puts her down to sleep in the middle of her and Fergus's bed, clutching the blue wool blanket that has been packed for her.

Stephanie finally returns at ten to nine.

'Don't say anything,' Fergus whispers, as Jane goes to answer the front door. 'I mean, don't give her a hard time about being late.'

'I wasn't going to,' she returns through gritted teeth.

'Sorry,' Stephanie mumbles, when the door is opened. 'Took longer than I thought.'

Her face is pale, and she seems stressed. In fact, she looks awful, as though she's seen a ghost. 'Is everything okay?' Jane asks.

'Yup,' she mumbles.

Fergus appears in the hallway. 'Hi!' he says brightly, extending a hand. 'I'm Jane's husband. You're Stephanie, right?'

The wan look disappears and now there's a genuine smile on Stephanie's face. In fact, she almost twinkles as she shakes his hand and says, 'Call me Steph... hi.' But then Jane is well used to people reacting this way to her husband, especially women. There's something reassuring about his presence, not to mention an abundance of charm.

'We put young Poppy down because she was tired,' he tells her easily. 'I'll go and fetch her, shall I?'

He comes downstairs again with the sleeping Poppy on his shoulder, her blue blanket draped over her. Steph smiles again at the sight of this handsome man managing her daughter so expertly, showing her perfect white teeth.

'She's a pretty little thing, isn't she?' Fergus observes once the front door is closed again.

'Who? Poppy, or Stephanie?'

'Both.'

Jane laughs with as much amiability as she can muster, but she feels drained and strangely out of sorts. 'I think I'll run myself a bath,' she tells Fergus, pouring a glass of wine and heading upstairs.

After a soak, she feels better. It hasn't been so bad, taking care of little Poppy, she tells herself, just this once.

Only it isn't just once. A few days later, Steph shows up on the doorstep with the same request: that Jane mind Poppy for an unspecified time. And, once again, she returns late into the evening. This time, Fergus has been up into the loft and dragged down the baby chair that used to clip on to the edge of the kitchen table and a box full of toys. Jane hopes that it doesn't look as though they're setting up a permanent crèche arrangement.

'Is your mother nearby?' Jane asks as neutrally as she can muster, when Steph makes a third request for her babysitting services the following week. 'Or any other family members? Only I'm not always going to be here when you need Poppy minding.'

'My mum's in Ireland,' Steph says. That's all. No explanation as to why, given that Steph herself is clearly a Londoner, nor any mention of any other relatives.

'I hope she's not going to make a habit of this,' Jane mutters darkly once the baby has been collected, asleep as before. 'I mean, Poppy's sweet, but I don't want to be treated like a free babysitting service. And what about when Joss and Evie are back home in June? What are they going to make of us acting like surrogate grandparents to someone else's kid?'

'I don't see why they should mind,' Fergus says calmly. 'The more the merrier.' He catches sight of Jane's frown and rolls his eyes. 'Come on, it's a few hours here and there: where's the harm?'

The harm, Jane reflects silently, is that they have no idea where Steph is going. Or why she's so ready to leave her precious daughter with strangers.

FOUR

MAY

The barbecue is held in the communal garden one Sunday afternoon in May, nearly a month after the Hamlins moved into number 12.

Trestles are covered with paper tablecloths, and boxes of hired plastic glasses and cases of wine and beer are arranged on them, along with a galvanised steel tub filled with ice. Rani and Xavier have ignored Irina's offer of help, sourcing a couple of white canvas gazebos themselves and erecting them in the centre of the lawn, although the forecast promises only a slight possibility of showers. At one edge of the grass is a large gas-fired barbecue that belongs to Robert and Danielle Salter, and Robert himself is standing in a swirl of smoke, wielding his tongs like a magician with his wand. Trish's partner, Tony, a red bandana knotted round his forehead, is acting as his sous-chef. Robert and Danielle's sons race around yelling at full volume, kicking people's drinks over, while Danielle applies all her attention to a bottle of rosé that she's annexed for herself.

'So where are the new people?' she demands tipsily, her stiletto heels sinking into the grass as she approaches Jane and Trish. 'Why aren't they here? I want to meet 'em.'

'They were invited,' Trish tells her. 'I put the invite through the letterbox myself.'

'Has anyone actually had a conversation with either of them?' Danielle sloshes another half-pint of rosé into her plastic tumbler.

Jane has minded Poppy on no fewer than four occasions, but is strangely reluctant to mention it. Steph will be gossiped about by the likes of Danielle if she does and, much as Jane is exasperated and puzzled by the girl's secretiveness, she doesn't want that. She has no wish to see Stephanie Hamlin shamed. They would probably speculate that she was having an affair, something Jane had mooted to Fergus, after the third afternoon she had dropped Poppy with them.

'Nah,' Fergus said, without hesitation. 'She's not the type.'

'How do you know?' Jane demanded, 'What *is* the type?'

He didn't elaborate, but even though she still has her doubts, Jane doesn't bring up the babysitting arrangement now. Perhaps Steph will mention it herself, if she shows up at the barbecue. Both eventualities are looking unlikely.

A murmur goes up among the group nearest the gate, and heads turn in one movement. Hedge fund supremo Michael Kovacic pushes the gate open with a masterful shove, his phone pressed against his ear with his other hand. He's wearing a polo shirt with the collar turned up and in his Italian suede loafers, his feet are bare. His arrival counts as a rare sighting, since he spends most of his time on business trips, flying between European capitals on private jets, discussing multimillion-pound investments with his clients. Behind him comes Irina, in a floaty white dress and espadrilles, her expensive tumble of hair pinned up to one side with a diamond slide from Chanel. She's leading their older daughter, Kamila, by the hand, and their Filipina nanny follows in her wake, holding the younger girl, Paulina.

Michael, who is at least fifteen years Irina's senior, accepts a glass of wine but ignores everyone and continues talking into his phone. Irina fusses over the children's immaculate outfits until a swaying Danielle homes in and starts engaging her in conversation. Irina plays along, nodding occasionally, but her eyes are roving over the assembled guests. She makes no attempt to pretend she's not bored.

Fifteen minutes later, his glass drained, Jane sees Michael indicate to his fiancée with a sharp tilt of the head that he has done his neighbourly duty for the year and is leaving. Irina looks around for the children and the nanny as though she intends to join him, but then something happens.

'Oh look!' Trish mutters under her breath. 'Isn't that Richard Hamlin?'

Sure enough, Richard Hamlin is strolling over towards the barbecue, alone. He's dressed in a smart pair of designer jeans and a pink dress shirt with a white windowpane check. The sleeves are rolled up and the buttons strain over his pectoral muscles. And, although the late afternoon light is fading fast, he wears a pair of aviator shades. His hair is freshly cut; shaved short at the sides and swept back from his forehead, and he looks quite different from the tracksuit-clad man who arrived with the pickup truck on moving day.

He grins genially at the assembled company, then helps himself to a beer and walks over to a sweaty Robert Salter, engaging with him over the heat of the charcoal. They're soon laughing, presumably over the age-old thrill of burning coals, that force that draws men together at outside parties. There's a definite confidence about him, a swagger.

'Hi, Richard,' Jane says, walking over to him. 'Steph not with you?' She doesn't know if Steph has told him about the Headleys minding Poppy, so for now decides not to mention it.

'Baby's a bit off colour,' he says, his tone casual. 'Probably her teeth and that, you know.'

'Probably,' agrees Jane. She suddenly finds herself

wondering why Richard couldn't have come to collect his daughter from them on the occasions she'd minded her, when he got back from work. Which, since he has an office job, was probably a lot earlier than eight thirty or nine in the evening.

'You're an accountant, yes?'

'That's right,' he says. He's still wearing the sunglasses so she can't read his expression. 'By training, yeah.'

Jane waits for him to embellish, and with a slight jut of his chin, he goes on.

'I don't work as an accountant any more, I run my own business, you know?'

'Ah, I see. Doing what?'

'Property development. Mainly.'

That might explain the late hours, Jane thinks. She's just about to question him further on exactly where he works, when she senses someone hovering at her shoulder. Someone wearing expensive scent.

She turns to the new arrival, on her own now that her fiancé has left the party. 'Irina, this is Richard Hamlin. You know; half of the lucky couple who won number twelve.'

It's perhaps a little bitchy to point out the Hamlins' lottery-winning status, thereby underlining that they are only at this exclusive gathering due to dumb numerical luck. But Richard doesn't react. He's staring at the woman next to her.

'Irina Semenova.' She extends a tanned hand, her wrist jingling with a series of gold Cartier love bracelets. The left hand sports a diamond the size of an egg on the ring finger.

Jane can't think what on earth the two of them would have to talk about, and she has no desire to find out, moving away to join Fergus, who's deep in conversation with Rani and Xavier. But glancing over at them, Jane can see a lot of macho posturing from Richard and hair flicking and giggling from Irina. You don't have to be a genius to work out that there's a flurry of nascent flirting going on, and Irina stays on at the barbecue for at least an hour after the nanny has taken the children home to bed.

By the time Jane and Fergus leave, the fairy lights have all been switched on and Richard has swapped his shades for his regular glasses. He takes them off frequently, chewing on one of the arms.

'He's actually a bit of a hunk,' Danielle whispers to Jane when she goes over to say goodbye. 'Looks like he spends a lot of time in the gym.' She has designated herself event photographer and is darting about taking pictures with her phone, with slurred cries of, 'Come on now; it's for the 'gram!'

'D'you think we should call in on Steph?' Jane asks Fergus as they walk back to number 5. 'I'm a bit worried about her being all alone with a teething baby.'

'She's a mum.' Fergus gives a derisive snort. 'Teething babies are par for the course. And I'm sure she won't appreciate the suggestion she can't cope. Anyway, you're the one who thinks we've done more than enough for Poppy already. For all we know, she's got a friend over. Leave her to it, I say.'

A few weeks later, at the end of her university exam period, Evie comes home to London and Joss takes the train up from Brighton, staying in Sycamore Gardens for a couple of days to spend time with his sister.

It's good to have both children at home, but also lovely for Jane to spend one-on-one time with her daughter. Jane and Evie take a trip to Covent Garden together to browse the shops and eat brunch, which Evie insists has replaced lunch for everyone under thirty.

'Are you and Dad okay?' Evie asks, as they sit on a pavement table drinking Bloody Marys and eating something that features avocado and eggs.

'What do you mean?' Jane's tone is sharper than she intends

it to be, but she's immediately on the defensive. Evie has always been very empathic, very sensitive. She picks up on things.

'I don't know; there's just a weird vibe between the two of you. You don't seem to be gelling, you know? And he's out all the time.'

'We're fine,' Jane insists, bending to drink her cocktail so that she won't have to meet her daughter's eye as she tells an outright lie. 'He's just very stressed at work at the moment. He always is at the end of the academic year: you know that.'

'Okay, if you say so.' Evie gives her mother a hard look, but lets the matter drop.

Evie leaves after three weeks to take up a temporary flat-share with a friend in Edinburgh, where she will be earning money working at the Festival. During the time that she's at home, Steph Hamlin asks Jane to babysit on a couple of occasions and Evie cheerfully helps out, declaring Poppy 'adorable' and 'insanely cute'. Jane is only too happy to have her daughter's help, and Evie makes the most of the light evenings by taking the buggy for long walks around their South London suburb, returning with Poppy fast asleep on both occasions.

'Did you say that silver pickup belonged to the Hamlins?' Evie asks on the second occasion, letting herself back into the house and leaving the sleeping Poppy parked in the hall.

'It's Richard's,' Jane tells her, coming up the stairs from the kitchen to greet them. 'The little red hatchback is Steph's.'

'Only it's parked out there now, outside their house. Rather than disturb the princess by hauling her out of the buggy, why don't I just push her round there? Then her dad can put her straight to bed.'

It's impossible to argue with Evie's logic, yet still something makes Jane hesitate. If Steph is doing something Richard doesn't know about during her absences from home, wouldn't that just draw attention to it? She glances over at the sleeping baby, her cheeks flushed, her blue blanket clutched in her chubby fingers.

'She's spark out; let's just leave her here while we eat. If Steph's not back by the time we've finished our supper, one of us can pop her round to number twelve.'

'Okay. Sure.' Evie clatters down the stairs after her mother, and before the three Headleys have finished eating their moussaka and salad, Steph rings the doorbell.

She's back a few days later, asking if Jane can babysit Poppy the following afternoon.

'Sorry... I'm afraid I can't this time: I've got a dentist's appointment.' Jane pulls a face to show that she's not happy at this prospect. 'But, you know, there's a really nice little nursery just on the other side of Clapham Road. Maybe you could think about booking her in there for the occasional session. I know people who've used it, and apparently the staff are all lovely.'

Steph shakes her head vigorously. 'No. He... I... Richard doesn't want me doing that. He wants me to look after Poppy myself.'

Jane's reflex is to look askance at this, but she tries to maintain a non-judgemental expression. 'In that case, why don't you ask Rani Moreno? She's on maternity leave, so she's got time on her hands, and it will be nice for you to meet another young mum. I'll give you her number.'

She is sincere about Rani, but not about the dental appointment. She doesn't have one. There's another reason she's not going to mind Poppy. She's going to follow Stephanie.

FIVE

JUNE

By now, Jane has a rough idea of how Steph's absences are scheduled, and she's ready to leave and watching the front of number 12 from three thirty onwards. Evie is out for the afternoon with her former schoolfriends.

Sure enough, at three thirty Steph drags the buggy down the front steps and walks to Regency Court, where she rings one of the bells and disappears into the building. A couple of minutes later, she emerges alone. It's a warm day and she's wearing shorts, a seersucker top and sandals, her long dark hair dragged back into a scrunchy. She has a small crossbody bag slung over her front, and is shouldering a full tote bag, which looks quite heavy.

Feeling slightly foolish at adopting a cliché straight out of a thriller, Jane has put on dark glasses and a baseball cap, with her fair hair tucked underneath. She maintains what she hopes is a discreet enough distance as she follows Steph out of Sycamore Gardens and up the main road to the tube station. It's busy, and Jane has to jump the queue for the ticket barrier so that she can keep Steph in her sights. She descends the escalator and turns right for the northbound Victoria line platform.

Getting into the same carriage would be far too obvious, Jane realises, so she steps onto an adjoining one and remains standing so that she can continue to view Steph through the window in the carriage door. People crowd onto the train at every stop, and she has to continually shift her position to maintain her view. After ten minutes, they pull into King's Cross, and Steph stands up, repositioning the tote bag over her shoulder.

On the platform, she follows the signs for the St Pancras exit, continuing straight into the station, past the row of tempting shops and turning right for the ticket hall. Once she has bought a ticket from one of the machines, Steph stares up at the departures board, working out which platform she needs.

Jane, who has followed her with ease through the broad concourse, feels a frisson of panic. If she is to continue to follow, she will have to have a ticket too, but how can she buy one if she has no idea where Steph is going? The next train due to leave is the 16.12 to Ashford International from Platform 12, so she buys a return ticket for Ashford, reasoning that the ticket will at least get her through the barrier, after which, if she's challenged by a member of staff, she can always claim she has innocently boarded the wrong train. It will be true, after all.

Her hunch is right, however. Steph heads for Platform 12. Making a note of which carriage she has climbed into, Jane darts into the supermarket concession and buys a bottle of juice and a magazine, which she thinks will be useful to keep her face obscured. She gets into the carriage behind Steph's, choosing a forward-facing table seat that allows her a view of the back of Steph's head. As she sits down, Fergus phones her, but she cuts the call. At least it only takes thirty-eight minutes to get to Ashford. She hasn't yet decided what she's going to tell her husband about where she's been, but, with luck, she won't be home too late anyway. If she were to admit to Fergus she's been following Stephanie to try to get to the bottom of her mysterious absences, at the very least he would tell her she was being ridiculous. At worst, he would threaten to tell Steph. Either way, he would strongly disapprove.

Jane is just immersing herself in an article about some soap star's new home in Marbella when in her peripheral vision she picks up movement in the next carriage. After less than twenty minutes, they're pulling into Ebbsfleet International, and Steph is disembarking. Her heart pounding, Jane jumps to her feet and, in her haste, she knocks her juice bottle all over the table. It drips into the lap of the woman sitting opposite her, who squirms in her seat as she tries to avoid the deluge of sticky liquid. Some people might be able to ignore it and bolt, but Jane's polite, middle-class reflexes are too ingrained.

'Oh my God, I'm so sorry!' She hands the woman the paper napkin she picked up at the shop till and rummages in her bag for a packet of tissues, thrusting some in the woman's direction and using another to dab at the table. By the time the tide of juice has been stemmed, the train has lurched forward and is leaving the Ebbsfleet platform behind. It's too late. Steph has gone. Jane has lost her.

Once she's arrived at Ashford, Jane has just over half an hour to wait before her train back to St Pancras.

At she paces fretfully up and down the platform, she asks herself what on earth Steph could be doing in Ebbsfleet. As far as she knows, there's nothing there except for a rail terminal that connects with Paris, Lille and Brussels. Is she heading to Europe, with a few of her possessions in that tote bag? But if she were running away in such a dramatic fashion, wouldn't she take her daughter with her?

Jane gets back to Sycamore Gardens with ten minutes to spare before Fergus returns from his office, and he finds her chopping onions and listening to the radio in the kitchen, just as on any other evening. She leans in to accept his kiss and the glass of wine he proffers, grateful that she won't have to lie to him or to go into any awkward explanation.

But once supper has been cleared up and it has gone dark, her mind strays back to Steph. If she failed to return to collect Poppy, surely Rani would have phoned her, as the person who'd introduced them? Or would she or Xavier simply take the baby back to number 12 and hand her over to her father, no questions asked? Jane resolves to phone Rani in the morning on the pretence of checking that the babysitting went to plan, but, in the end, she doesn't need to. While she's drinking a coffee in the sitting-room window, she sees Steph pushing the buggy along the pavement, her face pale and drawn.

So if she wasn't running away to mainland Europe, surely she must have been going to Ebbsfleet to meet someone, Jane reasons. Or someone in nearby Gravesend, perhaps. And the regularity and secrecy of these assignations suggests that she's meeting the same person over and over, and behind Richard's back. In other words, she's having an affair. Next time she's asked to babysit, Jane resolves, she will ask more direct questions about why Steph needs to be away for so long.

But she doesn't get the chance. After that afternoon in June when she followed Steph to Kent, she expects daily that she'll appear on her doorstep, but she does not. For now, at least, the requests to mind Poppy have dried up.

'Fancy a spritzer?'

Danielle Salter turns up on her front step a couple of weeks later, brandishing a tumbler the size of a small bucket. Jane is trudging wearily back from school after a day of trying to keep Year 2s from developing heatstroke in 33 degrees centigrade.

She knows that Danielle will only be asking her in because she wants – or is in possession of – gossip, but Jane is sweaty and exhausted and the clinking of the ice cubes in a glass is a lure she's powerless to resist.

She follows Danielle into the kitchen, and once she's been supplied with an equally huge glass crammed with orange slices, ice cubes and a green olive, she heads out into the Salters' garden. An oversized paddling pool had been set up, along with a water slide, and Hayden and Otis are racing around in swimming shorts brandishing super-soaker guns, their bodies dripping wet.

'It's the only time the little darlings are happy,' Danielle observes, 'When they're drenching each other in water.'

'It's good that you've got this set up already, with the summer holidays coming up.'

'Oh God, don't remind me.' Jane can't see Danielle's eyes behind the gold-trimmed Fendi sunglasses, but from the tone of her voice, she's sure they're rolling. 'I can't lie: I'm dreading it. No idea how I'm going to keep them occupied.'

Since she's offered childcare assistance to Stephanie Hamlin, Jane briefly wonders if, in the name of fairness, she should offer to help Danielle too. But no; the Salter boys are a step too far.

'Will you be going away anywhere?' she asks instead, gulping gratefully on the chilled glass of Aperol spritz.

'We've got a villa in Corsica for a couple of weeks.' Danielle sighs. 'I mean, I'd like to go away for a bit longer, but Rob won't take more time away from work.'

'Maybe I could keep an eye on the house for you while you're gone.' That would be a doddle compared to taking care of Hayden and Otis, Jane thinks. 'I could pop by and pick up the mail and water the plants.'

'That's very kind, Jane, but it's fine. Irina's housekeeper keeps our spare key and she'll come over and sort anything that needs doing.' She lowers the rim of her sunglasses and her voice at the same time, although the children are shrieking so loudly they'd never be able to hear a word. 'Speaking of Irina, you know Michael's away in Antwerp.' She gives a hammy pantomime wink.

'What do you mean? Michael's always away on business. Pretty much every week, as far as I can tell.'

'Yes, I know, but this time I think Irina's been making hay while the sun shines, if you get what I mean. Playing while the cat's away.'

Jane stares back at her. 'You mean she's seeing someone behind his back?'

Danielle nods with satisfaction.

'I see.'

'Aren't you going to ask me who?' Danielle's tone is tinged with impatience.

'Are you saying you know who it is?' Jane is genuinely intrigued now.

'Yep.' Danielle sucks up some Aperol through her straw, unable to conceal her grin of satisfaction. 'It's only our new neighbour.'

'You mean?' Jane is staring again. A jolt of shock fizzes in her innards. 'Richard Hamlin?'

'Come on, don't tell me you're surprised. You saw how they were all over each other at the barbecue. You could have cut the sexual tension with a blunt knife. And you've got to admit, he's pretty sexy. In a "bit of rough" kind of way.' She makes air quotes.

'I suppose so. I hadn't really thought about him that way.'

'Oh Jane, come on!' Danielle sneers. 'Don't tell me you haven't noticed! You must be the only one who hasn't.'

'So how do you know? Did Irina tell you?'

Danielle shakes her head. 'Oh God no, she's way too up herself to do that. But when I went to put the recycling out a couple of nights ago, late, I saw him coming out of number seventeen, and her standing in the doorway wearing nothing more than a kimono thingy.'

'That doesn't necessarily mean anything,' Jane points out, a touch defensively. But as she leaves Danielle's house to head home, it occurs to her that she has been so busy focusing on Stephanie's behaviour, she has genuinely not given Richard much thought. Perhaps it's not Stephanie Hamlin who has embarked on an affair, but her husband.

SIX

JUNE

From: j.headley
To: z.clifford
Subject: CONGRATULATIONS!!

*So thrilled that little Clemmie arrived safe and sound...
she's absolutely gorgeous! Hope the delivery all went
smoothly and you're enjoying the luxury of maternity
leave.*
Lots of love to you both, Jane xx

From: z.clifford
To:j.headley
Subject: Re. CONGRATULATIONS!!

*Awww, thanks J. The good news is that it all went very
smoothly and she's divine, if a bit of a diva! The bad
news is I've decided I need a lot more time at home with*

her, and I won't be coming back in September after all,
or for the foreseeable.
Zoe xxx

'So have you thought about what you'll do instead? Go back to working in the law?'

Fergus and Jane are sitting in the garden on a beautiful midsummer evening, and she's just told him that Zoe's announcement that she's not returning from maternity leave has helped her make up her mind: she's going to hand in her notice at Danepark.

Jane takes a sip of her gin and tonic and lets her gaze wander over the walled garden. The trellises are slightly rotten and sag under the weight of overgrown climbing roses, and the lawn is a little yellow in patches, mossy in others. Neither she nor Fergus are exactly dedicated gardeners.

'I'd like to, but the problem is I've been away from the profession for over a decade. I'm thinking I perhaps ought to do a bit of retraining before I look around for something permanent.'

'Good idea,' says Fergus, nodding. He approves of any sort of academic self-improvement.

'There's something called a Level 7 Diploma which would bridge the gap between my practical experience and a proper law degree. It would mean I could take on the paperwork for conveyancing and divorce.'

'Handy if we ever decide to split,' Fergus says with a wry grimace. 'Save us some money.'

Jane looks at him sharply, not completely sure how to take this. The saying 'many a true thing said in jest' comes into her mind, and she can't quite shake it. 'Don't be silly,' she says eventually, deciding not to lend too much weight to his statement.

'So I think I'll probably apply for that. But if I don't get in, I'm not sure what I'll do, to be honest. I've spent so much time making sure the kids are happy, I'm honestly not sure what it is that makes me happy.'

Her husband gives a little frown and turns to face her. 'Come on, darling, I'm sure that's not true. What subjects did you enjoy when you were at school, for example?'

'Nothing but PE, to be honest,' Jane says, but with a smile to show she's not entirely serious.

'Well, the last thing the world needs is yet another bloody personal trainer.'

'True,' Jane agrees. 'But I have been thinking I should do more exercise. Get in shape before I get too creaky at the joints.'

'Good idea. Tennis? Squash?'

'Maybe.' Jane takes another gulp of her drink. 'Perhaps I'll just start by running again.'

'Good plan.' Fergus gives her leg a vague, affectionate pat and hauls himself out of the deckchair to go and refill his drink.

In the spirit of seizing the day, Jane digs out a pair of yoga leggings and a sports bra on her next day off from school. Stiff-limbed and a little self-conscious, she sets off at a slow jog towards the leafy expanse of Myatt's Fields Park.

What she has not reckoned with is the weather, however. The sun is high in the sky, the baking pavements radiating a wave of heat, and before she has run half a mile, she's red-faced and pouring with sweat. She turns back to Sycamore Gardens, feeling foolish at her lack of forward planning. At this time of year, there's no point running during the hottest part of the day. After stripping off her sweaty kit and showering, she resolves to try again in the evening.

'You going somewhere?' Fergus enquires at 9 p.m., as she comes downstairs in a fresh set of sports gear.

'Don't you remember?' Jane asks, perching on the bottom stair to tug on her trainers. 'I'm going to start running again.' She decides not to mention that she has already tried earlier and nearly collapsed from heatstroke.

He does a double take. 'But it's almost dark.'

'So?'

'So just take care, all right? Make sure you have your phone with you.'

She brandishes it at him, before letting herself out of the front door.

Parks will be closing now that it's dusk, so she runs the streets aimlessly with no route in mind, gradually starting to rediscover her stride and enjoy the feeling of rhythmic forward motion. As she reaches the turn to Sycamore Gardens again, it's completely dark and the place is still and silent, apart from the background hum of traffic on the main road and the tweeting of a solitary song thrush in the elm trees.

Then her eye detects movement as she rounds the curve of the cul-de-sac. Someone is walking briskly along the pavement. Jane can see that the figure is a man of athletic build, dressed in shorts and flip-flops with a lightweight hooded jacket obscuring his face.

He stops outside number 17 and looks up at the front of the building. The house shared by Michael and Irina is the oldest and largest on the street and when it was first built had sole rights of access to the central gardens. It's a three-storey detached villa built in the late 1820s in the style of Nash, its imposing frontage rendered pale cream like the terraces that border Regent's Park.

As the sensor is triggered on an outside security light, Jane gets a quick glimpse of the man's face, although she has already guessed his identity. Richard Hamlin.

He presses the doorbell and glances over his shoulder warily as he waits for it to be answered. Jane attempts to duck behind a gatepost, but it's too late; he has seen her. She gives him a self-conscious little wave of greeting and starts to walk more quickly towards number 5. As she reaches her own house, she turns round and sees the door of number 17 being opened to admit Richard, before being briskly closed again. Jane just catches a glimpse of bronzed limbs and a skimpy satin negligee. So Michael Kovacic is away again, then.

Michael is back a few days later. Jane sees him take Kamila out to play on her micro-scooter, his phone clamped to his right ear as always, his facial expression one of irritation.

The following weekend, the Salters depart for Corsica. Their boys are at private school and therefore break up earlier than Danepark. When Jane returns from her evening run on the Monday evening after they've left, she notices immediately that there's an upstairs light on in number 6. Her first thought is of the spate of burglaries that plagued the previous summer, houses being targeted when the occupants were away on holiday. But why would a burglar risk switching on a light like that? she wonders. She's pulling out her phone to call the police when she remembers that Danielle has asked Irina's housekeeper to look after the house in their absence. That must be it.

But as Jane replaces her phone in her pocket, the side gate to number 17 is opened and the same housekeeper comes out with a large black bag of rubbish, which she puts in the wheelie bin.

'Bernila!' Jane calls to her. 'Hi!'

The other woman looks up and gives a timid wave.

'I wondered if I could have a quick word with Irina?'

'Miss Irina is out,' Bernila says. 'Mr Michael in. You want to talk to him?'

'No, thank you.' Jane shakes her head. 'It's okay.'

She turns back, looking up at the lit window at number 6 as

she does. The Salters' spare keys are in Irina's control. And what better place for an illicit tryst than an empty house?

Irina is out in the communal garden the following afternoon with her children, as composed and immaculate as ever. She's wearing cream linen trousers with a white wrap-around top that shows a strip of tanned midriff, and gold leather sandals that reveal crimson-painted toenails.

Jane has taken a rug and a book with the intention of soaking up some sun, since her own garden is north-facing. She gives Irina a little wave when she spots her and is rewarded with a cool nod. After twenty minutes or so, she's starting to sweat and the words are blurring on the page in front of her eyes. She hauls herself to her feet, folds the blanket and goes to sit on the bench next to the Russian woman.

'Is Michael still away?'

Irina merely nods.

Jane points to the huge oval diamond on her left hand. 'Any plans for the wedding yet? Have you decided when it will be?' As far as she's aware, Irina has been engaged for at least a couple of years but shows little sign of wanting to walk down the aisle.

'It's not that important, honestly.' Irina shrugs. 'We live like we are married.' The tone of voice suggests this is not necessarily a good thing.

'I suppose marriage just provides some security for the children... in the future.'

Jane is aware this sounds crass and a little old-fashioned.

'Not really— Pauli, no!' Irina waves her arm at her younger daughter, who is squatting down next to a flower bed and shovelling soil into her mouth. 'Kamila! Stop her please!' Her gold bangles clink as she gesticulates. 'Michael and I already have a prenup agreement, and it gives me two point five million for each child I have, whether I am married or not. Cash.'

Jane nods, as though this enormous sum is entirely run-of-the-mill, but inwardly her mind is whirling with astonishment.

'How much do hedge fund people earn?' she asks Fergus over supper that evening.

'Depends how senior they are, as in most professions.'

'Someone like Michael Kovacic?'

'As I understand it, he's senior partner at Onyx Asset Management. So probably anywhere between three and six million a year. With bonuses and profit sharing on top.'

'Bloody hell!' Jane gapes.

'I know, it's eye-watering, isn't it? Why, were you thinking of upgrading from a university associate professor, with his modest high five figures a year?'

Jane laughs, only too happy that he's employing a playful tone for once. 'If I could find one who'd have me, of course I would.'

But then I'm not a trophy like Irina Semenova, she thinks. No wonder Irina has been so casual about getting round to a wedding. It turns out it's not as though she needs the financial protection of marriage. Even if she and Michael split before making it up the aisle, she stands to be a very rich woman indeed. But then does it still apply if Irina has been unfaithful? Jane wonders. She can't see the very alpha Michael Kovacic taking kindly to being cuckolded.

SEVEN

JULY

As the end of the Salters' holiday fortnight approaches, so the heat intensifies. The nights become unbearably humid and stuffy, and even with the windows open and an electric fan churning away, Jane finds it difficult to sleep. Fergus slumbers heavily next to her, while she tosses and turns, throwing the sheet off, then pulling it on again.

During one of these disrupted nights, as the digital display on the alarm clock shows 01:02, she heaves herself off the bed and goes down to the kitchen to fetch a glass of iced water, relishing the sensation of the cool tiles under her bare feet. Outside, the night sky is a deep, velvety blue.

On her way back up to the bedroom, she pauses next to the window on the mezzanine landing, her peripheral vision picking up some movement outside. If she positions herself at a forty-five-degree angle, she can see over the wall and into the back garden of the Salters' house. At first she assumes the brief flash of movement was probably cats, or foxes, but as her eyes adjust to the darkness, she can make out the outline of two distinctly human shapes. One of them she can only see from the rear, but the luxuriant cascade of curls leaves her in no doubt as to their identity. It's Irina, wearing only the skimpiest of slip dresses, her legs and feet bare. The other, facing in Jane's direction, and for once devoid of hat or hoodie, is Richard Hamlin.

He glances up in the direction of the Headleys' house before very slowly and very deliberately cupping the sides of Irina's face and kissing her hungrily. His hand pushes up her back, hitching up the tiny dress and exposing a patch of naked buttock. Jane wants to look away, and yet she can't. She just can't.

Richard's hands roam over Irina's body and she arches her back, pressing her groin against his body. Her enjoyment, her abandon could not be any more obvious. He's not having to persuade her into anything; she wants it; that much is all too obvious. He manoeuvres her backwards so that she's resting against the wooden picnic table and starts fumbling with his flies. Now Jane really does look away, with a little gasp, but as she rounds the landing onto the next flight of stairs, she can't help seeing that the couple are now lying on the grass and engaged in animalistic coitus. They must have both waited until their respective partners were asleep before sneaking out in the heat of the night, like characters in a Tennessee Williams play.

The reason the Salters house is being used has already been established, but why in the midnight garden, when there's so much more risk of being seen? Or is that merely part of the thrill?

By the time she has got out of bed the following morning, tired and groggy from disrupted sleep, Jane has already decided she will say nothing about it to Danielle. The woman is an incorrigible gossip, and Jane feels a degree of distaste at the two of them sharing such a powerful secret. They are hardly close friends, after all.

Should she say something to Irina, though? Just to warn her

that she's not being as discreet as she thinks she is. Or does she not care? After a couple of mugs of coffee, with her brain firing more efficiently, Jane decides against that too. Whatever her intentions – and she believes they come from a good place – it's ultimately none of her business if Irina Semenova is having an affair with a neighbour. She can afford to if she wants to: literally. The phrase 'shoot the messenger' also comes into Jane's mind. It's unlikely her interference would make a difference, but it almost certainly would be unwelcome. No, silence is the best policy, for the time being at least. She resists the temptation to tell Fergus. He would just tell her off for getting involved.

That night, the sultry spell is broken by a thunderstorm. The chance to sleep properly is particularly welcome for Jane, since the following evening her colleagues at Danepark Primary are throwing her a leaving do. She protested strongly that she doesn't want any fuss made, but Zoe insisted that after Jane's many years in service to the school, they have to mark the occasion somehow. A drink and tapas in nearby Little Portugal is the compromise that has been reached. And Zoe has texted to say she has arranged for her mother-in-law to look after her newborn daughter for an hour, so there's no getting out if it now.

Once she's changed into her favourite green linen dress, and spent twenty minutes perfecting her make-up, Jane walks the half-mile to the tapas bar. The table is easy enough to spot, since a large gold helium balloon with the words 'SORRY YOU'RE LEAVING' floats above it. Jane is ushered into a seat at the centre of the table next to Zoe, and someone pops open a bottle of *espumante* to loud cheers; the first of many drunk during the evening. There are a couple of speeches, the presentation of an elegant Dartington glass vase and vouchers for a spa day, then things descend into increasingly rowdy chatter and laughter.

Eventually, Jane gets unsteadily to her feet. 'I'll miss you all, you lovely lot,' she pronounces to a round of cheering. 'Now let me out of here while I can still walk in a straight line.'

'In your dreams!' someone heckles, prompting more applause.

She feels distinctly tipsy as she walks back along South Lambeth Road with her gift bag and the bobbing gold balloon, but the night air and the exercise quickly sober her. It's only as she reaches the junction with Clapham Road that she becomes aware of footsteps behind her. Nothing unusual about that on a busy London street, but Jane senses that this person is deliberately keeping pace with her. Instead of pressing the button for the pedestrian crossing, she swivels round on her heel so she's facing whoever is following her.

It's Richard Hamlin.

'Hello.' She's the first to speak, since saying nothing seems ridiculous. The word comes out as a high-pitched gasp.

He doesn't say anything in return, but just looks at her, his indolent grin revealing slightly crooked front teeth. His grey-blue eyes behind the glasses are fringed with dark lashes, his jaw square, his cheekbones angular. Is that what Irina is attracted to? Or is it the muscular shoulders and flat abdomen? A couple of feet away from him, Jane is struck most of all by how young he looks. Perhaps that's the appeal, given Michael Kovacic must be around fifty.

'Can I help you?' Again, her words sound ridiculous.

'Should be the other way round, shouldn't it?'

Jane glances around her, but the few pedestrians and motorists in the vicinity are paying them no attention. 'I... I'm not sure what you mean.'

'What I mean is...' The trace of a smile is still there, but he lowers his voice a little. 'It's you who seems to want something from me.'

'No, I don't,' Jane retorts. She wonders if the colour rising in her cheeks is visible in the street light. 'What on earth gives you that idea? I did what any good neighbour would do welcoming new people to their street. And I certainly didn't go looking to babysit your daughter!'

'I'm not talking about that.' Richard's voice is cold, his words dropping like poison into the night air between them. 'I'm talking about you following me about, spying on me.'

'I don't spy on people.' This is said with more conviction than Jane feels. She has followed his wife across London and down to Kent on a train, after all. Has Stephanie seen her, and told Richard?

'I'm talking about watching through windows.' In his strong South London twang, it comes out as 'win-ders'. 'Looking into other people's houses. And gardens.'

So that was it. He has seen her looking out into the Salters' garden, watching him seducing Irina. Having sex with her.

'Look,' she says firmly, pulling herself up straight and going into teacher mode. 'Despite what you might think, I don't care what you get up to behind Stephanie's back. Your private life is your own concern.'

'Good.' He's smiling now, but the menace in his tone remains. 'And it better stay that way. You understand?' He cocks his head slightly, indicating that he expects a response. The light from the street light bounces off the lenses of his glasses, making his facial expression unreadable.

'Yes. I understand.'

'Your old man needs to keep you under better control, know what I'm saying?'

His words, and the image they suggest, are coldly shocking. And how are they now going to walk back in tandem to Sycamore Gardens? This fresh thought roots Jane to the spot, clutching the crystal vase to her chest in its beribboned gift bag. But Richard has already strolled off, and she sees that his pickup truck is parked on a double yellow line a hundred yards away. As he unlocks it, he turns back to stare at Jane for a few seconds, before climbing in and driving off into the night.

She shivers violently, as if it's December rather than a warm night in July.

EIGHT

JULY

'Good do last night?'

Fergus is munching on a piece of toast while looking at the news headlines on his phone.

'Yes, it was great.' Jane forces a smile as she loads mugs into the dishwasher. 'And a bit sad too, of course, after all these years.'

She tells him about the leaving gifts she received, and they speculate about when would be a good time to take the spa break. She doesn't mention her encounter with Richard Hamlin: of course she doesn't. Fergus would be angry on her behalf, and would probably march round to number 12 to speak to him, making things worse. Not only that, but he would repeat his opinion that she was taking far too keen an interest in the comings and goings of their new neighbour. If he were to find out about her trip to Ashford, he would say she'd taken leave of her senses. And after her unsettling experience the previous evening, Jane thinks he would probably be right. She says nothing more, and conversation turns to their upcoming trip to Suffolk for a week's holiday.

However, the need to speak to someone about what has

happened is strong, and after Fergus has left for work, she pays a visit to Trish Oldenshaw. It's Thursday; Trish's day off work.

'Come in, come in, my love!' Trish greets her warmly, her dogs scampering round her ankles. 'I was just about to take these two lunatics for a walk, but it can wait half an hour. Coffee?'

'Yes please.'

She follows Trish into her sunny minimalist kitchen and tells her, without preamble, about being followed by Richard Hamlin.

Trish lets her mouth fall open. 'Good God, Jane!' She rests a hand on her friend's forearm. 'He threatened you! Are you okay?'

'I'm fine,' Jane assures her. 'Well, a little freaked out, obviously.'

'But why on earth would he say that? I don't get it.'

Jane flushes slightly. 'I saw him with Irina. They're having an affair. Well, a sexual fling, at least. Not sure it goes any further than that.'

'So you saw them... by accident?'

'Pretty much. Danielle Salter mentioned something about spotting them together, so I was perhaps being more observant than I would have been otherwise, but I was on my way back from a run the first time, and I saw him going over to number seventeen. While Michael was overseas.'

Trish purses her lips. 'Does that necessarily mean anything fishy's going on, though? He could have just been borrowing the proverbial cup of sugar.'

Jane sighs, shaking her head. 'The next time I saw them they were actually... you know... at it.'

'Oh my God!' Trish's eyes widen. 'Where?'

'In the Salters' back garden. While they were in Corsica. I went downstairs to the kitchen in the middle of the night, and I could see them through the window. Irina and Richard.'

'And he saw you, presumably?'

She nods. 'He must have. But honestly, Trish, it was as if they were putting on a display. Like they wanted to get caught.'

Trish pours them both coffee, shushing the yapping dogs with a shrill 'In a minute!' She turns to face Jane again. 'Have you told the police?'

Jane shakes her head.

'You know what I think? I think you should talk to Tony.'

Her boyfriend, Tony, was an inspector with the Met before he retired and now works part-time as a security consultant for major banks.

'Maybe.'

'Not maybe, definitely,' Trish tells her firmly, 'This Hamlin guy can't go around behaving like that, like he's some kind of gangster. Who knows what sort of company he keeps.'

'He trained as an accountant,' Jane reminds her, with a wry smile.

'So he says!' Trish snorts. 'Tell you what, why don't you and Fergus come round for a bit of supper with us this evening? You can ask Tony about it then.' She catches sight of her friend's expression. 'Ah. He doesn't know, does he? Fergus.'

Jane shakes her head. 'And I'd like to keep it that way. For now, at least. He's got a lot of stress at the moment with the end-of-year exams; I don't want him worrying.'

'Fair enough.' Trish finishes her coffee and bends down to clip leads onto the dogs' collars. 'Tony's playing golf at the moment, but he'll be back this afternoon. Why not pop round later?'

Tony Waddesdon is a short, vigorous man with a shaved head and a perma-tan who looks younger than his fifty-eight years. In contrast to Trish's feistiness, he's cool, calm and seemingly impossible to ruffle.

'Come in, come in!' he booms when he finds Jane on the doorstep. He's still dressed in his golfing wear of pale blue polo shirt and khaki chinos. 'Trish is out, but she told me you were coming.'

For the second time that day, Jane finds herself in Trish's immaculate kitchen.

'How about a little sharpener while we chat?' Tony asks. 'Or is it a bit early for that?'

She shakes her head. 'That would be nice, actually.'

'It's six o'clock somewhere in the world, right?' Tony pulls a bottle of chilled rosé from the fridge and waggles it in her direction. 'How about a shot of Her Indoors' lady petrol?'

'Perfect.' Jane grins, accepting the glass and enjoying the feel of the icy cold against her palm.

Tony opens a bottle of lager and seats himself on one of the stools on the opposite side of the kitchen island. 'So Trish tells me you've had a spot of bother with this Hamlin character.'

She nods.

'So how exactly did it happen?'

Jane recounts Richard following her back from her leaving party and confronting her.

Tony taps the beer bottle against his lower lip. 'Can you be certain that he was following you? Given you live a few doors away from each other, could he just have been heading home via the same route?'

'I suppose so...' Jane falters, uncertain. 'But he wasn't heading home on foot like I was, because he had his truck parked nearby... Honestly, I can't be sure either way.'

'And what exactly did he say? Did he say, "If you do x, then I'm going to do y to you"?'

She shakes her head. 'No, it was much more vague than that. I told him I didn't care what he got up to behind his wife's back and he said something to the effect of, "It better stay that way."'

'So would you say his manner was threatening?' Tony is in police officer mode now.

'Yes, definitely.'

Tony leans back on the stool, drumming his fingers on the edge of the island, thinking. 'The trouble is, unless he makes a specific threat to harm you in some way, there's not really much the police force can do about it. It's only classed as threatening behaviour under law if Hamlin leads you to believe that immediate violence is going to be used against you. D'you see what I'm saying?'

Jane nods, and takes a gulp of the chilled wine.

'Which doesn't, of course, mean that he's not a wrong 'un, and that he's not capable of putting you in fear. But if saying it would be a good idea if you minded your own business was a crime, the prisons would be even more crowded than they already are.'

Jane feels the blood rising up her neck as she remembers her amateurish attempts to find out the reason behind Stephanie Hamlin's absences from home. 'So you're saying I should just stay well away from him? And his wife.'

'Not exactly. I mean, don't go getting in their way for the time being; that's just common sense. But as an ex-cop, my approach is always to try to find out more about who you're dealing with. I mean, how much do we actually know about this man?'

'Not a lot,' Jane admits.

'So, I'll tell you what I'm going to do.' Tony leans forward again, spreading out his broad, tanned hands on the shiny surface of the island. 'I'm going to get one of my former colleagues who's still in the job to run some checks on the PNC, off the record. See if he's got any form. Not sure how long it will take me to organise, but leave it with me. And while we're waiting for that, it might not hurt for you to see if you can find out a bit more about him. Discreetly. While staying as far away from Hamlin as you can, given he's less than a couple of hundred yards away from you most of the time. Okay?'

'Okay,' agrees Jane. Tony's calm rationality is so reassuring that she feels herself relax a little.

He drains the remains of his beer and climbs down off his stool. 'And now, if you'll excuse me, I'm about to go and have my post-golf shower.'

Jane follows him into the hall and kisses him on the cheek. 'Ferg and I are going away on holiday,' she tells him as she opens the front door, 'so keeping out of his way will be a whole lot easier.'

'Good,' says Tony, approvingly. 'That's a spot of good timing, then.'

It will be a relief, Jane realises as she walks home, not to have to have any further dealings with Richard Hamlin.

NINE

AUGUST

Whenever they talk about their summer plans, the Headleys always refer to going 'to Suffolk', but the fact is, they always go to the same village and the exact same holiday rental, year in, year out.

Driftwood Cottage is a compact brick building with terra-cotta pantiles, overlooking Thorpeness Meare. The interior is dark and a little damp, with a distinctive smell of mothballs and old cardboard and wood varnish that would transport a blind-folded Jane straight to that place, wherever she happened to be. Downstairs, there is an open-plan kitchen with a stable door out to the garden and living room with a log burner. Upstairs are a small bathroom and two bedrooms, one of which has bunk beds and which Joss and Evie reluctantly shared until Joss declared himself too old and insisted on using the sofa bed in the living room.

This time, it's just the two of them, and Jane feels a heavi-ness, almost a sadness, as she unlocks the front door of the cottage with the key hidden under a loose brick, inhaling that familiar smell. She can picture the two children racing to the pine dresser and dragging out the collection of slightly mouldy jigsaw puzzles left by previous holidaymakers. At home they would not have bothered with them, but here in Driftwood Cottage they were always satisfied with a lot less, leaving their precocious metropolitan identities behind to play with board games and a tattered old pack of cards, to dig in the sand and run to the Italian ice cream kiosk on the seafront, always choosing their favourite flavour from the tempting ranks of coloured tubs. Will they ever holiday as a family of four again?

She puts this question to Fergus as they sit over a scratch supper of reheated lasagne and salad, while squally rain lashes at the windows.

'I shouldn't think so,' he answers flatly. Their first bottle of wine is already finished and unusually he reaches into their half-unpacked boxes for a second one, pouring himself a glass without offering one to Jane. 'I mean, why would they? Now that they're technically adults. Unless we're offering all expenses paid to the Caribbean, or Australia. Then it would no doubt be a different story.' He gives a bitter little laugh and tops up his glass again.

'Steady on, we're already a bottle to the good!' Jane makes to pull the bottle towards her, but Fergus blocks her with his forearm.

'What are you, the alcohol police?' he sneers.

'No, it's not that... I just don't want you spoiling a day of holiday with a horrible head tomorrow, that's all.'

'Why not? The weather forecast is foul anyway.'

'Because, apart from anything else, we're seeing Kat and Adam tomorrow. For lunch.'

Fergus merely shrugs, and once they have cleared the table and loaded the dishwasher, he takes the bottle of Merlot over to the sofa with him and sits there nursing it, his body hunched, his expression unreadable.

. . .

Katherine Dowler has been friends with Fergus since their undergraduate days at Cambridge, and she and her husband, Adam, own a holiday home in Aldeburgh. A long-standing tradition dictates that the families make sure that their time in Suffolk coincides, so that they can spend some time together every summer.

Jane has always gone along with this arrangement because Amelia Dowler is close to Evie in age and it was a bonus for her daughter to have a playmate while they were on holiday. But with Amelia away on a gap year in Cambodia, this time it would just be the two couples, and privately Jane is less than thrilled about this. The truth is that she dislikes Kat. She finds her bossy and sententious, and struggles to understand why she and Fergus ever became such good friends. Adam Dowler is pleasant enough, if a little insipid; browbeaten by his over-bearing wife.

Today they're meeting in the Blue Crab Café, one of their favoured venues, halfway between their two cottages.

'I've got them to put us over here,' Kat booms when Jane and Fergus arrive. She has spotted them through the window and is already standing up when they enter the café. Immediately, she waves her arms in a peremptory movement, indicating where they should go as though she's directing traffic. Her frizzy brown hair is streaked with grey and looks permanently untidy, and she's gained weight in middle age. 'Sturdy' is the euphemism Jane's mother would use to describe her build. 'They had us at that table right by the loos, but I told them that wasn't good enough, didn't I?'

Adam smiles weakly in assent.

'Anyway, I've ordered us a bottle of that Muscadet we like, and I think we should order the sea bass. It's caught locally, so it should be good.'

God help us if it's not, thinks Jane.

'Fine,' says Fergus without enthusiasm, reaching across the table to give Kat a swift kiss on her cheek.

'Well, this is nice!' Adam rubs his hands together vigorously as though trying to create a flame.

Jane smiles at the banal platitude and accepts the glass of the wine that Kat has ordered for them.

The conversation starts with the disappointing weather, ranges through work and career news ('Taking a bit of a risk, aren't you?' Kat demands when Jane's resignation from Danepark comes up) and settles inevitably on their children. This, at least, is a relatively safe topic, although Kat never misses the opportunity to brag about Amelia's academic achievements. She works her daughter's straight A*s from the previous summer and upcoming place at Oxford into the conversation, even though Jane and Fergus already know about them.

'Is Fergus all right?' Kat demands after he leaves the table to go to the bathroom. They've all finished the sea bass that Kat lobbied for and, to her credit and Jane's relief, it was very good.

'He's just a bit hung-over,' Jane says, giving what she hopes is a reassuring smile. 'We laid into the red wine last night.'

'Only he seems a bit subdued.' This is levelled as an accusation, as though her husband's mood is entirely within Jane's control.

'It's been a busy term, and he's tired. He just needs some time to decompress.'

'Well, he's in the perfect place for it,' ventures Adam, earning himself a glare from his wife.

'I'm not sure that's all he needs,' she says with a disapproving sniff. 'But, still, it's better than nothing, I suppose.'

In bed that night, Jane reaches for Fergus, running her fingers up and down his back, massaging his shoulders. This, he will understand, is a signal that she's in the mood for sex. But he merely mutters, 'Not now, I'm tired,' shrugging the duvet around his neck and inching away from her.

The wet, squally weather persists the next day.

After a late, silent breakfast, Fergus tugs on his cagoule and announces that, rain or no rain, he's going out for a long walk. The implication is that he will do this alone, so Jane sets about tidying the already tidy cottage and making herself more coffee.

There was no reason for her to bring a laptop, since Fergus has his, but she does have the tablet that she uses, loaded with holiday reading, and she now fetches it from her nightstand and sits down at the table with it propped up next to her mug of coffee. She clicks on the search engine and types in: 'Richard Hamlin accountant'.

It doesn't take much sifting through the web results and images to find him. He still appears on the website of Stevenson Hunter Paine LLP, as a junior partner. There he is in a group photo, wearing a suit but no tie, smiling confidently.

She's about to search for his resumé on LinkedIn when the door bounces open and Fergus walks in, his hair slicked wet and his face streaked with rain.

Before she can close down the window, he has covered the ten feet between door and table in a single stride and is staring over her shoulder. 'What the hell are you doing?' he demands.

'I was just...' Jane reaches for some witty riposte, but is too flustered to come up with anything. Her face reddens as though she's been caught looking at hardcore pornography. 'I was just finding out a bit more about—'

'Well, bloody don't!' Fergus snaps. 'This preoccupation with the Hamlins is getting out of hand. In fact, it's now coming across as a bit unhealthy.'

'I'm not preoccupied,' Jane protests, although this feels like a lie. 'I was just—'

'Just stop it, okay, Jane?' Fergus has turned away, pulling his mobile out of the pocket of his wet coat, before hanging it up to dry. 'For God's sake, pack it in!' He stamps up the stairs, calling, 'I need a shower to warm up,' over his shoulder.

Jane closes the tablet case with a sigh and goes to the fridge to work out what she can make them for lunch. Fergus's phone, still on the worktop, starts to vibrate with a call. Her eyes widen when she sees just a single initial on the screen. Was that right?

She looks again to make certain, but by now the call has cut out. Even so, she's quite sure she didn't read it wrong.

S calling.

TEN

AUGUST

It's a relief to be back in London five days later.

The weather improved drastically from the third day of the holiday, allowing for plenty of outings to the beach, boat trips on the mere and walks to the Thorpeness windmill. In other words, all of the Headleys' favourite Suffolk activities. Adam Dowler broke his wrist playing frisbee, forcing him and Kat to head home early, so they were also spared any more awkward socialising as a foursome. Fergus's mood lifted with the rain clouds, and their last few days together were relatively harmonious.

And yet Jane can't help being glad to get home, and to have time to herself when Fergus is at work. He has not mentioned her 'research' again after his outburst, nor has she questioned him about who 'S' is. For some reason the first name to pop into her head is Steph. But why would Steph Hamlin be trying to contact him? Perhaps something to do with them minding Poppy? Perhaps Steph called round to number 5 to see her while they were gone and was only contacting Fergus because it was obvious Jane wasn't there. To find out when they would be back. She can't think of any other reason for Steph to phone her husband. Once, Jane would have called round to number 12 to check this theory herself, but since Richard's warning, it seems like a bad idea.

'What are you going to get up to next week? Now you're a free woman,' Fergus asks as he unpacks the boxes of groceries they've returned with, and she loads laundry into the washing machine.

'I still haven't heard about the Level 7 course, but I thought I might approach a few firms about what kind of post I could apply for once I've got the qualification,' Jane tells him. 'See if I can get face-to-face meetings with a few HR people.'

'Good plan,' Fergus smiles approvingly. He's acquired a tan from the time spent on the beach and looks a lot better for the time away. 'I'm sure you'll get credit for being proactive.'

Jane's intentions may be genuine, but they are quickly set aside the next morning when she gets a text from an unknown number.

Hi, Trish gave me your number, hope that's okay. Just to tell you I got my mate in the Met to run thorough checks on Richard Hamlin and he's completely clean. Not so much as an unpaid parking ticket. Hope this helps.
Tony.

After she has replied thanking Tony, Jane fires off a text to Danielle Salter.

Can you send me photos from the night of the barbecue?
J x

She then continues changing from her shorts and vest top into a plain navy linen dress, puts on some make-up and walks to the tube station. She catches a Northern line train to Monument, then the District line to Tower Hill and, as she had planned before receiving the text from Tony, walks to Prescot Street.

It's a hot, humid August day, with heat bouncing from the pavements, and by the time she reaches the offices of Stevenson Hunter Paine LLP, her hair is sticking to the back of her neck, and there are dark sweat marks on her dress. The building is a modern five storeys built from sandstone slabs and with a tall glass entrance door leading to a spacious lobby. As Jane stands staring up at it, a teenage boy on an electric scooter collides with her, grazing her ankles and taking off without apology. There are now dirty grey marks on her shins, and as she bends down to inspect the damage, blood oozes onto the hem of her dress. She dabs at it ineffectually with a tissue, smearing it over her skin, before straightening up and pushing on the revolving door.

'Can I help you?' The blank-faced receptionist takes in Jane's dishevelled appearance. 'You're here to see…?'

'You'll have to do me a favour and fill me in on their name,' Jane has rehearsed this speech while she was crossing London on the tube. 'But I need to speak to your head of HR.'

The receptionist starts running her finger down a printed list. 'That would be Yvette McGraw. But if you don't have an appointment, I'm not sure you'll be able to see her. She's most likely in meetings all day.'

'Please phone and ask,' Jane is firm. 'I don't mind waiting a bit, but it really is very urgent.'

'Take a seat.' The receptionist waves to a central seating area with pale grey sofas and a huge planter of orchids on a low table.

Jane fetches a plastic cup of water from the cooler and sits down, picking up a copy of *Accountancy Age* which she flicks through without really reading anything. After forty minutes, just as she is about to embark on an article about proposed changes to research and development tax relief, the receptionist catches her eye and beckons her over.

'Yvette says she can give you five minutes. You'll have to fill this in, though.' She points to the visitor log on the desk. 'And I'll need to check photo ID, if you have anything on you.'

Jane takes out her driving licence from her wallet and fills in her details on the log.

'Fourth floor. She'll meet you at the lift.'

Yvette McGraw is a short, plump woman with bright red hair and a strong Northern Irish twang. No, she doesn't personally know Richard Hamlin: they have over two hundred people working there, including support staff and trained professionals, and he was with the Recovery and Insolvency team, who work on a different floor. From his record, she can see that he resigned from the firm four months ago and did not work his notice.

'Is that usual?' Jane asks.

'No, it is not.' McGraw maintains an expression of professional impartiality, but there's disapproval in the narrowing of her eyes.

'Any idea why he would leave so suddenly?'

'I can tell you that he cited personal reasons, but because of data protection, of course I can't go into them.' She gives Jane a tight smile. 'Now, if you don't mind, Mrs...'

'Headley. Jane Headley.'

'I need to get back to my meeting. Any future queries are probably best dealt with over email.' There's a cursory handshake and she marches off.

Instead of taking the lift, Jane heads through the door marked 'Exit' and down the stairs. A member of the clerical staff is walking up with a large filing tray of post in his arms.

'Recovery and Insolvency?' Jane blocks his path. 'Which floor?'

'Second,' the man replies, barely looking at her.

'Thanks.'

The second-floor offices are open plan, with widely spaced

desks and an atmosphere of quiet concentration. Jane stands there awkwardly, willing someone to make eye contact. Eventually, a young Asian man stands up, smiles politely and asks: 'Hi... are you okay? Can I help you?'

'I'm looking for someone who worked with Richard Hamlin.'

'Sure; no problem. I worked with him.'

'Could we have a quick word. In private?'

He looks surprised, but leads Jane into a side meeting room and sits down at the table, extending a hand for her to shake. 'I'm Tom. Tom Chen. How can I help?'

Jane sits down opposite him and once again reaches for a rehearsed speech. 'I'm a neighbour of Richard's, and since he left Stevenson Hunter Paine, his behaviour has been giving cause for concern.'

'I see.' Chen looks thoughtful.

Jane starts flicking through the photos on her phone. She holds out one of Richard at the barbecue, wearing his pink shirt and sunglasses. He's being engaged in conversation with Xavier Moreno, but his gaze is directed over Xavier's shoulder. Sure enough, in the corner of the shot, there is a patch of gauzy white. The dress Irina was wearing that night. She points to Hamlin. 'We're talking about this man, just to be clear.'

Chen gives her an odd look, taking the phone from her and studying the picture. 'Yeah, that's him.'

'You're quite sure about that?'

'Absolutely. I remember that checked shirt. He used to wear it all the time.'

Jane takes her phone back. 'And at the time he stopped working here, he seemed okay to you? As in, acting normally?'

'He seemed absolutely fine. Although it was odd that he left so suddenly. We were told it was for health reasons. He's not... There's nothing seriously wrong, is there?'

'No. He's not ill at all. He's running his own business now.'

Chen raised his eyebrows. 'I guess he lied to HR then.'

'And that's out of character?'

'Yes, I'd say so. He always played things pretty straight. Although he did talk about setting up on his own from time to time.' He shrugs his shoulders. 'Sorry, I don't know what else I can tell you.'

'Thanks, you've been very helpful.' Jane smiles.

'Listen, things in a top 50 firm like this can get pretty pressured, pretty stressful, especially in this department. It's not unheard of for people to, you know, crack. Have a bit of a breakdown and end up leaving. It happens, you know?'

'Yes,' Jane assures him, as she stands up. 'I'm sure it does.'

After she leaves the offices of Stevenson Hunter Paine LLP, Jane heads back towards Monument and calls in at a legal recruitment agency on Lower Thames Street. She could easily have registered with them online, but this way, if Fergus asks, she'll be able to justify a trip into the City. Without the need to mention visiting Richard Hamlin's offices.

When she gets back to Sycamore Gardens, feeling grimy and in need of a cool shower, she spots Danielle Salter pulling up outside the house in her car. She gets out and attempts to shepherd Hayden and Otis into the house while simultaneously carrying in the bags from a supermarket shop.

'Stop it! Otis, stop hitting him! And you, you give that to me! I didn't say you could have those!'

Danielle snatches a large bag of crisps from Hayden, then sees Jane and grimaces in response to her look of sympathy.

'Oh, Jane...' she calls as Jane climbs the steps to her own front door. 'Have you heard? About number twelve.'

Jane swings round. 'Heard what?'

'Apparently they put the house up for sale a couple of weeks ago. So soon after moving in! And guess what... a mum from the boys' school made enquiries about it with the estate agent and was told that since they had a house to sell, the vendors wouldn't let them even look around the place. Strictly cash offers only! What do you make of that?'

'I don't know,' Jane says, though she has the inkling of an idea.

'It can only mean one thing, surely,' Danielle crows triumphantly. 'That they're in a tearing hurry to get away from this place.'

ELEVEN

AUGUST

The 'For Sale' sign appears outside number 12 a couple of days after Jane's conversation with Danielle Salter.

'They'll be lucky,' Fergus observes grimly. 'The market's dead as a dodo at the moment. Especially for larger properties. But I guess having won the place, it's a debt-free asset and they want to cash out.'

'According to Danielle, that's exactly it: they're looking for cash offers only,' Jane tells him.

'That'll be an even tougher ask then.'

Jane reports back to Tony and Trish that Richard Hamlin was indeed formerly working as an accountant at a very well-respected London firm.

'If he checks out, and he's got no criminal record, I think you have to leave it,' Tony advises her. 'Put it down to you having caught him at a bad time. Who knows what stresses people are under? Maybe he's having a hard time with his new business. That's probably why he wants an injection of cash from selling the place. Makes sense to me.'

Tony is right, and part of her knows she should really heed both her husband and Richard Hamlin's warnings to mind her own business. So he's having a bit of a fling with an attractive neighbour: he's hardly the first man to do that. And yet there is still something that nags away at Jane. Something that doesn't feel right.

As she tackles a mountain of ironing in the sitting-room window, with the radio murmuring in the background, her attention is attracted by a flurry of movement outside. A pair of identical black limos with tinted windows slide past, followed by a black people carrier. Is there a funeral procession going on? And if so, who has died?

But when she looks out again, she realises that the cars are pulling up outside Irina and Michael's house and that this is the transport bringing them back from their holiday. Irina and Michael get out of the first limo, the children and their nanny the second. Bernila helps the driver of the people carrier unload at least half a dozen large Louis Vuitton suitcases and various smaller bags.

As the empty cars slide silently away again, around the oval of the Gardens, Jane thinks she sees Richard Hamlin watching them, but then realises it's his brother, Elliott, who not only looks exactly like him, but is a frequent visitor to the house. He rings the doorbell of number 12, and as the door is opened, he starts talking rapidly and gesticulating in a very agitated manner. After going inside for a minute or two, Elliott emerges to more shouting and strides out to the street as the door is slammed behind him. He climbs into his dusty Jeep Renegade and drives off at speed.

As Jane is turning to go back to her ironing, the door of number 12 reopens, and this time Stephanie emerges, alone, wearing denim cut-offs, a cheap-looking top and trainers, clutching her phone and keys. She too turns and shouts something angrily over her shoulder, then walks briskly in the direction of the main road. Only seconds later, once Stephanie is no longer visible, Richard Hamlin comes out of the house. He's wearing combat shorts and a tight T-shirt and his favoured aviator shades. Jane watches as his pickup truck also drives away.

And then it comes to her, like cold water being trickled down her spine. Where is Poppy? If Steph and Richard are both out, who is looking after their daughter? Didn't Steph tell her that she has no family or friends nearby who can babysit? And that Richard doesn't want her leaving Poppy in a nursery.

She snatches up her phone and fires off a quick text to Rani.

Are you minding Poppy for S? x

Rani replies a couple of minutes later.

Working on my thesis today. I offered a while back to have her again and Steph said she would like that, but then never heard anything back. Why? All okay? x

Jane is looking out of the window at the façade of number 12.

Tell you later, she types, adding: *Nothing to worry about.*

This is obviously not true. She *is* worried. Steph didn't have a bag with her and so was possibly not planning to be gone for long... would she leave Poppy alone in the house? Asleep in her cot, perhaps, but still alone?

Jane hesitates for a minute or so, Richard Hamlin's words of warning to her ringing in her head. But this is different, surely? This is a matter of child safeguarding.

Slipping her feet into her Birkenstock sandals, she scoops up her own phone and keys and walks over to number 12.

'What the fuck are you doing?'

Jane has her hands cupped on either side of her face to cut

out the glare as she presses her face against the ground-floor sash window.

She feels a jolt of shock run through her, and swings round to face her accuser.

Fergus.

'Rani was supposed to look after Poppy, only Steph never showed up.' This half-truth comes out in a rush. 'And I offered to come by and check for her. Only nobody's answering the door.'

'Well, presumably, that would be because they're out.' Her husband is looking at her with a mixture of incomprehension and disdain. He went to get his hair trimmed earlier in the day, and the shorter cut combined with his tan makes him look hand-some; dashing even. Like a twenty-first century Mr Darcy. 'Jesus, Jane, I thought we'd been over this. Interfering in the Hamlins' lives like this, snooping on them... it's simply not on. Not a good look, as my students would say.'

Jane explains that no one has seen Poppy for a while, and that both parents have just left the house without her.

'Then surely the obvious explanation is that she's some-where else, with someone else.'

By now, Fergus has grabbed her by the wrist and is pulling her down the path.

'I don't think so.' Jane tugs her wrist free angrily. 'She doesn't have anyone else.'

'In that case, if you're really worried that they've left the baby in the house alone, then it's a matter for the police. Not nosy neighbours.'

They are outside their own house now.

Jane points up the road towards the entrance to the cul-de-sac, where Steph Hamlin is now retracing her steps. 'Look, she's coming back. We can ask her.'

At first glance, she thinks that what she's seeing is Steph

pushing the buggy, but as the girl gets nearer, it's clear that the large object in her hand is a wheeled suitcase.

'No,' states Fergus firmly. 'We can't.' He half pushes, half herds his wife up the steps to the front door and unlocks it swiftly, pulling them both inside before Steph has the chance to spot them. 'Leave it, Jane,' he says in a low, cold voice. 'I mean it.'

'Or what?' Jane spins round to face him, her cheeks hot with fury. She and Fergus rarely row, but she has been on edge with him since before their holiday, plagued by the disconnect she can't quite make sense of. 'What exactly are you planning to do if I don't?'

It's Fergus's turn to be startled, but Jane is unable to hold back now that her temper has well and truly been lost.

'Or perhaps what we should really be asking is why? Why are you so keen to keep me away from Steph Hamlin? Is it because you want to keep her all to yourself?'

Her husband's face grows pale beneath the tan. 'What the hell are you talking about? You really have lost your mind, haven't you? It must be your age or something. Steph Hamlin? She's half my age!'

'She phoned you,' Jane hisses. 'When we were in Driftwood Cottage. I saw the call on your phone.'

He stares at her for a few seconds, shaking his head, then pulls his mobile from the pocket of his jeans and brings up the call log. 'Look,' he says, thrusting the screen so close to her face that she can't see.

She wrenches it from him and scrolls back through the last few weeks.

'I saw it,' she mutters. 'I know I saw it. And this doesn't mean anything. You can easily delete a call.'

Exasperated, Fergus points to a missed call from the week they were in Thorpeness. A call from 'Seb'.

'Seb Johnson, from my department phoned me – look. That's probably what you saw.'

Jane is squinting at the screen, trying to read the exact time of the call, but he snatches it away from her.

'Seriously, my love, you ought to think about seeing the GP.' He turns as he heads up the stairs. 'You need to get your hormones sorted out or something. I don't know what's up with you at the moment, I really don't.'

The day after their argument, there is a young man standing on the pavement outside number 12. A young man in a shiny suit and tan shoes with a pointed toe, clipboard under one arm as he frowns at his phone screen, a man who any switched-on London resident would instantly recognise as an estate agent. Sure enough, a pale blue hatchback branded with 'Baxter & Marsh' logos is parked close by, but not so close that it would obscure the frontage of the house or diminish its kerb appeal.

'Those must be the buyers,' says Trish, pointing through the sitting-room window of number 5. She has called round to have tea with Jane on her way back from walking her dogs.

Jane stands behind her and peers out over her shoulder, still mindful of Fergus's no-snooping mandate. An early-middle aged couple have just pulled up and got out of their car, shaking the hand of the estate agent and peering up at the handsome symmetrical façade of number 12. She is wearing a green dress and retro horn-rimmed glasses that make her look like a 1950s secretary. He is stringy and fit-looking, dressed in the designer jeans and loud shirt that suggest a job in the creative industries. The estate agent produces a key and lets them into the house.

'Doesn't look like the Hamlins are home,' says Trish. 'Mind you, I can't really blame them. Having strangers tramping round your home is pretty soul-destroying.'

'They've barely been there long enough to make it into a

home,' Jane points out.

'True.'

'Speaking of the Hamlins, have you seen much of Stephanie recently?' Jane turns away from the window and pours tea from the pot she has just made, handing a cup to Trish.

'Seen her a couple of times, I think. Just walking in the direction of the shops.'

'With her baby?'

'No, I don't think so... why?' Trish frowns.

Jane sets her own cup down. 'Rani said she'd not brought Poppy round for an agreed babysitting session. I don't want to worry her by bringing it up with her again, given she's getting close to giving birth herself, but... she hasn't asked us to look after Poppy for ages either. And I haven't clapped eyes on the child for a while. Come to think of it, I haven't seen that dog of theirs either.'

She tells Trish about the evening when both the Hamlins went out alone.

'But there was no sign Poppy was alone in the house? You couldn't hear crying or anything?'

Jane shakes her head.

'Well, there you are then. If they're aware that their neighbours are taking an interest in what they're up to, then they've probably asked someone else to look after her. He's got family, hasn't he? A brother at least. Maybe the sister-in-law has her for them. Especially if they're about to move away. Maybe they've even bought a new place already. They could have taken out a loan against number twelve easily enough.'

'I expect you're right,' Jane says slowly. Feeling a little foolish now, she manages a self-deprecating smile.

Trish gives Jane's shoulder a little squeeze before reaching for one of the biscuits on the plate between them. 'I think your imagination's running away with you, darling. Or maybe it's your maternal instinct going into overdrive.'

The implication is that the childless Trish, who has only ever been responsible for small canines, is being more objective, more logical. And her analysis of the Hamlins' situation does make perfect sense.

'Trust me, darling,' she smiles, reaching down to pet one of the bichon frises slumbering at her feet, 'it'll be something and nothing.'

Jane returns to Trish's words as she is going to bed that night. She did – in the kindest way possible – imply that Jane was overreacting. Fergus was less kind with his suggestion that she was becoming menopausal, but perhaps they were both right.

When she reaches the first-floor landing, the sound of voices and car doors slamming make her stop in her tracks. Fergus is already in bed, so instead of turning left into the master bedroom, she turns right into the unlit spare room and peers out of the front sash window.

Richard and Steph Hamlin are on the street outside their house, their voices raised in furious argument. Richard is holding several full refuse bags, and he turns away from Steph to toss them in the back of his truck. Its engine is running, and there's already someone in the driver's seat; probably Elliott Hamlin. Steph in turn marches to her red hatchback and gets into it, driving off with an angry crunch of the gears.

Jane hears the crash of the cat flap downstairs as Oreo races inside. He's clearly been spooked by a fox, because now there is the distinctive sound of one screeching in the front garden. The same noise alerts the Hamlin brothers, who turn to stare in the direction of number 5. Jane takes a step back from the window, but not before she catches sight of Richard Hamlin. He looks directly at her, before raising his right hand to his neck and making a throat-slitting gesture.

TWELVE

AUGUST

Kiaan Santiago Moreno is here!

Jane can't help but smile at the birth announcement when it pings on her phone. In the photo, Rani is cradling a blanketed bundle against her face, her expression one of pure joy, the baby's dark eyes both inscrutable and unknowing.

We would love to invite you to a traditional Naamkaran ceremony to welcome baby Kiaan to the world. Love, Rani and Xav.

The date is Friday of that week. Jane, who can't imagine wanting to host a social event so soon after giving birth for the first time, texts Rani with congratulations and an offer to help with the catering.

The aunties will do all that, don't worry xx

Having consulted a Hindu colleague from Danepark and been assured that bringing alcohol is okay, Jane arrives at the party with a bottle of champagne, a baby blanket for little Kiaan and a box of Fortnum's biscuits for Rani, who she knows has a sweet tooth. Fergus was invited, but refused on the grounds that he's too busy at work marking dissertations. Not that his absence makes a difference, since the flat is crowded with relatives, friends and neighbours. A huge flower-strewn table stands at one end of the living room, laden with plates of flatbreads, pastries and desserts and silver tureens filled with steaming rice and curry.

'Are you sure you're up to this?' Jane asks an exhausted-looking Rani, who has the new arrival draped over shoulder, a muslin protecting her orange silk sari. 'I don't think I could have coped.'

'It's the eleventh day, so that's when his naming ceremony has to take place.' Rani touches Jane's arm, her own wrist jangling with its many gold bangles. 'I've had plenty of help, don't worry. But thanks for asking.' She lowers her voice slightly, 'To be honest, I've been stressing more about getting my doctoral thesis finished by the deadline.'

Jane goes to help herself from the buffet, and is instantly collared by Danielle. She's dressed as if she's attending a wedding, in a stiff, shiny cocktail dress, towering heels and a feathered fascinator in her bleached blonde hair.

'Jane, glad I've caught you... can I ask you a teeny-weeny favour?'

'Sure.' Sighing inwardly, Jane forces a smile.

'Only the in-laws are having the boys this weekend, so Rob and I thought we'd take off for a couple of days. He's booked a five-star place in the New Forest, you know: that one with the Michelin-starred chef off that telly programme.'

Jane doesn't know, but nods anyway.

'You know Irina's Bernila usually keeps an eye for me, but

she's on her annual trip home to the Philippines apparently, and I don't want to bother Irina with it. Michael's home, and I know he likes to have her all to himself when he is... Anyway, would you mind just taking the other spare key until we're back? Nothing needs doing, it's just in case of if there's an emergency. You know, burst pipe or gas leak or something.'

'Sure,' Jane tells her. 'No problem.' She hasn't mentioned the Salters' home being used for Richard Hamlin's trysts, and has no intention of doing so.

Wasting no time, Danielle rummages in her Chanel bag and pulls out a set of two door keys attached to a diamanté-studded fob. As she pockets them, Jane becomes aware of Xavier trying to catch her eye.

She winds her way through the press of cooing relatives and raised glasses of cava towards him.

'Congratulations, Daddy!' She kisses him warmly. 'Kiaan's absolutely gorgeous.'

He cups her elbow and guides her to the space in the bay window, out of earshot of anyone else. 'Jane, you know what's going on around this place, so if you don't mind, I'm going to ask you.'

Xavier's English is fluent but heavily accented. He's short with a wiry frame and sparkling brown eyes above a well-trimmed hipster beard.

Jane gives a little shrug and chases a samosa around her plate with her fork. 'Not sure about that, but I'll help if I can.'

'You know this man, Richard Hamlin?'

She nods warily, anxiety making her stomach lurch.

'Okay, so I hear he is an accountant. And I have a query about my corporate tax return.' Xavier has recently set up and manages a small artisan coffee business. 'So, when I see him walking past, I ask if I can, you know... how d'you say?' He taps the side of his head.

'Pick his brains?' prompts Jane.

'Exactly. So I was asking him about the deadline for filing the first accounts to Companies House, and if the deadline is flexible.' He pauses, and runs his hand through his luxuriant beard. 'You have to submit your first return within twenty-one months; I know this now. But this guy, this Hamlin, he just tells me the deadline is the thirty-first of January. But that's for an individual's personal return with HMRC. For business, the deadlines are different, and they depend on different factors. It was clear he didn't know any of this.'

'That's strange.' Jane sets down her plate carefully on the windowsill. 'Look, don't tell anyone this, but I went to his previous employers' offices to check him out. And he definitely worked there. It's a prestigious accountancy firm too.'

Xavier crosses his arms, his body language stubborn. 'But I'm telling you he didn't know something any qualified accountant would know.'

'Perhaps he misunderstood the question.'

'I thought of this, because I know my English is not perfect. So next time I saw him, I asked him something to catch him out. Rani's brother is a graduate trainee at one of the top ten London accountancy companies. Because I'm doing my own accounts a lot of the time, he's talked to me about the software they use in-house. You know, when he was advising me what to install myself. So I asked Hamlin which was better: Xero or FynSync. They're the most used software at the top end of the industry. And you know what?'

'What?' asks Jane, although the sinking feeling in her stomach tells her what's coming.

'He didn't know what the hell I was talking about,' Xavier says triumphantly. 'That man is no accountant!'

Jane glances around to make sure no one is listening to them. A beatific Rani is carrying her son in their direction, clearly wanting Xavier to take over parental duties. 'Look,' she says quickly, keeping her voice low, 'I'm glad you told me about this. And I'm not saying you're wrong, but—'

'Can you take him for a bit?' Rani holds out the sleeping baby to her husband. He has a white cotton cap on his head and a bindi at the centre of his forehead.

'Listen, I'd better get going,' Jane says, kissing Rani on her cheek. 'It's been wonderful.' She gives Xavier a meaningful look. 'Let's continue the conversation soon, yes?'

'Didn't you say the Salters were away?'

Jane hears the front door slam as she's in the kitchen preparing supper the following evening. Fergus thunders down the stairs and gives his wife a swift, perfunctory kiss on the cheek.

'They are, but just for the weekend.' Jane tips chopped salad greens into a bowl and holds out the bottle of white wine towards Fergus.

He shakes his head and goes to the fridge to take out a can of lager instead. 'Only there's a light on in their house.'

Jane keeps her expression neutral. 'I expect they left some on a timer, for security.'

'Probably.' Fergus snaps the tab off his can and carries it with him to the foot of the stairs. 'Have I got time for a shower? It's sweaty as anything out there.'

'Sure.'

As soon as she hears the water running, Jane darts up to the open mezzanine window and looks out. Not only is there light spilling over the lawn, but she is sure she can make out the sound of voices. She goes up to the master bedroom, tugs off her linen shorts and blouse and pulls on the leggings and sports bra that are on the chair, removing her phone from the pocket of her shorts. Then she taps on the door of the en suite.

'Ferg – supper's just salad, so it will keep... I'm going to go and have a quick run before we eat.'

The door is yanked open and Fergus's head appears, wearing a crown of shampoo suds, water dripping down his neck and shoulders. 'What – now? It's still bloody hot!'

'I don't want to do it on a full stomach.'

Before there can be further debate, she snatches up her running shoes and heads downstairs to the hall, reaching into her handbag, not only for her own door keys, but also Danielle Salter's.

It occurs to her that Fergus might be watching her through the window, so she turns away from the Salters' house and jogs in the opposite direction towards the end of the Gardens. After waiting at the junction with the main road for a few minutes, she doubles back and walks briskly towards number 6.

Then, her fingers trembling slightly, she pulls out the diamanté key ring, unlocks the front door and pushes it carefully open.

THIRTEEN

AUGUST

She recognises the first voice at once. Richard Hamlin. The second, low and female, is a bit harder to pick up.

Jane presses herself against the wall of the Salters' hallway for a few seconds, listening, hardly daring to exhale. The voices are coming from the kitchen, at the far end of the ground-floor lobby. She needs to get a bit closer to hear what they are saying, but not so close that they realise they're not alone. She edges forward around six feet.

Now she can pick out the husky, accented tones of Irina Semenova. She's agitated, speaking fast, and Jane can only catch a few words. They sound like, 'Simply not fair.' Then the strident, aggressive voice of Richard saying something like, 'You're fucking joking.'

She edges a few feet nearer to the half-open kitchen door. A floorboard creaks slightly, and she freezes, her heart thudding hard against her ribs.

'Did you hear something?' Richard asks.

'What?' Irina seems distracted. 'No, I hear nothing. You are imagining.'

With exaggerated care, Jane scrolls through the apps on her

phone until she finds 'Voice Notes'. She presses record, and hold the phone as far as she can in the direction of the kitchen.

'All I need is if anyone asks where I was last night, to say I was with you. It's not that deep, you know?'

'You say is not deep, but it's a problem for me. You were supposed to be with me *last* night and you don't show up last minute. You don't tell me where you're going. And tonight I'm supposed to be going to dinner with Michael, so I have to pretend to him to be ill. What is he going to say if he finds out?'

'Sort it, okay? Lie to him! Fucking drug him if you have to, so he loses his memory: I don't give a shit. Only for the time being, you've got to say that we were together, here. Last night. Okay?'

'Here... in this house?'

'Well, I could hardly be tucked up in bed with you and your old fella, could I?'

'I don't know, what if Michael—'

'You're going to have to tell him sometime, babe, you know? If we're going to be together like we planned. You've got to get the ball rolling sometime anyway, if you're going to get the money you're owed.'

The money you're owed? Is he referring to Irina's non prenup? The one that makes her a very wealthy woman if she leaves Michael?

'Look, it's not's that easy, you know? These things, they take time to organise,' Irina is saying now. From what Jane has heard, she can be quite fiery. Does Richard Hamlin know what he is dealing with? That, for all her status as a trophy girlfriend, she's no pushover.

'Fuckin' 'ell, Rina, you're doing my fucking nut!' Hamlin is loud now, and there's the sound of scraping as a chair is pushed back. 'We don't have fucking time, don't you get it? Not if we're to get away free and clear. You're going to have to find a way to hurry things up, for fuck's sake! And for the time being, you've got to say that we were together, here. Last night. Okay?'

There's a muffled gasping sound, and Jane realises with slight shock that Irina – cold-eyed, supermodel Irina – is crying.

'Come 'ere...' Footsteps, followed by the sound of a kiss. 'Sorry, okay. Didn't mean to heavy you.'

'I'm scared. I don't know how...' The rest of the sentence is inaudible.

'It'll be all right, babe, I promise. Sweet as a nut. Now, I'm going to have to get going.' There are more kissing sounds.

Like a street mime artist, Jane tiptoes backwards with exaggerated care, retreating as quickly as she can while ensuring every movement remains silent. She has left the front door ajar and she slips through it now, clutching her phone to her chest as she turns and runs off into the night.

As soon as Fergus has left for work the next day, she texts Trish.

> *Got time for a quick coffee?*

> *It'll have to be v quick, heading into the office in 30 mins x*

Jane arrives ten minutes later to find Trish, dressed in a smart lightweight trouser suit, thrusting papers into a document case.

'Coffee's made,' she says briskly, pointing to a pot on the kitchen counter. 'But I'm afraid you'll have to drink it with Tony.' As she speaks, he ambles into the kitchen in a towelling dressing gown. 'Something's come up at the office and I've got to shoot.'

Trish puckers her lip-sticked mouth into an air kiss, grabs her bag and papers and leaves.

Tony shrugs and pours them coffee. 'Sorry, but you're stuck with me.'

'Actually, you'll do just as well as Trish; better even.'

Jane refrains from mentioning her recording of Irina and Richard's conversation (after all, wasn't recording people without their consent illegal?) but tells Tony about the conversation she had with Xavier.

Tony makes a double-take gesture. 'But, hold on, didn't you say his employment as an accountant checked out?'

'Stevenson Hunter Paine confirmed they employed him, yes. But Xavier was so adamant that Hamlin didn't know stuff any chartered accountant would know.'

'Maybe he just wanted to avoid having to do someone's accounting for free,' suggests Tony. 'I mean, I used to find it infuriating when people found out I was a copper and wanted me to tell them how to deal with the neighbourhood scumbags. Case in point.' He grins at Jane, who smiles sheepishly. 'And Trish's brother... he's a doctor, and having to make dinner-party diagnoses drives him mad.'

'So you're saying he was pretending to be no good to get Xav off his back?'

'Maybe. It's the only obvious explanation I can think of.'

Jane stares down into her coffee mug.

'You don't agree?'

The silence lengthens between them. Jane is weighing up telling him about the conversation she overheard; and about when Richard Hamlin saw her watching him and pretended to slit his throat.

'I don't know,' she sighs eventually. 'I just have a strong sense that there's something about him we're not getting, something... off.'

'Well, in that case...' Tony gives a little grimace as he lifts his coffee mug to his mouth. 'You're going to have to find a way to dig deeper, aren't you?'

. . .

Late on Monday morning, while Fergus is at work, Jane takes the Northern line to the City and heads back to the offices of Stevenson Hunter Paine.

This time, she doesn't go into the building, but waits at one of the tables outside a coffee shop on the other side of the street, spinning out a frappuccino while she watches the front door. After an hour or so, employees start coming outside for their lunch break. They are in ones and twos and sometimes small groups, putting on their sunglasses and shedding jackets as soon as they are in the strong sunshine.

Eventually, Jane sees Tom Chen come out with a female colleague. They exchange a few words, then she raises her hand in farewell and heads east down Prescot Street. Jane snatches up her bag and darts across the road.

'Tom!' She waves her arms to attract his attention as he's turning to walk in the opposite direction. 'Tom, wait!'

He pauses, his smile polite but hesitant. He recognises her but clearly has no idea from where.

'It's Jane – Jane Headley. I spoke to you the other week. About Richard Hamlin.'

'Oh yes. Hi.'

'Sorry to be a pain, but could you spare me another five minutes?'

'I was just...' He flaps an arm in the direction of the sandwich shop further across the street.

'I realise you're on your break, but this will really be very quick. I just need you to listen to something for me.' Jane points to the coffee shop table she's just vacated and steers Tom Chen briskly across the street. 'Sit down here a second.' She takes out her mobile, opens the voice notes app and presses play, holding it close enough for him to hear the audio above the background rumble of traffic.

'*...You're going to have to tell him sometime, babe, you know? If we're going to be together like we planned. You've got to get the ball rolling sometime anyway, if you're going to get the money you're owed.*'

'Recognise the voice?' she asks. 'Here – I'll play it again.'

Tom Chen is looking puzzled. 'Sorry, I don't. I've no idea.'

'It's my neighbour, your former colleague – Richard Hamlin.'

Now he's shaking his head. 'No,' he says firmly. 'That's not Richard Hamlin.'

'Are you sure?'

'One hundred per cent certain. Richard Hamlin is from Swansea. He has a strong Welsh accent.'

The last person Jane wants to see as she unlocks her front door is Danielle Salter.

Her body and brain are both still flooded with adrenaline from Tom Chen's revelation. The man at number 12 is definitely not Richard Hamlin. So, who is he? Where is the real Richard Hamlin? And what part does Stephanie play in all this?

'*...and I'll have the key back when you're ready!*'

Danielle's grating voice cuts into her thoughts.

'Sorry, what?'

'I was just saying we had a fab weekend away, and thanks for keeping an eye on the place.'

'Oh, right... it was nothing, don't worry.' Jane rummages in her bag for the diamanté key ring, thrusting it in the other woman's direction and turning to go.

Danielle is still hovering: a sure sign that she has some gossip to impart. 'Have you heard the news?' she crows.

'No, what?'

'The Hamlins. They're not at number twelve anymore.

Fiona Collins from number nineteen went outside to let her dog out for a late-night pee on Saturday, and she says she saw him loading some stuff onto the back of his truck. No sign of her red car, so she must have already left. Then he took off.' Her heavily made-up eyes are sparkling at the drama of it all. 'They've done a moonlight flit.'

'Not necessarily,' Jane tells her. She keeps her voice measured, though her pulse is racing at the implication of this news. 'They could have just been going on holiday.'

'Well,' Danielle crosses her arms triumphantly over her silicon-boosted cleavage. 'That's where you're wrong. Because I checked. I phoned the estate agent, pretending to be a buyer, but they've accepted an offer on the place, and they're due to exchange this week. "The current owners have already vacated the property" is what he said. Wouldn't tell me any more than that. No one has a clue where they've gone.'

'I see,' Jane's voice comes out as barely more than a whisper.

'No sooner than they've appeared, they've disappeared.'

PART TWO

KEREN

FOURTEEN

MARCH

Keren Stockley is late for work.

She's frequently late for work, but a few days ago, the manager of the day care facility saw fit to warn her about this frequent lateness. And Keren can't afford to lose her job. It's a crappy job, in her opinion, but she still needs it.

'I need to go in the shower first, for fuck's sake!' she rages at her boyfriend. Dressed only in a pair of white Calvin Klein boxers, he's admiring his abs in the bathroom mirror while he lazily brushes his teeth. 'I'm supposed to have left ten minutes ago!'

Liam spits out the white foam, shrugs and wipes his mouth on the back of the bathroom's only towel, ushering her past him into the bathroom with an exaggerated gesture of courtesy.

She showers quickly, skipping a hair wash and instead dragging her dark curls into a bun on the top of her head. Once she emerges, wrapped in the same towel, Liam drags it off her and pushes past her and into the bathroom again, but only after delivering a playful slap on her naked backside.

'Ow!' Keren complains. 'Jesus!'

Given her mood, she would dearly love to get into a full-blown row. There have been many of those of late, as their eighteen-month-long relationship slowly but inevitably sinks like a passenger liner disappearing under the waves. But here and now, there simply isn't time. She tugs on her work uniform of black leggings and a plain yellow polo shirt embroidered with her name and starts sifting through the piles of clothes and shoes on the floor of their messy bedroom in an attempt to find the beaten-up trainers she uses for everyday.

On the night stand, Liam's phone starts buzzing with messages. Keren glances at the notifications on the screen, then taps in his passcode, which she happens to know is made up of the shirt numbers of his three favourite Crystal Palace players. She then scrolls back through the history in the phone's notifications centre.

SCORE-BET: Your account is in arrears. Please pay £400 in order to keep your account open.

SCORE-BET: Your account is in arrears. Please pay £550 in order to keep your account open.

SCORE-BET: Your account has now been closed. Please contact member services immediately.

CASINO-STARS: Top up your balance, insufficient funds in your account.

CASINO-STARS: Account debit still outstanding. Please pay in immediate funds to prevent debt recovery.

And so on. There are a lot of them, stretching back over the past few weeks. His gambling habit is one of the issues sinking the metaphorical vessel of their relationship, chiefly because Liam doesn't see it as a gambling habit. To him, it's a legitimate side hustle, a second job. Only, as Keren sees it, to represent a bona fide source of income, there has to be some actual money coming in. And Liam only ever seems to lose. He crows about winning fifty quid and spends it on drinks or new clothes, completely ignoring the fact that to win that fifty he's thrown away around six hundred on bad bets.

At least she has her own bank account, even though they share household expenses. She's deliberately kept it that way. She realised at the outset of their relationship that this small icon of independence would make it easier in the event that she decided to leave Liam.

Placing his phone back on the nightstand, she tugs on her trainers and sets off to work.

Ruth Buckby intercepts Keren as she's shrugging on her blue polyester tabard in the staff rec room. Blue tabards indicate that you work in the baby room, red is for toddlers and green is pre-schoolers.

'Keren, can I have a word please? If you wouldn't mind?'

The Stepping Stones nursery manager is a thin, miserable-looking woman with lank mousey hair and an underbite. She dislikes Keren, and the feeling is mutual.

'I know I'm late,' Keren says as she follows Ruth into her office. She checks her watch: it's 7.40. 'But it was literally only five minutes. And no one from the baby room has done drop-off yet.'

'This isn't about your timekeeping.'

Keren stares at her, distracted by the piece of what looks like tomato skin caught in her prominent upper incisors.

'We've had a complaint from one of the parents. About what she termed your "sloppiness".'

'Which one? Hilary da Silva?'

'No. It was Mrs Hamlin. Apparently Poppy had a... situation... with her nappy...'

'Yeah. A poo blowout,' Keren supplies helpfully.

'Exactly. And she needed changing into her spare clothes. Only when she was picked up, you'd put her in some other child's clothes, not the spare set provided by the Hamlins. And it said on her daily log, Poppy had sweetcorn for lunch, when that's on the list of foods she's not to eat. As she said – sloppy.'

'Sorry,' mutters Keren, biting her lip.

'Is that it?'

'Well, what d'you want me to say? I didn't mean to do any of it, I was probably just rushing.'

'Exactly. Better time management in general would be a good idea.'

'Sorry,' Keren repeats.

'Yes, well, there's not time to go into it now: we need to get breakfast underway, but perhaps a discussion at your performance review might be an idea. It's coming up soon, I believe.'

Keren escapes back to the baby room and starts slamming cereal bowls on the table, throwing a handful of plastic spoons after them.

'Jesus!' says Chloe Dockerill, who works with her in Babies and is the closest she has to a real friend at Stepping Stones. 'Had a row with that hot boyfriend of yours?'

'He's not that hot,' Keren mumbles. She's still furious with Liam about the money he's been wasting on betting apps.

'Well, I would do him, I tell you!' Chloe cackles. She's a heavyset girl with a mass of wavy blonde hair, heavily stencilled brows and eyes that are never without long false lashes. 'What's up?'

'Just been called into Buckteeth's office. Apparently, there's been a complaint about me.'

'Really?' Chloe looked startled. 'Shit. Who?'

'Bloody Stephanie Hamlin. Bloody snooty cow.'

'Oh, you mean your sister!' Chloe laughs again.

'She's nothing like my bloody sister.'

'You know what I mean: you look exactly like her. You and she could be twins. You've got the same hair, the same skin, the same figure.'

'She's tons older than me!' Keren insists angrily. She hates these references to the similarity between herself and Stephanie Hamlin. There may be a physical resemblance, but they're not really alike at all. Their two lives are worlds apart. She also hates herself for being mildly obsessed with the high-achieving, poised Stephanie, who is everything she's not. The comparison of their looks just makes this all the more galling. 'And how dare she say I was "sloppy". Bloody stuck-up cow. What if that goes on my permanent staff record?'

What if I end up losing my job, she thinks. The only steady income she and Liam have at the moment.

'Well, it's Tuesday, so Poppy's not here today. Just chill out and try to forget about it, yeah?'

Keren manages to forget about the complaint, but she cannot 'chill out'. Her mind keeps going back to the messages on Liam's phone. Because she knows Liam well enough to know that this will only be the tip of the financial iceberg.

As she gets off the bus at Tulse Hill that evening and walks down Knight's Road to the flat, she checks her account balance on her banking app: £957.91.

Their rent and council tax, totalling just over £1,300, are due in a couple of days. A utilities bill of £367 and water bill of £273 are now several months overdue. Since there's no way she can cover these outgoings alone, she has no choice but to raise it with Liam when he comes in from work an hour later.

'Yeah, yeah, I know. I'll sort it,' is his only response. He's sitting on the edge of the sofa, fiddling with his phone. He does this constantly. A glance at the screen tells her he's playing online poker.

'What does that mean?'

'It means I'll sort it, yeah?' he snaps. His blue eyes are unnaturally bright, and he's pursing his lips in concentration. Keren knows from bitter experience that it's unwise to cross him when he's in this frame of mind. When he's gambling, it's as if he's in a trance, and any attempt to break him out of it makes him lose his temper. So, for now, she bites her tongue and goes into the tiny kitchenette, switching on the oven to heat some chips.

The doorbell rings. Liam, of course, ignores it, so it's Keren who goes to let in his twin brother, Lance. Lance, who everyone jokes is the beta version of Liam. Very similar, just slightly less in every department. Less clever, less brash, less good-looking. They're non-identical twins, but still look similar enough to confuse people who don't know them well.

'All right, Kez,' he says with a cursory nod, loping into the living room.

She brings the brothers a bowl of oven chips and ketchup, and after they have been consumed, Liam abruptly announces that he and Lance are going to the Golden Lion to play pool. The twins don't live together, but Keren often thinks that they might as well, given the amount of time they spend together. They exist in a mysterious universe of twin co-dependency: frequently arguing but both unable to take any decision without the backup of the other. Liam needs to control and dominate his twin, Lance to be controlled and dominated.

You can't afford to go drinking, Keren wants to say, but she doesn't. Instead, she puts on the Netflix dating show everyone has been talking about at work and scrolls mindlessly through her phone.

The doorbell rings again ten minutes later, but this time she doesn't recognise the man standing in the hallway, staring down at her. He's big and burly like a bouncer, with a shaved head and a leather bomber jacket, and he has a leather attaché case under one bulky arm.

'Liam Devenish,' he says in a low, rasping voice. 'He at home?'

'He's out.'

'But he does live here? He your boyfriend?'

Keren nods slowly.

The man hands her a business card. 'BTS Recovery Ltd,' he rasps. He sounds as though he smokes three packs of cigarettes a day, and smells like it too. 'I'm here to collect payment on a debt he owes.' He reaches inside his jacket and pulls out a typed letter, which he hands over, stabbing at a figure with his huge thumb. 'See – says here what he owes.'

Keren stares. The sum is £2,760.

'Are you in a position to make payment now? Only if you don't, I have to inform you that my client will be commencing court proceedings against him.'

'I haven't got anywhere near that much in my account.' As soon as she's said it, Keren realises she shouldn't have. She shouldn't have mentioned her own bank account.

'How much you got, darlin'?'

She makes a quick mental calculation of what she would need to survive until her next payday if she eats two of her three meals a day at work. 'I suppose I could give you about £800 but—'

'That'll do for a start.' He has stepped past her into the flat now, and his eyes are roaming around the living room. He pulls a card reader from his attaché case and holds it out towards her, waiting. 'Otherwise that boyfriend of yours could wind up in prison, and you don't want that, do you?'

Keren hands over her debit card, which the man slides into the machine and thrusts back at her.

'PIN please, darling.'

He gives back the card with a receipt for £800, then pulls out another printed sheet of paper.

'This explains that I'm legally entitled to take possessions up to the amount of the debt. Got a car, have you?'

'No,' lies Keren. Her ancient hatchback and Liam's pickup are both parked out on the street somewhere.

He turns and points at Liam's prized PlayStation 5. 'I'm prepared to reduce the total debt by another £300 if you let me have that.'

Is she allowed to refuse? Keren wonders. She knows that Liam paid over £500 for it. On the other hand, surely it would be better to reduce the debt as much as possible.

'Okay,' she says weakly. 'But I'll need something in writing. You know, to say it's made what he owes less, by that much.'

'No problem,' says the man easily. He's already unplugging the console and untangling the leads. Once it's tucked under his arm, he points to the business card, which Keren is still clutching. 'Make sure you tell that boyfriend to get in touch as soon as possible about the rest of the debt, all right?' He gives her a satisfied smile and saunters back through the front door, leaving behind a cloud of stale cigarette smoke. 'You have a nice night now, darlin'.'

FIFTEEN

MARCH

'You should never have let him bloody take it. You're a real moron sometimes, Kez, you know?'

Twenty-four hours later, Liam is still complaining bitterly about Keren handing over his PlayStation to the bailiff. 'There are procedures that those grasping bastards are supposed to follow. That don't include just helping themselves!'

'He was going to take the cars otherwise,' Keren protests. 'You'd have been a lot more upset if you came back and found he'd taken your truck!'

'You could have given him yours,' Liam reasoned. 'It's a heap of junk anyway. Bloody money pit.'

'Well, if it's so worthless it wouldn't have reduced what you owe by much anyway,' she spits. They're sitting on the sofa with cans of lager and a takeaway. 'As it is, I've spent every penny I've got and you still owe over fifteen hundred quid!' She stabs angrily at her spring roll with a plastic fork.

'And the rest,' Liam mutters.

'What d'you mean?' She shifts on the sofa so she's facing him.

'I mean I owe on other accounts too, not just that one.'

'So how much? What's the total?'

He shrugs. 'Somewhere between six and eight.'

'Thousand?'

'Of course it's thousands. Jesus, you're so thick, sometimes!'

'And what about interest?'

He just shrugs.

'But, Liam, what about—'

He stands up, throwing an empty can across the room. 'Christ's sake, woman! Get off my back! You do nothing but fucking nag!'

He snatches up his hoodie and pulls it on, reaching for his phone and his keys.

'Where are you going?'

'Out.'

Two seconds later, the front door slams.

Not for the first time, Keren wishes she had someone to talk to about her relationship with Liam. Her mother lives in Ireland, and contact with her is virtually non-existent, has been since she left London with her latest man six years ago. She's a little closer to her half-sister, Siobhan, who lives in Essex, but hasn't seen her in person for a couple of years. Siobhan has never met Liam, but when she heard that his father was in prison for armed robbery and that Lance has served time in a young offenders' for petty crime, she wasn't exactly supportive. As for her father, she's never even met him. He was a Ghanaian student who impregnated her mother and disappeared within the space of six months. There's Chloe, at work, but she's blinded by the fact that she fancies Liam rotten. She's therefore not going to be giving an unbiased opinion.

Not that Keren can blame Chloe. When she first met Liam, in a nightclub in West Croydon, she was floored by the primal attraction she felt for him. He's above averagely good-looking, but that wasn't what caught her attention, or at least not solely. It was his confidence, his swagger, his sheer animal magnetism.

Her eyes had followed him around the crowded club, seeking him out wherever he went. She returned to that same club week after week, hoping to catch a glimpse of him again. When eventually she did, he asked her if she was stalking him, paralysing her with embarrassment. Then, to her shock, he asked her out for a drink. It was pretty much a disaster. She was tongue-tied with shyness and went to bed with him to avoid the awkwardness of struggling to make interesting conversation. Three months later, they moved in together. It had been Keren who pushed for this – she was living in a hostel at the time and desperate to get out – but Liam had gone along with the suggestion willingly enough. He liked having someone to clean up after him.

In the eighteen months since then, she has discovered that, for all his sex appeal, Liam is selfish, petty and frequently bad-tempered. If she had somewhere to go, she would leave. But she doesn't. With her mother abroad and her father out of the picture, she has no family home to move back to. And each time she reaches the end of her last nerve with Liam, he turns on that irresistible charm of his and pulls her in again. They row, and then they end up in bed having angry make-up sex. Over and over in an endless cycle.

Perhaps Siobhan will offer support, given that she has strongly disapproved of the relationship from the start. Keren flicks idly through her phone, pulls up her sister's WhatsApp and types.

Was thinking maybe could come visit

She adds a heart emoji, hesitates a few seconds, then presses the send icon.

Siobhan replies a few minutes later.

Hey stranger?! Yes sure sis, let me know times.

This is followed by a kiss-blowing emoji.

Keren puts her phone down with a sigh. If she plans a trip to see Siobhan, Liam will only kick off. He knows that her sister thinks he's a lowlife and, as a result, they've not seen each other since the relationship began. He's pretty much banned it.

Keren hasn't raised the issue of the unpaid rent with him, but she does so when he eventually returns. He's had a few drinks, and this always mellows him enough for her to be able to tackle him without him flying off the handle.

'Ah, forget about the fucking rent,' he says. 'What are they going to do about it?'

'Can you do some extra shifts, get the money that way? Because I don't get paid again for another three weeks.'

Liam works shifts as a warehouse supervisor, and does the occasional small removal job, using a transit van that officially belongs to Lance. He did well at school and constantly surprises Keren with how clever he is, but has never managed to hold down a decent job, mostly because he ends up falling out with – and sometimes fighting with – his superiors. He simply can't toe the line: any line. 'Doubt it,' he sniffs. 'I mean, it's a zero-hours contract, isn't it? They only use me when they absolutely have to. They're cutting back right now anyway, not handing out more work.'

A few days later, a letter arrives from the landlord's solicitor, demanding they cover the unpaid rent arrears immediately. Keren does as Liam says and forgets about it. She tears up the letter and thrusts it to the bottom of the kitchen bin.

Returning from the nursery the following Friday, she goes to insert her key in the Yale lock and it immediately sticks. Only then does she notice the heaps of black bin bags on the communal landing, overflowing onto the staircase. She peers into one and sees a selection of her underwear, one of Liam's shoes and a tub of hair gel. The TV and the triangular dumb-bell stand are propped in a corner. She tries the key again and sees the bright, shiny brass of a new lock barrel.

'Oh shit!'

She fumbles at her phone with shaking fingers. Liam picks up straightaway, but his response is a barked 'What?' He hates her calling him while he's at work.

'I'm at the flat. The locks have been changed and all our stuff has been taken out.'

A volley of expletives follows, and half an hour later, Liam returns to find Keren sitting miserably on the top step amid the forest of black bags.

'What the fuck?' he demands, as though this is somehow of her doing.

'The landlord must have waited till we were both out and then done it.'

Liam swears again, but no amount of his swearing and blustering about finding the landlord and 'shanking' him, as he describes it, is going to change the situation. According to the letter of the law, he should have given them formal notice of eviction, but without being able to pay the rent arrears, they have no hope of getting their tenancy reinstated, and they certainly can't afford to start legal proceedings.

'So now we're bloody homeless,' Keren says, wiping away tears with her sleeve.

'I'll chuck our stuff in the back of the truck and we can doss at Lance's. Just till we can get somewhere else.'

'But we can't get somewhere else without money!' Keren wails.

'Got any better ideas?' Liam snarls, snatching up a fistful of the black plastic bags and charging down the stairs with them.

Keren thinks of Lance's squalid one room flat. It's barely more than a bedsit and smells of weed and bad drains. The grimy nylon carpet, which they will have to sleep on, is stained and embedded with stale toast crumbs.

I'm going to have to leave him now, she thinks, as she wearily carries a couple of bags down to the street. *I'm really going to have to do it.*

SIXTEEN

MARCH

'Sweet for you to crash here,' says Lance, who despite his criminal past is more good-natured than his brother. 'Only, tomorrow, I'm having a couple of mates over.'

A 'couple of mates' turns out, in the end, to be a full-blown party, with at least thirty assorted bodies crammed into the tiny flat, smoking weed, spilling beer and playing music so loud that at least two of the other residents of the block hammer on the door to complain. The last of the guests finally leaves just before four and Keren, who has been pressed miserably against a wall all evening, shuffles the grimy sofa cushions onto the floor and lies down next to Liam, her limbs spilling over the edge of the cushions onto carpet sticky with drink and powdered with cigarette ash.

They sleep until ten. Desperate for a decent cup of tea, Keren volunteers to buy breakfast for them all at the greasy spoon a few doors away. Liam sits morosely swigging from a mug of coffee and staring at his phone, while Lance tucks into a full English and shares a pot of strong tea with Keren.

'You two seen this?' Liam asks suddenly, showing them his screen. 'This ad keeps popping up on my Facebook feed.'

Lance sets down his fork and squints, then shows it to Keren.

Prodomus Million-Pound House Draw

Become a millionaire overnight! Spring is here, so why not celebrate by giving yourself the chance to win this fully-furnished house in one of South London's loveliest roads, worth £3 million. Beautifully designed and decorated, it features five bedrooms, four of which are en suite, and a wonderful garden. Not ready to move? No problem, you could rent it out for £15,000 a month. Or you could sell and become a multimillionaire overnight. The choice is yours!

Draw closes in: OD 8H 36M 51S

Keren looks at the picture of what to her is a rather severe detached period house with eight big sash windows and a porticoed front door.

'Mug's game, innit?' Lance sneers. 'Like the National Lottery.'

But Liam is reading the small print.

'How much money you got in your account?' he asks Keren.

'Only about a hundred and fifty quid, why?'

'And I've got about a hundred cash for a clearance job I did...' He pulls five twenty-pound notes from his jeans pocket and thrusts them at Keren. 'It says here the maximum number of entries is 450, and that costs £200. So here's my half of the stake. We'll each pay a hundred and buy the maximum. Using your card.'

'Mug's game,' repeats Lance, shovelling baked beans into his mouth.

'I don't know...' Keren is frowning. 'I mean, there must be millions of people entering.'

'What have we got to lose?' asks Liam.

'Everything,' says Lance with a grin. 'Pretty much. If you've only got £250 between you and nowhere to live.'

'Yeah, but what if we win,' Liam exhales, and he has that trance-like look on his face. 'Think how fucking awesome it would be.'

'Oh my God, oh my God! I don't fucking believe this!' Three days later, Lance returns from his job at a print shop in Catford and barrels through the door of his flat, waving a copy of the local newspaper. Then he stops in his tracks, staring down at the page more closely. His brow furrows. 'Oh wait... hang on.' He tosses the paper down onto the stained sofa. 'I thought for a minute you two had won that bleeding house, but it's just a couple who look like you.'

'Let me see,' Liam snatches up the paper.

'I know we haven't won it,' Keren says flatly. 'I had to put my email on the form, and the draw was yesterday. I'd have been told already if we'd won it.'

'I see what you mean, though,' says Liam. 'They do look a bit like us. Quite a lot like us, actually. She's mixed race like you, and if you add glasses and take away all the shredding from the gym, I could totally be him. Look, Kez!'

But Keren's not interested in reading about the lucky winners. Instead, she's withdrawn into herself, her brain chewing over and over how she's going to live on £50 until the end of the month, like a dog with a bone. She shakes her head and bats the paper away.

'Look!' Liam insists, tapping her arm with it.

Reluctantly, she takes it from him and looks at the article.

Parents win dream home in fundraiser for children's cancer charity

Richard Hamlin (31) and his wife Stephanie (29) have won a multimillion-pound property in South London in the Prodomus fundraising draw for Young Cancer UK. The couple entered the draw, which has raised over half a million pounds for the charity, in February with the purchase of a £25 ticket. Stephanie, a part-time visual merchandiser, and Richard, a chartered accountant, are parents to nine-month-old baby Poppy.

'Oh my God!' Her hand flies up to her mouth. 'That is so weird!'

'What?' demands Liam, taking the paper back from her and looking at the photo again.

'I know her. The wife. Her kid's at Stepping Stones, in the room I work in. Remember I told you one of the mums had made a complaint about me the other week? Well, it was her: Stephanie Hamlin.'

'Mental coincidence,' Lance agrees.

'From the sound of it, they've got money already,' Liam spits angrily. 'Why do they get to win it and not us, when it's us who really needs it?'

'I don't think they've got loads,' Keren points out. 'I know they're living in a rented place while they save up the deposit to buy. I heard her talking to one of the other mums about it.'

'They're still loads better off than us. So why do they deserve it?'

'Because they were the ones that bought the winning ticket,' Keren says flatly.

'Yeah, but they only spent the minimum, and we bought as many as possible. Two hundred pounds' worth!'

'You don't know that,' she says hotly, but Lance points to the line in the article where it says they bought a £25 entry.

Liam isn't listening to her anyway. He rants on and on about the injustice of the situation, becoming more and more worked up and increasingly angry about an imaginary bias in the system. Keren has seen him like this so many times before. Within a few minutes, he's pretty much convinced himself that he and Keren are the rightful winners of the house and the Hamlins have somehow taken it from them.

He fetches a six-pack of lager cans from the fridge and tosses one to his brother before cracking one open for himself.

'But, listen, there's obviously one very good thing here, yeah?'

'What's that?' Lance demands.

'The fact that these people... the Hamlins... they look weirdly like us. It's almost uncanny.' Liam scrapes his fingertips through the stubble on his chin, thinking. 'I mean, one way of looking at it is that it's a coincidence, right? But the way I see it, it's like fate. It's the universe saying this is meant to be.'

'What is, bruv?'

'If the house has been won by a couple exactly like us... why can't it *be* us?'

Keren feels a curdling sensation in her stomach. 'Liam!' she warns.

But he's on a roll now. 'And the fact Kez works at their nursery... that's even better. It means we can find out their address.'

Lance's eyes flash in his brother's direction. He takes a swift gulp of his beer. 'Are you saying?' He draws his forefinger across his throat in a slashing gesture.

'Nah, I'm not saying we do them, no. But what if we can get them out of the way long enough to get our hands on the keys to that house...'

Lance grins, warming to the idea of a criminal enterprise. 'We could go over there one night with my van, get the Hamlins into it, then you two pose as them when the keys are handed over.'

'Nah,' Liam's shaking his head. 'Neighbours might see something, or might have CCTV. Too risky. Plus they've got a kid, haven't they? It might scream the place down. No, we've got to be a bit cleverer than that. We need to get some stuff printed at your place.'

Lance nods enthusiastically. 'Easy enough to do.'

'And we'd need to get our hands on a decent motor. Then all we have to do is go over there and convince them that we're from the charity auction company. Make it look legit.' He glances in Keren's direction. She's shaking her head. 'What's up with you?' he demands impatiently.

'I don't want to be involved, okay?'

'Come on, Kez. We're in this together, right? You're my partner: that means we do stuff together. We bought the house draw tickets together, remember?'

'But we didn't win!' Keren shouts. She rolls up the copy of the newspaper and hurls it across the room, knocking over the one lamp in the place. Then, since she no longer has a bedroom to call her own, she stamps into Lance's bedroom shouting, 'I'm not doing it!' before slamming the door with a violent crash.

Liam leaves her stewing in Lance's room for a while, then comes in and sits down on the floor next to her. There was no way she was going to sit in the balled, stained mess of Lance's bedclothes. He takes her hand.

'Look, don't you want a home, babe? A proper home. Not to sleep on the floor in Lance's lounge?'

'Of course I do,' she says fiercely without meeting his gaze. 'But not like this.'

'But like we've just said, when you break it down, we've got as much right to that house as those Hamlins have. More, given we bought more tickets. So what are we doing wrong?'

'Everything,' Keren says glumly. 'And you and Lance know it.'

Liam starts stroking her arm, up and down, up and down, caressing her shoulder. 'Tell you what, how about if we sell the house and share the money with them, fifty-fifty? That would be more than fair, right? 'Specially since they've got a lot more than we have to start with.'

The rhythmic stroking continues. 'But what would you do with them in the meantime? The Hamlins?'

'We'll find somewhere for them to stay for a bit, just while we sort out selling the house and dividing up the proceeds.'

Keren looks at him doubtfully. In her mind's eye, she's seeing a clean, comfortable bedroom, a spacious well-fitted bathroom. She doesn't want to stay with Liam, but she does want those things. And she can have a share of the money surely, once they've got it? Once she has money, she won't have to stay with him. She could head out to Ireland and join her mum. Or go to Ghana, where her father's family are from. She's always wanted to visit Africa. 'But the Hamlins aren't going to just, you know, go along with it. They'll report us to the house charity, or the police.'

Liam's fingers pause on her arm. 'That's just it; we'll persuade them not to. If they don't go along with it, we'll, you know... make things tricky for them.'

'I don't like it,' Keren's shaking her head. 'I just don't think it'll work. Even if we can make the Hamlins agree, other people are going to notice. People who know us.'

'My mum's dead and my dad's in the nick. You don't even know your dad, and you never see your mum or your sister. And Lance – he's completely on board. We'll just have to bung him a bit of cash and he'll be golden.'

'But the Hamlins will already have told people they're

moving to the house they've just won. People will want to visit; their friends and family.'

'There are ways of sorting that,' Liam says darkly. He squeezes her right thigh.

'All right, but I'm not doing it, not if I have to go with you when you... visit... the Hamlins.'

'Course not, you muppet. The wife'd recognise you.'

She scowls at him, edging her leg away from his.

'Anyway, we'll need you to deal with the kid.'

Keren lets out a long sigh, shaking her head.

'Come on, Kez, it's you and me against the world, right?'

That's what he always used to say when they first met. It isn't true, of course, as Keren discovered pretty quickly. Instead, it's Liam's world and you live in it according to his rules. But now he needs her, she realises. He needs her because without her his chances of pulling off this mad scheme are absolutely zero.

And with this realisation, a thrill courses through her. For the first time since they got together, it's she who has the power. The feeling is unfamiliar, but she likes it.

SEVENTEEN

APRIL

Keren's instructions are that she must go to work on Thursday and behave as if everything is absolutely normal. Only when she gets word from either Liam or Lance must she put her own part of the operation into practice. But she's jumpy and on edge the entire day, certain her co-workers must be able to hear the thunder of her heart slamming against her ribs. Getting through the daily nursery routine is made even harder by the fact that she's in the baby room with Chloe, who has a raging case of PMS and keeps snapping at her about the slightest little thing.

The plan has to be commenced on a Thursday because it's the only day of the week when Poppy Hamlin is at nursery and her parents are at home together. Going to their individual offices would be too complicated, given that one works in the West End and the other in the City. But in addition to knowing the Hamlins' home address, Keren knows their routine. So she knows that both Stephanie and Richard work from home on a Thursday.

This morning, she drove to work rather than taking the bus, making sure she was the first staff member apart from Ruth Buckby to arrive at the nursery. While Ruth was shut in her

office, Keren took the spare car seat that was kept in the storeroom for emergencies and carried it out to her red Citroen.

Eventually, just after five o'clock, the text arrives, from
Lance's phone.

All sorted. Over to you.

It's followed by another message, one that makes Keren's
pulse race even faster. It's a location pin, giving the address of
the house. The million-pound dream house.

Poppy is usually collected at around five thirty on a Thursday. Keren leaves the baby room for a believable interval, then
comes back in and gathers up the changing bag containing
Poppy's spare nappies, a bottle, baby food and her favourite
blue blanket, hoisting the baby up onto her hip.

'Stephanie Hamlin's outside on a double yellow,' she tells
Chloe. 'She's asked if I can take her out to the car. Won't be a
sec.'

Chloe, in the midst of changing a dirty nappy, grunts assent
without looking round.

Keren carries Poppy to her own car and clips her into the
seat. Climbing into the front seat, she strips off the yellow polo
shirt with 'Keren' embroidered on the front and pulls on a spare
T-shirt left on the front passenger seat. Then, without going
back into the nursery to clock off, and ignoring the baby's cries
of distress, she drives away.

Liam has told her that he and Lance won't be arriving at the
dream house until at least seven thirty, so she drives aimlessly
around in the South London traffic, with Poppy dozing in her
seat. When she finally wakes up, Keren takes her to McDon-
ald's and passes some more time feeding her fries and spoonfuls
of McFlurry. Eventually, she puts the baby back in the car seat
and drives to the address she was sent by text before she left the
nursery.

She recognises the house from the promotional material, but what she wasn't expecting was how grand the surroundings would be: the sweeping curve of the crescent, the park-like green space at the centre of Sycamore Gardens, the grandeur of the architecture.

I don't belong in a place like this, is her first thought. Then she catches sight of Liam's pickup truck pulling up, and the two brothers unloading bags of their belongings, the bags that had been tossed out onto the landing of their old place. *We don't belong here*, she corrects herself.

She stares for a minute, then removes the grizzling Poppy from her seat and carries her up the front path and into the house.

'Amazing, innit?' grins Liam, waving a hand around the huge kitchen with its newly fitted teal-blue units and state-of-the-art appliances. 'Can you believe it, Kez, us living in a place like this?'

Keren glances into the ground-floor reception rooms. The furnishings are tasteful but bland, in shades of cream and beige. It reminds her of the décor in a hotel lobby. Personally, she can't imagine ever feeling at home in a place like this. But then, they're not going to be living here, not for long. They've got to get it sold as quickly as possible and move on.

'You should see the bathroom, Kez, the en suite. It's like something out of a movie.'

'Is there a baby's room?' she demands.

'Nah, not as such. There's a couple of rooms with kiddie beds in.'

'But no cot?'

Liam shakes his head, and Keren tips her head in the direction of the squirming child on her hip.

'What are we going to do with her, then? We're supposed to be her parents, remember... so where's she going to sleep?'

'We'll figure something out tomorrow, okay. Just chill out for now. Come and have a beer. Or you can have some champagne. Prodomus have left a bottle in the fridge for us, with this.' He waves a letter. 'Says all the final checks have been carried out, and we're now free to enjoy our new home.'

Stephanie props Poppy on one of the sofas in the family room end of the huge kitchen and finds a rusk for her in the changing bag. She made sure she brought enough food, milk and nappies to tide them over the first night at least.

The doorbell rings, and the three adults glance at each other, alarmed.

'Go see who it is, Kez,' says Liam. 'And if it's anyone official, get rid of them.'

Keren opens the door to a middle-aged woman, holding flowers and what looks like a lunchbox. She's wearing the sort of jeans Keren's mum wears, and a flowery top. Her shoulder-length blonde hair is wispy and untamed, and her face has a sort of faded prettiness. Keren looks down at the stranger's feet, which have unvarnished nails emerging from battered Birkenstocks. Imagine not painting your toenails, Keren thinks.

The woman smiles broadly and holds out the flowers and the plastic box. 'Hi, I'm Jane Headley. We live at number five: my husband Fergus and I. I just wanted to come and say welcome to Sycamore Gardens, and to give you these.'

'Thanks,' says Keren. She turns and walks back into the kitchen, thinking the woman will just leave, but she follows. Keren puts down the flowers and plastic box of what looks like cakes on the worktop.

'How are you managing?' the woman asks. 'Moving's such a nightmare. I expect you'll be glad when your husband gets here to help you.'

Liam holds out his hand for her to shake, but doesn't bother to stand up. 'Richard Hamlin. Nice to meet you.' He indicates Lance, who's emptying the contents of a can down his throat, and Keren wonders what he's going to say. 'This is my brother... Elliott.'

'Oh, gosh, I'm sorry,' Their neighbour blushes, as though she's said something embarrassing. 'I thought... It's just that we saw your picture in the news and you were wearing glasses, so I...'

Liam pulls out some glasses from his tracksuit bottoms and Keren realises with a sickening sensation that he must have taken them from the real Richard Hamlin. 'Lenses,' he explains, pointing at his eyes. 'Only wear the bins sometimes. You know, for work and that.'

'I see, sorry.' Their neighbour appears to notice the baby for the first time. 'You don't have a highchair.'

Talk about stating the obvious, Keren thinks irritably. She just wants this woman, this Jane, to leave.

'That's awkward for you. I'm just trying to think which of the neighbours might have one you can borrow. The Perrys at number nineteen might: they've got a little one who's recently grown past that stage. I'm afraid my two are far too old for me still to have baby equipment.'

''S okay,' Liam says, the lies coming to him easily. 'We've got one, we just haven't brought it over yet. There's more stuff we need to go back and fetch.'

Keren goes and picks up Poppy, swaying her on her hip to quieten her.

Lance, oblivious to the drama, is reaching into the box that Jane brought and pulling out a piece of flapjack, which he shoves into his mouth whole

'Well, as I said, I'm at number five, and I'm sure I can ask around for baby stuff for you to borrow until your own gets here. Do you have a cot?'

'She'll come in with us, just till the cot gets here, you know,' Keren says, thinking *just go, will you?*

Finally, Jane takes the hint and heads back towards the hall, saying 'I'll leave you to get on with it, shall I? I expect you've got loads to do.' They don't show her out.

'Pretty slick, bruv,' Lance observes once they're alone again. He eats two more of the flapjacks. 'You handled that like a pro.'

'Next time, it'll be one of their friends or family, not just a neighbour,' Keren says darkly. 'What the hell do we do then?'

'Relax.' Liam rummages for his discarded hoodie and pulls out two mobile phones from the pocket. 'Got the Hamlins' phones, and we checked their social media. He comes from Wales, and her family are all up north somewhere.'

'What about their friends, though?'

'They haven't given anyone this address yet.' Liam sounds confident, happy almost. *He's loving this*, Keren thinks. *Loving it a bit too bloody much.* 'And anyone who wants to come and visit, we're just going to have to put them off.'

'What d'you mean?' Keren demands.

He tosses her one of the phones. 'Here – this one's hers. I've disabled the passcode. You need to stay on top of all her messages from her mates and her family, okay, just enough so that no one gets worried. Just give chatty answers, but don't commit to any meetups. Blame the move for being too busy. Stay engaged, but keep responses to the minimum, okay? Look at previous messages she's sent to see how she signs off: kisses and that. I'll do his. That way, we can keep everyone at bay long enough to get this place sold.'

Keren stares down at the phone.

'Okay, Kez?'

'Okay,' she agrees.

'And keep that bloody kid under control; she's doing my nut.'

Poppy has started shrieking again. Keren finds a bottle of formula from the changing bag and after a few false starts manages to heat it in the new microwave. She sits on the sofa with the baby on her lap, and Poppy falls asleep, the bottle teat still in her mouth. Poor thing must be so confused, Keren thinks, with a pang. And she's not the only one wondering where her parents have got to.

'What have you done with them?' she demands, as she stands up and carefully transfers Poppy from her lap to the sofa. 'The Hamlins. Where are they?'

'You don't need to worry about them,' Liam's slurring slightly now. He's drunk all the lager and is now starting on the complimentary champagne. 'They're right where they need to be for now. All tucked up, like their kid here,' he points a trainer-clad foot in Poppy's direction. 'Nice and safe.'

EIGHTEEN

APRIL

When Keren wakes the next morning, it takes her a while to work out where she is. Sunshine is streaming from a large sash window over a set of pristine white bedlinen. This bed is without doubt the most comfortable she's ever slept on in her life. And the biggest; she's sharing it with Liam and yet he's feet away from her.

She turns her head to the right and starts slightly at the sight of a single mattress on the floor next to her, with a primitive rail of cushions created round the edge. Poppy Hamlin is lying at its centre wearing a pink Babygro and clutching her blue blanket. Her eyelids start to flutter open, and she opens and closes her tiny fists.

'Here,' Liam pulls himself up against the opulent pile of down pillows and tosses her Stephanie Hamlin's phone. 'You need to check for messages and let her work know she's not coming in. I'll do his. The last thing we need is people they work with asking questions about where they are.'

Typical Liam; his mind already leaping forward a mile a minute.

'Stephanie doesn't work on Fridays,' Keren points out. 'She's part-time. And he's probably booked time off for the move.'

'Well, find an email address for her work and send her employers one anyway. Tell them she's resigning. You might be able to convince the people round here that you're Stephanie Hamlin, but you're hardly going to cut it at her office are you, even if you do look just like her.' He gives a little snort of derision and holds up Richard Hamlin's phone. 'I'm just emailing his HR to tell them he's leaving. I'm saying he's ill so they won't expect him to work out his notice.' He goes back to scrolling, 'Oh, and you'd better quit your own job at the nursery too. And email them from Stephanie's account telling them you're going to be a stay-at-home mum, so to take her' – he points in Poppy's direction – 'off their list or whatever.'

'But I—'

'Look, you can hardly go back there, not now we're lumbered with the kid.'

'*I'm* lumbered, you mean,' Keren counters sourly.

As if on cue, Poppy rolls over and pulls herself up to sitting, her lower lip wobbling when she looks for the faces of her parents and fails to find them. Keren reaches down for her and hauls her up onto the bed, playing shadow puppets with the blue blanket until she elicits a hesitant smile.

'If I jack in my job, what am I supposed to do for money?' She starts looking through the contents of Stephanie's phone.

Liam points to a tallboy in the corner of the room, where he's put the keys and wallets that he took from the Hamlins. 'We'll use their bank accounts to withdraw cash. It'll only raise the alarm anyway, if they're not used at all.'

Keren looks up again. 'There's a text here from Stephanie's mum asking for the new address so she can send flowers. And her sister's asking when she can come down for a visit.'

'Put them off,' Liam says tersely. 'Whatever you do, don't let them know the address. It'll be game over if they rock up.'

'But what shall I say? If I refuse to tell them, it's bound to make them suspicious.'

'Say you're getting change-of-address cards printed up and sent out.' Liam scratches his chin. 'And say they can come down and visit in the summer, when the weather's better and they can make the most of the garden.'

Not for the first time, Keren is astonished by how Liam's brain works. Too clever for his own good, that's what Siobhan once said about him, and she was right.

He climbs off the bed and walks naked towards the en-suite bathroom, scratching his backside with one hand and frowning at the screen of Richard Hamlin's phone. 'Shit. There's an email from the landlord of their old place, thanking them for giving notice that they're moving out.' Liam exhales hard, a sort of whistling sound. 'We're going to have to get back round there and clear the place out, or this geezer's going to wonder what's going on.'

'We need to go and get the baby stuff anyway,' Keren points out, tugging on her threadbare towelling bathrobe and lifting Poppy off the bed. 'The neighbours will think it's weird if we don't.' She sets off in the direction of the stairs.

'Lance will have to help us,' Liam calls over the banisters. 'We'll need his van.'

'Just make sure it's this morning,' Keren shouts back as she flicks the kettle to boil. 'I'm never going to manage unless we have a buggy.'

She makes tea for herself and a bottle for Poppy, then composes a text to Ruth Buckby.

I'm afraid I won't be able to come to work until further notice, as my mother has been taken very ill and I have to go over to Ireland.

Displeasure is evident in the one-word reply: *Noted.*

The Hamlins' former home is a spacious first-floor flat in an Edwardian conversion in Herne Hill. Before Lance has even got the key in the front door, they're deafened by a volley of barks. Poppy squeals with pleasure.

'A dog?' Keren demands. 'You didn't say they had a bloody dog!'

'To be honest, I forgot about it,' Liam says, with a shrug.

'How could you forget?'

'Oh, you know, maybe because we had one or two other things to think about.' He's sarcastic now.

'I put down some food for it,' Lance tells her.

The dog clearly remembers this act of kindness because it barrels out and starts jumping up and licking his face. It's an ugly, brutish sort of beast, and not at all the sort of pet that Keren would have paired with the Hamlins.

'I reckon he must be a rescue,' Lance says as though reading her mind. He bends down and examines the tag on its collar. 'Says he's called Buster.'

Poppy is wriggling to get down, having recognised the toys neatly stacked in one corner of the sitting room. It's a bright, cosy place with stripped wooden floorboards, lots of house-plants and shelves filled with books, some of which have already been placed into open packing cases.

Liam grimaces. 'What the hell are we going to do with all of these?'

Keren ignores him, finding a large backpack in the hall cupboard and setting about filling it with Poppy's toys and clothes. 'I don't care what you do with any of it, as long as you bring back the cot and the highchair, okay?'

Once she's gathered as much as she can carry, she dresses

the baby in clean clothes and straps her into the expensive, all-terrain buggy that takes up most of the space in the hall.

'Right, we're going to get the tube back. See you at the house.'

'Guess we'll just have to take all this lot down the tip,' Lance reaches into the fridge and pulls out a can of Coke and a chocolate bar. 'At least they've made a start on packing it up.'

'You can't do that,' Keren says hotly. 'The Hamlins are going to want their stuff back.'

'We'll take it to my mate Derren's lockup then, okay?' suggests Lance.

Keren has already turned her back to wheel the buggy out of the front door, so she doesn't see the look exchanged by the two brothers. A look that says, 'And pigs might fly.'

As she rounds the curve of Sycamore Gardens, pushing a sleeping Poppy in the buggy, Keren passes number 5, and remembers it's where the nosy neighbour Jane said she lived.

Two people are standing on the top step outside the front door: a man and a younger woman. The man is tall and greying, but although he's old enough to be Keren's father, she can appreciate that he's good-looking in a conventional way. The girl certainly isn't Jane. She's much younger; petite and fine-boned, with olive skin and balayaged hair styled in a very on-trend wavy bob. His daughter perhaps? Didn't Jane say she had grown-up kids?

Then he bends his head and kisses the woman on the mouth. Not the daughter then. It's a hasty kiss, but there's real passion and intensity in the way it's delivered. Keren's kissed enough boys in her time to know that you don't kiss someone like that unless you really fancy them. He immediately retreats behind the closed front door, leaving the girl to run down the steps and onto the pavement. Keren watches the girl walk quickly down Sycamore Gardens, glancing around as though she's afraid of being seen. So who is the man? Keren wonders. It could be Jane's brother, or a friend who's staying with them. But even as she's deciding this, her gut instinct is telling her she's wrong. If he lives there, then that man has to be Jane's husband.

NINETEEN

APRIL

The next morning, all Keren wants to do is have a long lie-in in the huge and comfortable bed. Then she wants to amble to a coffee shop to meet a friend and enjoy an iced caramel frappuccino with extra cream, followed by a bit of aimless shopping.

What she doesn't want to do is drag herself up at six-thirty to deal with a leaky nappy, a cranky baby and a change of cot bedding. Even if she does now have a fabulous utility room with brand new washer and dryer.

'Don't bring that bloody kid back in here,' Liam grunts from under the duvet, once she's sorted the poo-smeared Poppy and put clean sheets on the cot.

'But she's up now, she can come in here with us.'

'No!' Liam snaps.

With a sigh, Keren takes Poppy downstairs to the kitchen and puts her in the highchair, distracting her with a handful of Hula Hoops while she puts the kettle on. This is it for the foreseeable, she realises. She's stuck with looking after the Hamlins' child round the clock. She likes children, otherwise she wouldn't have applied for the job at Stepping Stones in the first place, but not all the time. She's certainly not ready to have a baby of her own, and yet here she is, with a baby. When she's tried to push Liam on the subject of the baby and what on earth they're going to do with her, he just says that he'll sort it. Nothing more.

While Liam and Lance disappear to do God knows what, Keren pushes Poppy around in her buggy, trying to get her to sleep. She can't remember when she last felt so miserable. Here they are amidst all these beautifully manicured gardens and blossom-filled trees, living in what would once have been her dream house, and yet this is as far from a dream as she can imagine. She's never wanted to break up with Liam more, and yet she's never been so tied to him. Having a bank account in her own name means absolutely nothing now, she thinks, as she trudges up Sycamore Gardens in the direction of the main road.

She heads past number 5 and catches sight of Jane Headley. The woman is watching her through the window, even though she ducks out of sight and pretends not to be.

Sure enough, when Keren comes back from the shops, with Poppy now not only awake but in full-blown tantrum mode, she's barely just let herself in the front door, when Jane rings the bell.

'Hello again. I saw you going past just now and...'

Keren folds her arms and says nothing, hoping the woman will take the hint and go away.

'I wondered... I know it's a bit of a nightmare getting everything sorted out when you first move... is there any help you need?'

Keren catches sight of Liam's truck turning into the Gardens. Behind her, Poppy lets out a wail.

'Got to go,' she says quickly, and closes the door.

But, of course, Liam has seen. He always does.

'What the fuck did she want?' he demands as soon as he's inside. 'Bloody busybody.'

'Just offering help.' Keren carries on unpacking the groceries she has just bought with Stephanie Hamlin's debit card.

'Well, stay away from her, okay? And the other neighbours. We can't afford to let people get too close, or they'll start asking awkward questions.'

He snatches a can of lager from the fridge and takes it out into the garden, gazing around at its magnificence. He lights a cigarette and lies back on one of the rattan loungers with it, looking every bit at home in these upmarket surroundings. Keren would like to go outside and join him, but she's got the baby to deal with. *Bloody Poppy*, she thinks as she plonks a crate of building blocks in front of her with a resentful slam.

'What I don't get is why the baby can't be with the Hamlins.'

After she's finally fed Poppy and put her in her cot, Keren opens the sliding door and goes to join Liam in the garden. He's still drinking beer, smoking and scrolling through his phone – or, more accurately, phones – since he also has Richard Hamlin's handset with him. She's poured herself a can of Coke and added a generous slug of vodka. Brushing blossom petals off the seat first, she sits down on one of the garden chairs.

'Because, firstly, where they are isn't suitable for a kid.' Liam blows an aggressive jet of smoke in the direction of the sky. Now that the sun's going down, it's growing cold outside. 'And, secondly, think about it: all the press stuff says that this house has been won by a young couple with a baby daughter. We rock up here without a baby and people are going to think it's a bit suss.'

'So where are they?' Keren demands.

'In a safe place, that's all you need to know.' He waggles Richard Hamlin's handset in her direction. 'I hope you've been checking her phone, Kez. Keeping on top of messages, liking stuff on her socials. Making things look normal.'

She takes a long swig of her vodka and Coke. 'Are they

somewhere in London?'

'Like I said,' Liam mutters darkly. 'You don't need to know.'

On Monday morning, while Liam is taking an age under the en-suite's walk-in rain shower, Keren takes his phone off the charger by the bed and enters the passcode. She goes straight to his mapping app and checks on the location search history. She knows that Liam uses it as a navigation tool when he's driving somewhere, and that he or Lance will almost certainly have entered where they've been into the map's search function. She immediately recognises the street address of the Hamlins' flat in Herne Hill, and above it there's one more recent entry.

Eastmeade Fort

She checks the location on the map. It's on the far edge of the North Kent marshes, on the southern bank of the Thames east of Gravesend. The sidebar next to it tells her that East-meade is a disused artillery fort once used to protect the Thames from attack by the French, but now semi-derelict and not open to the public. And then she vaguely remembers Liam telling her about having an aunt and uncle in Kent and playing with his twin brother on the mudflats of the wetlands during school summer holidays. He's talked very little about his family life, and that particular anecdote stuck in Keren's mind. Maybe because the idea of a happy, carefree Liam seemed so far removed from the angry, resentful man he is now.

She puts Liam's phone back on the charger, dresses in jogging bottoms and a sleeveless Lycra top, and with the shower still hissing loudly behind the bathroom door, she fetches Poppy from her cot. Once she's given her a rusk and strapped her into her buggy, she pushes it briskly to the Headleys' house.

'Hiya,' she says when Jane answers, arranging her features

into what she hopes is a friendly expression and gives a self-conscious little wave.

Apparently, Jane has a job – something that didn't occur to Keren – and is on her way to it now. She says she won't be back until the afternoon.

'Only you know you said you would help? Well, I need someone to mind the baby for me. I have to go somewhere. Somewhere I can't – you know – take her. Because you said you'd had kids of your own and that...'

'Of course,' Jane smiles, but it looks a bit forced. 'I don't see why not.'

'Thanks. See you here later, yeah?' Keren turns the buggy around, but Jane is following her.

'Actually, wouldn't it be better if I came over to you? All Poppy's stuff's there... save you dragging it over here.'

Shit. That's the last thing she needs. There's no way she wants Liam twigging what she's up to. 'No,' she says quickly. 'He... Richard... my husband... he wouldn't like it. Having a stranger in the house.'

So Jane agrees to have Poppy at her own place after she gets back from work that afternoon. It's later than ideal, given the distance Keren needs to travel, and she's on edge for the rest of the day, using the time to do some unpacking and tidying, checking out train times and withdrawing more money from the cash machine using Stephanie's card.

At four o'clock promptly, she returns to number 5 and hands over Poppy, who immediately makes a beeline for the Headleys' cat. Jane seems highly organised and acts as though she can take care of a ten-month-old with her eyes closed. She'll probably make a much better job of it than Keren does, and it's this thought that allows her to walk off down Sycamore Gardens with a spring in her step, unencumbered at last.

And then she remembers where's she going. And how afraid she is of what she's going to find when she gets there.

TWENTY

APRIL

There are direct trains to Gravesend every hour, and Keren arrives at St Pancras with about two minutes to spare before the 16.25 pulls out of the platform.

The train may be fast, but from her online research earlier that day, she's calculated that from the edge of the town nearest the marshes, it's still at least a forty-minute walk to Eastmeade, and the only way to get there is on foot, along something called the Saxon Shore Way. If her hunch is right, and the Hamlins are hidden at the fort, then what on earth are they doing for food and drink? Surely Liam and Lance wouldn't have left them there with nothing at all. Unless....

Unless they're not alive anymore.

But, no, she pushes that thought back to where it came from. No, Lance may have a record for petty crime and Liam may be dodgy, but he's not that dodgy. They're not killers.

It seems wrong to go empty-handed, so Keren finds a supermarket near the station. Faced with the enormity of what this shopping list represents, her mind goes blank and she just stares at the shelves. Stuff in tins? But how will they open them? Cheese? No, rats might eat it. In the end, she buys water, crisps, energy bars, wet wipes and tampons and jumps on a bus that drops her at the very outskirts of the town.

The road ends abruptly fifty yards from the bus stop, and beyond it are just empty skies filled with shrill birds and wide bays of mud. It's not a romantic or pretty sort of landscape, just derelict industrial buildings, clumps of barbed wire and broken barges. She sees the occasional walker, but most of the time, it's just her and black-necked geese marching along the water's edge.

It's nearly six o'clock by the time she finally sees the low, hunched outline of the fort on the cliff's edge. It's built of pale granite and has openings like window casements, through which the guns must have been pointed. Keren's back is aching from trudging along with heavy shopping bags, and her shoes are soaked from the long walk across the marshy ground. She approaches the building uncertainly.

'Hello?'

There's no response. The information online had said something about underground munitions storage, and after walking around the perimeter for a while, she finds a set of steep stone steps with a door at their foot. The door is made of thick planks, partly rotted in places. Keren slides on the steps, losing her footing and almost dropping the bags of food. Can this bleak, forsaken place really be where the brothers decided to bring the Hamlins?

She pushes hard on the door and it gives way. There's another, shorter flight of steps, leading to a warren of different chambers. It takes a few seconds for her eyes to become accustomed to the darkness. It's not total darkness, because the storage areas are linked by a passageway that has purpose-built light wells, and outside, the sun has not yet set.

'Oh, thank God,' says a voice, and Keren's thought, before she's even seen who's speaking, is a terrible one. One that didn't even occur to her until this point.

They think I've come to rescue them.

For a few seconds, Keren's so dizzy with shock that she feels as though she'll pass out. She has to fumble to the side of her and use the wall as support. Because there they are, the Hamlins, in one of the purpose-built munitions stores.

Once she's calmed her breathing a little, she's able to take stock of the situation. There are large iron loops cemented into the walls, perhaps used long ago to secure the larger weapons. Chains have been looped through these and then attached round the ankles of Richard and Stephanie, secured with a high-security hardened steel padlock. Liam must have known about these loops, Keren realises, must have remembered them from playing here as a kid, and realised how useful they would be. Typical Liam, always thinking of the next problem, and then the one after that.

The chains he's used are long enough to allow the Hamlins to reach a bucket in one corner, being used as a primitive toilet. There are bottles of water scattered around the floor, most of them empty, and some food wrappers. Richard has several days of stubble, and deprived of his glasses, he's dazed and disorientated. Stephanie's face is puffy and tear-stained, but she seems more focused. Keren remembers how she was once both fascinated by and furiously resentful of her. That feels like another lifetime ago.

Instinctively, she realises that she can't speak with them, can't engage with them at all. Because although her instinct is to try to release the Hamlins, there's no way she will be able to do it. The chains are heavy and fixed to a solid wall; the lock substantial and sturdy. She can't undo them. And even if she were able to, all hell would break out. Her own life would fall down like the house of cards it has become.

Put down the stuff and go. She repeats the words in her head like a mantra, trying to quell her overwhelming guilt. *Just put down the stuff and go.*

They're saying things to her, pleading with her. Is it just the house they want? Richard is asking. Because, if it is, they can have the wretched house, just as long as they let them go.

Forcing their words out of her head, Keren unpacks the bags, making sure everything is within their reach, then turns quickly to go.

'I know you,' Stephanie's voice, though croaky, is insistent. 'You're the girl from Stepping Stones... Keren.'

Keren is at the foot of the steps now. *Don't look back. Don't talk to them.*

'Poppy!' Stephanie wails after her. 'Where's Poppy? What have you done with her?'

'She's fine,' Keren shouts, as she reaches the wooden door. 'Don't worry about her, she's fine.'

Then she runs outside and retches, bending double and gasping for breath.

By the time she's trudged back to Gravesend and hailed a passing cab to the station, it's almost eight o'clock. Nearly nine by the time she gets back to Sycamore Gardens and goes to fetch Poppy.

Keren can tell that Jane Headley is a bit annoyed with her for being so late. She can't really blame her, even though they didn't agree a definite time. But she does at least confirm that the tall, handsome man kissing that girl was indeed Mr Headley. Fergus, he's called; weird name. He seems nice, though. Super nice. She instinctively prefers him to Jane. He seems like someone she could confide in, a thought she mentally squirrels away for later.

Liam's out when she gets back, thank God, so she avoids questions about where she's been. After she's put Poppy to bed, she sits down and goes through Stephanie's phone, responding to messages, because she knows Liam will check up on that. It feels a bit of a weird thing to be doing anyway, but having seen the Hamlins, it seems even more so. Weird, and wrong.

And she realises with a gut-wrenching pang that she's going to have to keep going back to Eastmeade Fort. She can't just leave them there to rot, not now she knows.

TWENTY-ONE

MAY

Keren has something covering her face, and it's preventing her from breathing.

She's lying on her back in the dank, stony munitions store of Eastmeade Fort, and Stephanie Hamlin has one of the shopping bags she used to bring the water and supplies and is pressing it hard into her mouth, choking her.

Then she wakes from the dream and finds that Liam has thrown off his half of the duvet to try to relieve the warmth of an unusually sultry spring night, and it has landed over her face.

'You know the Hamlins?' she says to him, when he eventually wakes up too. She can hear Poppy complaining from the small bedroom where they've put her cot, but she ignores her.

'What?' Liam glares at her. 'You're giving me brain ache with all these questions, Kez.'

'You are going to make sure they have food and water, aren't you? I mean, it's been about a week now: you can't just leave them to starve.'

'Of course I'm going to feed them,' he scoffs. 'If we wind up with a couple of dead bodies, then someone will end up identifying them, and that'll lead the Old Bill right to this address, won't it?'

Keren's thinking that if they're found alive, or if they manage to escape, then the police will definitely come knocking anyway. But she doesn't want to start a debate that will risk revealing that she knows where the Hamlins are being detained. So she ends the conversation by going into the bathroom to pee, then shuffles across the landing to fetch Poppy and take her downstairs.

'Look at this,' Liam says, following her into the kitchen and holding up a piece of card. 'This just came through the letter-box.' He yanks orange juice from the fridge door and stands there in his boxers, drinking straight from the carton.

Keren takes the card from him and reads it. It's an invitation for a couple of weekends' time, to the annual barbecue and Pimm's in the communal garden.

'That's typical of this lot round here,' sneers Liam. 'Fucking Pimm's.'

'What even is Pimm's?' Keren asks.

'Poncey drink, that you stick strawberries and all sorts of crap in. Tastes of nothing, but I bet they love it. With their perfect bougie houses and their perfect bougie lives.'

'They're not that perfect,' Keren corrects him. 'That Jane – the one who came round here with the flowers – her husband's got a bit on the side.'

'You sure?' Liam eyes her sharply. 'How d'you know that?'

'Because I saw them together. This girl was coming out of their house while Jane was at work, and he kissed her.' She takes a jar of banana porridge from the fridge and starts feeding it to Poppy, who bangs her fists impatiently on the table of her highchair.

'Kissing someone doesn't necessarily mean he's knocking her off,' Liam says with a shrug.

'It does when you kiss someone like he was kissing her.'

'Is that right?'

Liam seems genuinely intrigued, and it now occurs to Keren that if she needs Jane to look after Poppy for her, the less interested Liam is in the Headleys, the better. In fact, she ends up wishing she hadn't mentioned it at all. Too late.

She returns to the fort again, as soon as she can, once again leaving Poppy with Jane Headley.

This time, in addition to food, Keren takes spare plastic buckets she bought in a cheap home goods stall on Gravesend high street. Gagging copiously, she drags the full one to the furthest empty chamber in the series of storerooms, and provides the Hamlins with a fresh one to use as their toilet. Stephanie weeps with gratitude at this kindness, but still Keren refuses to engage with them. She's concerned that Liam doesn't seem to have dropped off more food and water since her last visit. On her own, she can only bring what she can carry across the marshes, and it's clear that this isn't enough to properly sustain two adults. The Hamlins are both looking painfully thin, and ill.

For several weeks, it feels that her life consists of nothing more than juggling a teething baby and trips to Kent on the train to provide a lifeline to two people: one of whom she doesn't know and another that she once violently disliked. She can access the cash in Stephanie's account to cover the cost of the trips, but maintaining normality in the Hamlins' digital life is becoming more difficult. Of course she hasn't sent out change-of-address cards as promised, and Stephanie's mother and sister are starting to push her on her failure to do so. Her mother has started phoning to talk, and there are only so many missed calls that can be racked up before alarm bells start to ring.

Keren mentions this to Liam one afternoon when he's in the

bedroom sorting through a box of things he took from the Hamlins' flat.

'How much longer is this all going to take?' she asks, her tone sharp. 'I mean, someone's going to twig there's something wrong pretty soon.'

'Yeah, I know, babe.' Liam reaches into the box and drags out a pink checked dress shirt, inspecting it carefully. It's good quality, but not the sort of thing he'd ever wear. 'I'm on it, trust me. I'm just making some discreet enquiries with estate agents, trying to find one who'll handle the sale without running big ads and stuff. As soon as I've got someone who'll do it the way we want, we'll put this place on the market and get the hell out.'

'And what about them... you know, the Hamlins? What's going to happen to them then?'

He doesn't answer, simply giving a dismissive shake of his head as he strips off his vest and puts on the pink shirt. It's a little too tight over the chest.

'What are you wearing that for?'

'Going to that barbecue thing,' he says nonchalantly, admiring his reflection in the full-length mirror in the dressing room. They have a dressing room now, for God's sake. Keren's mind flashes back, as it does frequently, to the underground room in the munitions store at Eastmeade.

'Why?' she demands. 'Why on earth d'you want to go and drink the poncey Pimm's with the bougie neighbours?'

'The way I see it, it will look more weird if we don't make a bit of an effort. We don't want to be whispered about behind our backs.'

As if they aren't already. Keren mentally rolls her eyes.

'You coming then, Kez?'

'No.' She shakes her head firmly. 'No way.'

'Why not?'

'Because I'll have to bring the baby and she'll be a pain. She's cutting her molars and she's being a right cranky madam.'

And because if she goes with Liam and Poppy, it will be weird seeing the Headleys and not mentioning the favours they've done with the babysitting.

Liam shrugs. 'Suit yourself.'

Ironically, Liam finds out about Keren's trips to Kent on a day when Poppy has not been left at number 5.

Jane claims to have a dental appointment, but it's obvious that she just doesn't want to look after the baby, and Keren can't really blame her. Instead, she suggests asking Rani, the pregnant Indian lady who lives in the block of flats. By the time Keren has settled Poppy with someone new, she's running a bit late and just misses the fast train to Gravesend. Instead of waiting around at St Pancras for half an hour, she decides to catch the train that's just about to leave for Ebbsfleet. It's only a five-minute taxi ride from there to Gravesend and on this occasion she's already purchased the supplies she's taking at the local shops.

When she arrives, it's clear that Liam – or someone, Lance perhaps? – has been to the fort fairly recently. There are some empty sports drink bottles, a pack of loo roll and some packets of crisps that were definitely not delivered by Keren. The Hamlins have given up trying to make her talk now, and merely stare at her sullenly, their faces grey and hollow.

She just misses a train back to London and by the time she's waited ages for another and got stuck between tube stops for ten minutes, she's so stressed and distracted that she walks straight past Regency Court and heads for the Headleys' house. Then she catches herself in the mistake and turns around to walk back in the other direction. And as she does so, Liam's truck swings into the Gardens, heading straight towards her.

He wastes no time rolling down the passenger window.

'Where the fuck are you going? And where's the kid?'

Keren points in the direction of the block of flats. 'I left her with one of the neighbours for a couple of hours. I wanted to go and do some shopping, and to be honest, I just needed a break, okay?'

'But, babe, you can't be dumping her on the people round here. That's going to get them too involved in our lives, and once they're involved, they're going to start sticking their beaks into our business. We've been over this...' Then he looks her up and down and frowns. 'So if you've been out shopping, where is it?'

'Where's what?'

'The fucking shopping. The stuff you just said you bought.'

'I didn't see anything I liked.'

But he's shaking his head. 'Nah, Kez, that ain't how you operate. You always see some bit of tat you like. So' – he pushes his shades up on his head so he can make eye contact – 'where've you really been?'

Keren doesn't answer.

'I think we both know, don't we? Because I know some-body's been going down to Gravesend and taking stuff to the Hamlins, somebody who definitely isn't me.' He puts his shades on and revs his engine. 'You and me are going to need a little chat.'

And so it all comes out when she gets back to the dream house. That she has been to the Hamlins' makeshift prison several times, and that on all but one of those occasions, Jane Headley has taken care of Poppy for her. With the full knowledge of her husband, and even the help of her daughter while she was at home.

'That's just bloody great, isn't it?' he rants. 'Getting their whole bloody family involved in our business.'

'I never told them where I was going,' Keren protests, 'And

they never asked, neither. As far as they're concerned, we're Richard and Stephanie Hamlin.'

'But it's not going to stay that way for long, is it?' Poppy starts wailing from her cot, and Liam swears under his breath. 'We need to get something on them, something we can use to keep them quiet if we have to.'

'They're not those sort of people, though. They're squeaky clean. Not into anything dodgy,'

Liam pulls his cigarettes from the pocket of his tracksuit trousers and lights one, sliding open the kitchen doors so that the smoke can escape. 'Didn't you say her old man was playing around?'

Keren nods.

'Well, maybe we can use that to our advantage somehow. Who is she? One of the neighbours?'

She shakes her head. 'I don't think so. I've never seen her round here apart from that one time.'

'Well, I need you to find out who she is, yeah? Get on to it. Let's face it, you're going to have time on your hands now you're not going down to Kent anymore.'

'Who says I'm not?' Keren asks defiantly. She slams the kitchen door to shut out the sound of Poppy crying.

'I do.' Liam gets that glittery look in his eyes. 'Seriously, you'd better not, Kez. No more trips to Eastmeade, yeah? Or you'll regret it.'

He can't exactly report her to anyone for going, can he? Who would he tell? And besides, anything she's done, he's done the same, and way worse. And yet she takes his threat seriously because it's Liam making it. And with Liam, you just never know.

TWENTY-TWO

JULY

Keren knows that Jane's husband works at a college somewhere in the centre of London.

She googles 'Fergus Headley'.

Dr Fergus D. Headley, Associate Professor of Economics, London School of Economics Public Policy Programme

There's a black and white headshot of him grinning rakishly like an old-school movie star. She checks on the university website and finds that the building where he works is just off the Strand. If she's stuck with keeping Poppy amused all day then she may as well head into the West End, Keren reasons, as hang around here.

It doesn't take long to realise that this was probably a mistake. It's hot and humid and Poppy screams at the top of her lungs for the whole tube journey. She continues after they've emerged onto the dusty street, arching her back and twisting against the straps of the buggy as though she's being tortured. A biscuit offered is hurled to the ground. In the end, Keren buys a bottle of chilled blackcurrant juice with a plastic spout and lets Poppy suck on it. She knows this is terrible for her developing teeth, but she's out of ideas, and this at least silences the child while she's pushed along Aldwych and towards the imposing red-brick building in Houghton Street.

'I'm looking for Dr Headley,' she tells the woman at reception. 'Fergus Headley.'

'Are you one of his students?' the woman asks, looking doubtfully at the flushed, sticky Poppy.

'Yes,' lies Keren.

'His office is on the first floor – 107 – can I ask if you have an appointment?'

Keren has already turned and headed to the lift. Only once she's inside it does she realise that she has no idea what she plans to say or do once she finds Fergus's office. She starts rehearsing a little speech in her head, but, in the end, she doesn't need to use it. Because as she comes out of the lift and follows the arrow pointing towards 'Rooms 101–115', she sees her. The girl who was at the Headleys' house that day. She's coming out of room 107 and lingering for a few seconds in the doorway, her body language flirtatious; provocative. She kisses the tips of her fingers and waggles them in the direction of whoever is in the room, then turns to go down the stairs.

Keren hauls the buggy back into the lift and presses the button for the ground floor. As the doors slide open, she catches sight of the girl again. She's wearing a sleeveless white linen top and ripped jeans, and her mouth is a slash of vermilion. She heads down a corridor to an area where there are rows of wooden pigeonholes with names on them, and stops in front of one of them, extracting a sheaf of letters and thumbing through them. Then she pulls out her phone and carries on down the corridor, examining her mail with her free hand and talking quickly in a language that Keren doesn't recognise.

Once she's alone, Keren walks over to the pigeonholes and reads the typed name on the brass name plaque.

Selina Permeti

She knows she'll never remember it, so she takes a photo of

it with her phone and pushes the buggy back through the building's reception area and out onto the street. She's only walked a few steps before she hears someone call out to her.

'Stephanie?'

Keren has forgotten momentarily that this is now her name, so she doesn't respond until she hears it a second time.

'Steph?'

She turns round to see Fergus Headley. He smiles at her warmly, and Poppy, seeing someone she recognises, makes a squeal of delight and twists in her seat, trying to get out.

'What are you doing in these parts?' he asks, bending to chuck Poppy under the chin. 'That's where I work,' he explains, pointing back at the red-brick edifice. 'I'm just popping out to grab a coffee. The stuff in the staffroom machine is unspeakably bad.' He pulls a face by way of illustration and Poppy gurgles at him, reaching out her sticky fingers.

'Just going to Covent Garden to do some shopping,' Keren lies.

'Why don't you join me? There's a place just on Kingsway that does great iced lattes, if that's your thing.'

Keren doesn't think she should, given that she's only here to spy on him. But he does have such kind eyes, and she is hot and thirsty.

'Okay then.'

He takes the buggy from her and pushes it to the coffee shop, which astonishes Keren. Liam would never in a million years do that. He orders an Americano for himself, a caramel frappuccino for her and milk for Poppy.

'So, how are you settling into number twelve?' he asks in that easy way of his.

She shrugs. 'You know... okay.'

'Only it can't be easy for you, finding yourself suddenly in a completely new environment, with a young baby to look after.' His eyes narrow slightly. 'This may be speaking out of turn, but you don't seem to be getting a whole lot of support from your husband.'

A silence hangs between them. Keren looks down at her plate and makes a mumbling sound that might be assent, might be disagreement.

'For example,' Fergus sets down his coffee cup and looks at her directly, 'when Jane's agreed to look after this one' – he ruffles Poppy's curls – 'Richard never comes to fetch her, even though it's obvious he's at home.'

There's no point disagreeing, because everything Fergus has said is completely true. Keren considers, with a rush of reckless-ness, telling this kind man everything. That she's not really Stephanie Hamlin, and that she and Liam didn't really win 12, Sycamore Gardens in a lottery. That the real owners are being kept prisoner in an underground munitions store on the Kent coast. But she loses her nerve. It would be like deliberately deto-nating a bomb in her own life.

'Listen,' Fergus holds out his hand, 'give me your phone and I'll put my number in it. It might make you feel better having it, in case... you know... anything happens and you need help.'

She hands him her mobile, and while he's tapping in his details, he says, 'Oh and also, when our two were that age, we got a huge amount of mileage out of a paddling pool in the back garden. Why don't you think about doing that? Give her a couple of plastic buckets to play with and it'll keep her enter-tained for hours. We might even have our old one in the loft, though God knows what sort of condition it's in.'

Keren sucks up the remains of her iced drink. 'Thanks, but it's fine.' She stands up and takes the brake off the buggy. 'We've got stuff like that, we just haven't unpacked it yet.'

As she walks away, she tries to picture Liam's reaction if Fergus Headley showed up with a second-hand paddling pool and shudders despite the heat.

. . .

When Keren gets home, she switches on Stephanie's mobile to find several missed calls from both her mother and her sister. And a text from her sister:

What's going on Steph? We're worried about you! Xx

She shows this to Liam when he eventually gets home. He's been for a spray tan on his way back from the gym, and his gleaming bronzed arms have a strange biscuity smell.

'They're going to come looking unless I give them the address, I know it,' she tells him.

'And if you do give it to them, they're going to be straight round here anyway, babe. It's obvious.'

'So what do we do?'

'Tell them we're going away on a villa holiday that we won as part of the prize. For three weeks. I've got an estate agent lined up now, and by then we should have an offer and we can clear off out of here.'

'Can't we just go now?' Keren pleads.

'And go where exactly?'

'We could use the money in their accounts to stay in a B and B or something?'

But he's shaking his head. 'It'll look too odd if we vanish before the place is sold. Just tell her friends and family you're going away.'

'Where?'

'I dunno... a Greek island or something. Corfu, how about that?'

'They'll expect pictures.'

'So lift some off some random's Instagram account and use those. Jesus, Kez, do I have to do all the thinking round here?' He rummages in his jeans pocket for his cigarettes. 'Anyway, how d'you get on? Did you find out about that bird Jane's old man's shagging?'

Keren shakes her head.

'Come on now, I know exactly when you're lying: the right side of your mouth starts to twitch. You did, didn't you?'

She hesitates.

'So who is she?'

'I can't remember her name.'

'I don't believe you.'

Before she's had time to react, he's snatched her phone and started scrolling through the photos. He knows that when she's worried about remembering something, she always takes a picture of it.

'*Selina Permeti*... this is her?'

Keren nods reluctantly.

'Good,' he says thoughtfully, forwarding the picture to himself. 'Useful info, I reckon.'

Keren gathers up a pile of Poppy's laundry and shoves it into the washing machine, then roots through the fridge for something she can make for the baby's tea. Buster whines at her ankles.

'Dog needs walking,' she tells Liam.

'You'll have to do it.'

'Christ, Liam, I do bloody everything myself. It's a full-time job looking after the kid.' She picks up Poppy from the floor where she's banging a plastic bowl against one of the kitchen units and shoves her, rather more roughly than she should, into her highchair.

'Tough shit!' Liam snaps, grabbing his keys and wallet. 'Because I'm going out.'

He's been increasingly short and irritable with her over the past few weeks. He's also stopped pestering her for sex, which makes her suspect that he's seeing someone else. It's not the first time he's got up to stuff behind her back, but Keren decides – as she feeds both the baby and the dog – that it will be the last.

She lets Buster out into the garden and dumps Poppy on the

lawn with a washing-up bowl full of water and some toys, before pulling out her phone and starting to send some texts. She has stuff to organise now.

Because before she can be rid of Liam, she needs to rid herself of the Hamlins' child.

TWENTY-THREE

AUGUST

So what happened? Siobhan's text to Keren demands. *Thought you were going to visit ages ago but you went silent on me. Now all of a sudden you need to come round?! xx*

Keren lets out a loud sigh, which echoes around the empty kitchen. Buster, stretched out on one of the beige sofas, lifts his head briefly, then goes back to sleep. Poppy, for once, is also asleep and Liam is taking one of his interminable showers. She composes a text to her sister.

> *Yeah sorry, there's been a lot going on. Tell you about it when I see you. Tomorrow okay?*

Can't, we're away! Kids are on school holiday, remember?! xx

> *When are you back?*

At the weekend xx

> *I'll come Monday*

'Who's that you're messaging?' Liam demands, coming into the kitchen. His hair is still wet and he smells strongly of Tom Ford Noir. He's also wearing his favourite T-shirt, one that clings to his pecs.

'My sister,' Keren says, adding truthfully, 'She's just telling me about her holiday.'

Liam grunts, uninterested, groping through the mess on the kitchen counter to find his keys.

'Where are you going?'

'Just need to sort something. Something to do with the house.'

Keren looks askance at him. 'What kind of something?'

'Just something I need to get lined up before people start looking round. Which is going to be happening next week. Apparently, the agent's got plenty of buyers interested, which is sweet.'

He doesn't wait to be questioned further, but slips on the suede loafers he took from the Hamlins' flat and slams out of the house. As she looks up from her phone, Keren notices that he's left the key for his pickup behind. Liam never goes anywhere on foot.

She darts to the front door after him, pulling it open carefully so as not to make any noise and looking out into the darkening street. She can see Liam now, strutting along the pavement, hands in his pockets. He walks up to the front door of number 17; the biggest, smartest property in the street. All Keren knows about the people who live there is that they have a fancy car and domestic staff. Liam rings the brass bell on the shiny, black front door and after a few seconds, it's opened and he steps inside. Keren can just about make out the outline of the person answering the door. It's a female.

So she's right. He is fooling around again.

. . .

Keren's already in bed when Liam returns.

'Don't bother, yeah,' she murmurs, when he starts tiptoeing around the bedroom with exaggerated care. 'I'm still awake.'

When Liam comes back from the bathroom, she asks, 'So when the house is sold, what's going to happen then?'

He glances at her sharply. 'What you on about?'

'Where are we going to live? We're each going to have half the money, right?'

There's no reply.

'Right?'

'Well, it might end up being not exactly fifty-fifty. It was all my idea, after all.'

'Which you couldn't have carried out without me.'

Liam gets into bed and turns away from her. She can just make out the hunched shape of his right shoulder in the faint beam of the street light from outside.

'Are we going to have to go somewhere we can't be found, like abroad or something?' Keren says out loud into the darkness. 'Once the Hamlins have been let go?'

She can tell he's not asleep, but the question is met with silence.

On Monday morning, Keren packs some of Poppy's things into a bag and calls a minicab to take her and the baby – along with the buggy and the dog – to Liverpool Street station.

Poppy is hugely excited by the thirty-minute train journey to Chelmsford, standing on the seat and pressing her fat little hands against the window as first buildings and then trees and fields whip by. She doesn't want to get back into the buggy and is crying loudly by the time Keren arrives at the modern housing estate where Siobhan and her husband live.

'Shhh!' Keren tries desperately to quieten the child before she rings the doorbell, but she's too late. Siobhan has already opened the door and is standing on the doorstep with her hands on her hips.

'Keren! What the hell!'

'You knew I was coming,' Keren says meekly.

'Jesus, I'm not talking about that!' She points at the red-faced and hiccupping Poppy. 'A baby? Whose is it?'

'Am I coming in, or what?' Keren pushes the buggy past her sister and into the hallway, unclipping Buster from his lead, before bending down to release the wriggling Poppy. She holds the child out to her sister. 'This is your niece. Her name's Poppy.'

Siobhan stares, her mouth open as she takes the baby. 'Jesus, what... you never said anything! You didn't even tell me you were pregnant.'

'I wasn't, last time I saw you.' Keren has calculated that since the two sisters' last meeting there's been enough of an interval for her to conceive, go through pregnancy and give birth to a baby who is now a year old.

'I know, but you could have told me on the phone! Jeez, Kez. And a bloody dog, too? Thought you didn't like dogs!'

They go through into the living room, which has a pale laminate floor and sofas with lots of glittery and fluffy cushions.

Siobhan sets Poppy down on the rug, taking her in. 'She's gorgeous, Kez, she really is. But then I always said you and Liam would have good-looking kids, didn't I?' She rummages in a cupboard and finds a box of Duplo, which she puts in front of the baby, before turning to her sister, arms folded across her chest. 'So, come on then.'

'We didn't plan to have her,' Keren mutters. This is perfectly true, after all. 'Neither of us was sure about keeping her.' This is also true, in a way.

'But you could have said something once she was born!'

'Things weren't great between me and Liam. You know what he's like.'

Siobhan makes a scoffing noise.

'We've been going through some problems, so that's...' Keren tails off. She knows that what she's about to do is a huge gamble. But she also knows that her sister, a stay-at-home mum with two school-age children, has a nice house and time on her hands. And that Siobhan was desperately broody for a third baby, but her husband, Mick, vetoed it. 'Look, Shiv... I need you to take her for a bit, okay? Me and Liam, we're going through some really rocky stuff right now and I don't want her being around it.'

Siobhan is already on her knees playing with the baby, encouraging Poppy in her attempts to pull herself up to standing. 'How long for?' she asks.

'I don't know... a few days.' This is absolutely not true, but she has to let her sister think it is, at least until she's had a bit of time to get used to the idea.

'Okay, but make sure it is only a few, yeah?' Siobhan gets to her feet and starts going through the bag Keren has brought. 'There's not a lot here... but never mind, I've got a load of Melissa's old stuff bagged up in the spare room, and we can make a little trip into town, go to Baby Gap.' She runs her fingers through Poppy's dark blonde curls. 'Buy this little princess some new outfits, eh?'

'Is it okay if I leave the dog too?' Keren says in a rush. 'Poppy loves him; she'll settle better if he's here.'

Siobhan sighs. 'I suppose so. The kids are always on at Mick to get a dog anyway.'

Keren leans forward and kisses her sister on her cheek, avoiding looking directly at Poppy. 'Thanks, Shiv, you're the best.'

TWENTY-FOUR

AUGUST

Keren's chief emotion on the train back to Liverpool Street is one of relief. For the first time in weeks, she's not encumbered by having to look after the child of another woman. But being unencumbered raises so many questions that her relief is swiftly replaced with overwhelming anxiety. She's free: so now what is she supposed to do? Living with Liam is difficult at the best of times, but living with him while outwardly assuming another woman's identity is proving impossible. That means that she can't delay any longer: she has to go. But where?

Fergus Headley's words come back to her suddenly. '*If anything happens and you need help...*' She finds his number on her phone and dials it. It rings out.

When she gets back to Sycamore Gardens, she sees that the windows at number 5 are all shuttered and the Headleys' Volvo estate is not parked outside. They must have gone away on holiday, and their absence makes Keren feel strangely exposed, unprotected. It's also stranger than she expected to be back at number 12 without little Poppy. The place still smells of warm milk and baby lotion, and there are still babygros hanging on the airer in the utility room, freshly tumble-dried and fragrant with the hypoallergenic fabric conditioner that Keren bought to wash the baby clothes. She even misses the dog a little bit.

Liam is not at home, so Keren runs herself a bubble bath in the enormous tub in the en suite. She takes a highball glass, fills it with ice from the fancy dispenser on the fridge and tops it up with vodka and a carton of blackcurrant-flavoured toddler drink, before carrying it up to the bathroom. Siobhan has sent her a string of updates and photos chronicling what Poppy has been up to, plus some pictures of Jake and Melissa with Buster the dog. Keren ignores them, switching off her phone and sinking into the sea of scented foam with her drink. This is how she thought their dream life would be, she tells herself, back when she allowed Liam to talk her into it.

Twenty minutes later, he slams into the bathroom.

'What are you playing at? I've been trying to ring you!'

Keren ignores him too.

He marches out onto the landing, and she can tell from the direction of his footsteps that he's going into the small room where Poppy slept.

'Where's the kid?' he demands when he gets back.

'Not here.'

He stares at her, paling slightly under his tan. 'What have you done, Kez? Please don't tell me you've done something stupid. You've not been down to Kent again?'

Keren shakes her head, reaching for her vodka cocktail. 'I left her with Siobhan. And the dog.'

Liam sinks down onto the closed toilet seat, rubbing his hand along his designer stubble. 'How do we know we can trust her not to blab?'

'Because she thinks Poppy is ours. She looks like she could be. So what would there be for her to blab about?'

He shakes his head slowly. 'Yeah, well, it's probably for the best. Seeing as how you've royally fucked up.'

'Fucked up?' She hauls herself up in the bath, sending

foamy water sloshing over the floor tiles. 'What are you talking about?'

'The estate agent was here this morning measuring up and taking some photographs and he said a woman came up to him and asked him where Stephanie was. Turns out it's her *sister*.' He places a heavy emphasis on this last word. 'Her sister, Kez! Apparently she got the address from the company that runs the house draws. And straight away she's down to London to try and work out why the hell Stephanie's not letting her family visit. You were supposed to be on top of all of that!'

'I was!' protests Keren. She stands up and reaches for a towel, wrapping it around her dripping torso. 'I told everyone who contacted Steph that she's gone away to Corfu, like we decided. I posted pictures and everything. It's not my fault if people don't believe it.'

'Yes, it is, because you should have been more convincing!' Liam is glaring at her now.

Keren snatches up her vodka and juice and pushes past him, marching back into the bedroom.

He follows her, his tone patronising now. 'Fortunately, the agent's a clued-up kind of guy, and he wasn't about to start a family feud, so he just said as far as he knew the vendors were fine, just away on holiday somewhere. In the end, she accepted it and pissed off.'

Keren shrugs as she tugs on her underwear. 'So that's okay then.'

Liam gives an exaggerated sigh. 'Well, not really, is it? It's not going to take long before someone's back again.'

'What do we do?' She's not looking at him as she asks this, instead sorting through a jumble of T-shirts in the dressing area, thinking about packing her stuff and what she's going to put it all in. She's not really interested in what Liam thinks any more, now that she's decided she's finally going to leave him. She really will this time too: he's not going to charm his way around her. This plan of his has turned into a nightmare and all Keren wants is to get out.

'We need to speed things up. Obviously, it's harder to find a cash buyer for a place this size, but we've got to do everything we can now. I didn't want the agent to put up a sale board outside, for obvious reasons, but I'm thinking now we're going to have to.'

'Mmmhmm,' says Keren absently, selecting a vest top and pair of sweatpants, her back still turned to him.

'Like I said, it'll probably help that you've got rid of the kid and the dog, now that we need to move things on. And I'm thinking we should move out of here ourselves while we wait for a buyer to come along. If Stephanie's family are getting suspicious, and the neighbours are going to continually stick their noses in, it's probably for the best, right? That way, they might all think we've gone off on holiday for a bit.'

Keren turns round. 'So where will we go?'

Before he can answer, the front doorbell rings and Liam goes out onto the landing, peering through the window to identify the caller. Then he thunders down into the hall and a few seconds later, Keren hears Lance's voice.

Then she hears Liam saying, 'Better come through here, in case, you know...' She leans over the banister just in time to see the two brothers disappearing into the formal dining room and shutting the door. They never go into that room; haven't used it once since they've been here.

Still in her bare feet, she creeps along the landing and down the stairs, taking care to tread very lightly. Then she pauses outside the dining room, her ear to the door. Frustratingly, the two brothers are at the far end of the room and they're deliberately keeping their voices low so she can only make out eighty per cent of what they're saying. Liam says something that sounds like 'time to cut our losses' and Lance responds with, 'You mean finish things completely?' Then he asks 'When?' and

Liam mumbles something about 'it can't be tonight, but as soon as you've got hold of...'

Got hold of what? Keren wonders, straining to hear better.

Liam must have moved so that he's slightly nearer the door, because she can hear the next sentence more clearly. '...Someone other than me and Kez: we're too closely involved, obviously.'

What the hell does that mean? Keren wonders.

This is followed by something inaudible, then: 'This Thursday, then, okay?'

Footsteps indicate that Liam and Lance have finished their discussion and are headed for the door. Keren turns and scuttles back up the stairs, reaching the first-floor landing just as the dining room door is opened. Thursday is only three days away. So what's so special about that particular day? She's not going to say anything to Liam about leaving him, Keren decides. Not just yet. Not until after Thursday.

When Thursday arrives, it begins uneventfully.

She sees the Headleys return from their holiday, but otherwise nothing happens. Keren hovers warily, keeping Liam in sight at all times, but he stays in the house, gambling on his phone and playing video games on the new console he bought with Richard Hamlin's last accountancy pay packet. What was she expecting, she asks herself, already knowing the answer to that question. She was expecting him to go to the fort in Kent. To the place where the Hamlins, as far as she knows, are still being held. To 'finish things'. But he doesn't.

'Haven't you got anything to do?' he asks her at one point, his tone irritable.

She shakes her head, no.

'Well, do some stuff on Stephanie's phone then.'

But she can't. It's too late for that. The messages from

Stephanie's family are now threatening to phone the police if she won't make a voice call to them. And there's no way she can do that. She doesn't sound anything like Stephanie Hamlin and, even if she did, they'd be able to tell.

To keep Liam quiet, she picks up the phone anyway and pretends to be messaging with it. He finishes his game and walks to the living-room window at the front of the house, watching the street. Keren stands up, so she can see what he's looking at. He's watching the man from number 17 going past in the back seat of the chauffeur-driven limo that takes him to his business meetings. Then he goes upstairs and begins one of his long sessions in the shower, emerging half an hour later scrubbed clean and smelling strongly of his Tom Ford aftershave.

It's all too obvious what's coming next.

'Just popping out for a bit.'

Keren watches through the window as Liam walks around the curve of the Gardens, but she does so knowing exactly where he's headed. He rings on the doorbell at number 17 and is admitted, like he was last time. This time, her emotion is one of pure anger. She no longer cares that Liam's sleeping with someone else, but she's furious at his hypocrisy; his sheer arrogant stupidity. He's warned her against letting any of the neighbours get too close and yet here he is getting it on with not only a neighbour, but someone whose other half is the big man on this street. Their chance of getting this house sold and keeping the money is hanging by a thread as it is. Why is he taking such a ridiculous risk?

'I know where you've been,' she says in a low voice when Liam creeps up the staircase several hours later. He's taken to sleeping in the spare room recently, but she intercepts him on the landing.

He pauses as he's pulling off his shirt.

'You're shagging that rich woman, aren't you? The one that looks like a Barbie doll.'

'Kez...' He sighs, his hand on the handle of the spare room door. 'We both know you and I haven't exactly been getting on great.'

'So you're not denying it?'

'There's no point, is there? And you and me... well, pretty soon things are going to be very different, aren't they? We're going to be able to split the money and we'll each be in a position to do our own thing. It's for the best, yeah?'

She studies his face, only just able to make out his profile. Seeing him in the half-dark reminds her of that first time she saw him in Flames nightclub and she experiences a painful stab of nostalgia, remembering how she used to feel about him. How this was her first proper relationship. And yet even then, she knew she would never be able to keep pace with Liam Devenish.

'I suppose so.' Keren sighs heavily. 'But, like you said, we're not going to be here much longer. So why risk it all having a fling with someone like her? It's not like it can really be... you know... a thing.'

'Why not?' Liam's tone is belligerent.

'Because... because it's obvious, right? Because we're going to have to take off somewhere we can't be found... I mean, look at her. She's well out of your league. She's never going to be serious about someone like you.'

'Actually, Kez, that's where you're wrong.' Despite the dim light, she can easily make out his grin of triumph. 'It is serious. Very serious. Me and Irina are planning to be together.'

TWENTY-FIVE

AUGUST

Liam stays in the guest room for their remaining time at number 12, Sycamore Gardens.

He wanders around the house the next day, making endless calls and texting constantly. Keren fields several messages from Siobhan, including a video of Poppy taking her first unsteady steps. The baby's lovely, Siobhan says, but can she please have an idea of when Keren will be back to collect her and the dog? Keren ignores them as she cleans and tidies to prepare the house for viewings. The 'For Sale' sign has just gone up, and the agent has already told them he has a potential cash buyer for the property: a young couple who are just moving back to London from Toronto and planning to start a family. They're keen to complete the sale as quickly as possible, but even so, Liam is constantly chasing and harassing the agent and the lawyers handling it.

'So now we're getting rid of this place, what's happening to the Hamlins?' Keren asks, as she pushes a mop listlessly over the kitchen floor. 'You're going to let them go, right?'

'It'll all get sorted,' Liam tells her, adding darkly: 'Lance is taking care of it.'

. . .

But when Lance comes round later that day, things seem far
from 'sorted'. The Devenish twins never normally have serious
fallings out, with Lance permanently cast in the role of Liam's
yes man; his sidekick. And yet now, Liam seems furious with
Lance, shouting and swearing at him, before pushing Keren out
of the hall and away from the living room, slamming the door in
her face so she can't hear what's being said.

'Stop earwigging, okay?' he snarls at her, as though whatever's wrong is somehow all her fault.

After a further heated exchange on the front doorstep,
Lance jumps back into the Jeep he's borrowed from one of his
dubious friends, and roars off. Keren decides it will be best to
leave Liam to cool off alone, so she shoves her purse into the
pocket of her denim shorts, grabs her phone and keys and heads
out onto the baking hot street. If she's going to have to pack up
and leave, she's going to do it in a civilised manner, not like last
time when their landlord hurled all her possessions into plastic
bags.

She catches a bus down Clapham Road and walks to
Brixton Market, where she buys a pair of sleek black wheeled
suitcases, fitting the smaller one inside the larger one to make it
easier to transport them back again.

When she returns to number 12, Liam and his truck are
nowhere to be seen. She takes a can of Coke upstairs, finds an
upbeat playlist on her phone and makes a start on her packing.
She folds her clothes neatly and carefully into the shiny new
cases, determined to pack properly, even though she still has no
idea where she's going. She can't think of anywhere apart from
to Siobhan's house, but if she shows up at Siobhan's, she'll be
expected to take Poppy back. So that option's off the table. And
there isn't enough money left in Stephanie Hamlin's bank
account to rent somewhere of her own.

'How long till we get the money for this place?' she asks a frantically scrolling Liam the next morning as she opens up the sliding doors to the garden and sets the kettle to boil. He must have got back very late, because she didn't hear him unlocking the front door or heading to the spare room. The garden is heady with the smell of wallflowers and filled with birdsong. Keren realises with a sharp pang that she will miss this place. This dream house.

'I've no bloody idea,' he snaps. 'Hopefully just a few more weeks.'

'And I'm getting half, right?'

'What?' he says distractedly.

'I'm getting half of the money?'

'Okay, yeah, whatever.' Liam looks up at her and adds, 'You do realise you're going to have to get an anonymous bank account, yeah? One with a number, not a name. Because the first thing they...' He pauses a beat. 'You know, the Hamlins or whoever, are going to do is try to follow the money. So it can't just be transferred into an account in the name of Keren Stockley.'

This was not a complication Keren had anticipated, and a small knot of fear uncoils in her stomach. He is going to give her the money, surely? Given what she knows. 'So how do I do that?'

'They have them banks in Hong Kong, Panama, places like that.' He stands up and pulls on his trainers, searching around for his kitbag. 'Where are my trainers? I'm going to head for the gym in a bit.' He looks at her, adding 'You'd better head out too, just while the agent's showing those cash buyers.'

'But, Liam, I don't know anything about foreign banks—'

'For God's sake, Kez, just google it!'

. . .

Once they've both returned to the house, Keren gets to work on Stephanie Hamlin's phone, using it to research how to open a numbered bank account, when there's an insistent ringing on the front doorbell.

'See who that is, but don't open it unless it's Lance, yeah?' Liam calls from the living room where he's now engrossed in a game of Deathloop.

A quick glance out of the landing window sends a shiver of shock through Keren. A uniformed police officer is standing on the front step. She races downstairs and, with a finger to her lips, mimes frantically to Liam to switch off his computer game. Then she grabs him by the wrist and pulls him into the kitchen at the back of the house, before the policeman thinks to look in through the living-room window.

'Police!' She mouths the word silently.

'What the...' Liam hisses.

The doorbell rings again, and they stand frozen like a pair of statues for a few seconds until they hear the sound of boots retreating over the gravel path.

Stephanie's phone bleeps, still in Keren's hand. *Message from Mum.*

Whenever she sees that word on the screen, her stomach reacts as if the communication has come from her own mother, even though she knows it's from some woman she's never met. A woman whose name she already knows – from seeing the family contact list at Stepping Stones – is Linda Fairburn. A further alert on screen shows a dozen missed calls from Linda.

> *I didn't want to do this, but I'm genuinely worried about you now. Haven't been able to speak or FaceTime you or R for weeks so I've reported my concerns at the local police station. Not that they were particularly interested, but they did say they'd get someone down in London to*

do a welfare check. Hopefully you'll ring before that
happens. M xxx

Keren's stomach sinks as she reads it. Her first instinct is to
say nothing and just get her stuff and go. But if the police come
back, which they almost certainly will, then they could end up
arresting Liam. If that happens, then they'll probably also catch
up with her at some point. And there'll definitely be no money,
not after that. After months of being someone else, she can't
face the idea of returning to being the old Keren Stockley, broke
and desperate. So she reluctantly holds up the phone and shows
Liam the text.

He snatches it from her and reads it, issuing a volley of
expletives. 'Christ's sake, Kez, you were supposed to be keeping
the family sweet! I've not had any problems with Richard's.'

'I tried!' Keren protested. 'But they're obviously closer with
Stephanie than Richard is with his lot, especially since she's got
a baby. They can tell something's not right.'

He looks back at her, shaking his head slowly, then resumes
playing his video game.

'Liam! The police could be back any minute. We've got
to go!'

'They'll probably go and speak to some of the neighbours
and they'll tell them we're living here and everything's normal.'

Keren stares at him in exasperation. 'Except that we haven't
got the baby anymore! Someone's bound to notice that eventually, and tell social services or something. Are you really
prepared to risk it, after everything we've been through?' Then
a thought occurs to her. 'Or are you just wanting to hang around
so you can see your Russian hooker again?'

'She's not a hooker,' he snarls, pushing past her and going
back to his PlayStation.

'Whatever, I'm not hanging around here waiting to be

arrested.' Keren goes upstairs and puts the last of her belongings into the two cases, clearing her stuff out of the bathroom.

Liam appears in the doorway a few minutes later.

'Okay, look, you're probably right,' he says reluctantly. 'But let's not make a big show of driving off in front of all the neighbours, yeah? If the Old Bill do turn up again and start ringing on doorbells, it's only going to look more suspicious if they've all seen us legging it. Let's leave it till tonight, after it's gone dark, okay?'

Lance appears a bit later to help Liam load his things into his truck, apparently on speaking terms again after their furious row.

'So where are you going to go?' Keren asks, her own luggage now stowed in the boot of her car.

Liam just taps the side of his nose.

'Why won't you tell me?'

''Cause you don't need to know.'

'Of course I do! How am I going to get my share of the money?' Her voice is shrill now, strident.

'Jesus, Kez, will you stop pecking my head about the bloody money!'

Realising that their raised voices risk disturbing the neighbours, she drops her shoulders and says quietly, but with as much menace as she can muster: 'I'm leaving now, but if I don't get my share, then I'll be straight round to the police.'

The expression on Liam's face is blank, uncaring.

Keren stands there for a few seconds, waiting for him to say something, anything, that acknowledges the ending of their relationship. It doesn't happen. With a slight shake of her head, she walks over to her car and accelerates away as fast as she can. Past the handsome houses with their blank, darkened windows, past the looming outline of the trees in the shared garden, not daring to take a final glance at number 12 or the man who has been at the centre of her world for the past two years.

Don't look back. Don't look back.

TWENTY-SIX

AUGUST

Keren spends the weekend in a budget hotel near Waterloo.

Stephanie's bank accounts have been pretty much drained now, leaving too low a balance for a long-term hotel stay. Keren checks out at midday on Monday and after killing a few hours wandering along the South Bank, she drives the couple of miles to her former workplace and parks on a side street with a view of the front of the Stepping Stones nursery. The hotel room was stuffy and overheated, its insubstantial windows failing to block the roar of traffic and the scream of sirens, so she barely slept. She didn't have the energy to unpack and repack her cases either, so she's wearing yesterday's sweat-stained and grimy clothes, her hair unwashed. When Chloe emerges at four o'clock at the end of the early shift, at first she fails to recognise the dishevelled girl who steps out of the red hatchback and intercepts her.

'Keren, Jesus! It's you!' She hesitates a second, then draws her friend into an awkward hug. 'How are you? Are you back from Ireland for good? Don't tell me you're after your old job back.'

Keren shakes her head.

'Bet you haven't been missing the place either. Buckteeth is worse than ever.' She tugs off her blue tabard and frees her blonde mane from the mandatory hair tie the nursery nurses wear at work, swearing as she dislodges one of her false eyelashes. 'Let's go for a drink.'

'Okay, but listen, Chlo, I need to ask you a favour.'

'Ask me over a drink. Let's go to the Moon.'

They walk to the Half Moon pub at the end of the street and find space at one of the wooden picnic tables in the small rear yard. Chloe buys them each half a pint of cider and a packet of crisps, which she rips open and lays flat so that they can share.

'So how's your mum?'

Keren does a double take, glass halfway to her lips. 'My mum?'

'Buckteeth said the reason you left without working out your notice was cos you had to go to Ireland to look after your mum.'

'Oh yeah...' Only now does Keren remember the resignation text she sent to Ruth Buckby. 'She's fine now. All good.'

'So what else have you been doing?' Chloe asks round a handful of crisps, then, before Keren has chance to reply, says, 'Hey, guess what, the same day you left, the Hamlins pulled Poppy from the nursery. Something about giving up her job and spending more time at home. I wondered if it had something to do with you.'

Keren startles, a flush of colour creeping up her neck. 'What do you mean?'

'Well, she made that complaint about you, didn't she? Said she was unhappy with the level of care. So perhaps that's the real reason she removed her kid.'

'Oh, I see.' Keren gives what she hopes is a disinterested shrug. 'Who cares?'

Chloe washes down her crisps with a large mouthful of cider. 'You still with Liam?'

Keren shakes her head. 'No. We broke up. Which is why I need to ask you a favour. I need to stay at yours for a bit. Just till I sort myself out.'

Chloe still lives at home, in a large chaotic house in Sydenham. Her parents, Lorraine and Steve, used to foster children for the local authority and still welcome a tide of waifs and strays in the shape of friends and partners of their own three offspring.

'Sure, no problem.'

'Don't you need to phone and check with your mum and dad?'

Chloe shrugs. 'Nah, they'll be fine. Another round?'

'Just a Coke. I've got the car.'

'Sweet!' Chloe grins, exposing small teeth and an expanse of gum. 'You can drive us home.'

The Dockerills live in a pebble-dashed detached house built in the 1930s, in a nondescript street to the north of Crystal Palace Park. It's shabby and cluttered, but Keren is welcomed warmly and given a bed in a small top-floor room that doubles as a home office.

'Sorry, we've got a foreign exchange student in the guest room at the moment,' Lorraine Dockerill tells Keren. 'But Juanita's only here till the end of the month, then she's going back to Salamanca. So you can switch rooms then, if you like.'

Keren assures her that she doesn't mind being in the attic office, and she means it. Being tucked away out of sight suits her better at the moment. She also resists Chloe's offer of the other bed in her room, knowing that it will mean endless late-night questions about how she has spent the last four months. If she's tired and off her guard, she might let something slip that will give away where she's really been. And she can't risk that.

· · ·

During the hours Chloe is at work at Stepping Stones, Keren does her best to stay out of the house and out of reach of Lorraine Dockerill's well-meaning concern. For several days, she wanders the neighbourhood aimlessly, only returning to the house when Chloe is due back and she can make herself useful by helping prepare the evening meal. Chloe's two brothers and their girlfriends are often around in the evening, and there is the silent presence of Juanita, whose shyness and lack of English render her mute.

On one of these days, Keren heads into the City to try and open her numbered bank account, only to discover that a substantial deposit is needed before this is possible. She relays this problem to Liam, suggesting that once the house funds are paid to him, he can forward part of her share for her to use as the opening deposit. But he doesn't respond to her text, or pick up any of her calls. Checking her own phone constantly, obsessively, achieves nothing. The image of the For Sale sign outside number 12 comes to her then, pale blue with the name Baxter & Marsh on it. She finds the number for their South London office and, in the absence of information from Liam, phones them to request an update on the sale of number 12, Sycamore Gardens. Contracts will be exchanged this Friday, she's told, with completion scheduled for a fortnight after that.

After a few days, the Dockerills make discreet, gentle enquiries about her plans. Will she be looking for a new job now she's back from Ireland? Of course she says she is, because what else can she possibly tell them? That she's waiting for a sum of money that should total over a million pounds to hit her bank account? She accepts the loan of a laptop from Chloe's brother, Paul, and to keep up appearances sits crossed leg on her single bed scrolling through job sites, reading descriptions of jobs she would never want and could never do anyway.

On Saturday, the day after contracts are due to be exchanged on number 12, she messages Liam again. By now, she's in a state of constant, heart-pounding anxiety. Surely now that the money is actually on the way, he will get in touch with her. But there's still nothing, and now when she tries calling, his phone is switched off.

After supper, she joins the family in the lounge, an untidy, over-furnished room crammed with photos of both Dockerill offspring and foster children. Steve Dockerill switches on the television and, despite Chloe and Lorraine's protests, flicks to the news channel.

Keren is only half-listening, but when the newsreader's words register, her pulse races and she feels faint, gripping the edge of the armchair.

'*Police in Kent are appealing for help in identifying a body found in an area of uninhabited marshland near Gravesend. They are asking any witnesses or anyone with information to—*'

Chloe grabs the remote from her father and switches to Netflix.

Keren leans forward, hanging her head over her knees to try and counteract the nausea and the ringing in her ears.

'Are you okay, love?' Lorraine asks. 'Need me to get you anything?'

Keren stands unsteadily. She hopes no one notices her legs shaking. 'It's all right, thanks, I think I just need an early night.'

In the sanctuary of her temporary room, she crawls under the covers and lies on her back, staring at the ceiling while she listens to the pounding of her heart. She knows she should log onto a news site and try to find out more, but she can't. She's too afraid.

When Chloe gets back from Stepping Stones on Tuesday evening, Keren can tell straight away that something's happened. Her eyes are unnaturally bright, and she responds to the usual enquiries about her day in short, staccato sentences.

She catches Keren's eye and cocks her head in the direction of the stairs, indicating that they should go up to her room.

'Just going to change,' she calls, and Keren follows her.

'Oh my God,' Chloe pronounces, flapping her hands in a dramatic gesture. 'You'll never guess what happened at work today.'

'Tell me.'

'This woman came to see Buckby, right, and she was asking her about Poppy Hamlin. About what happened to her.'

Keren feels a chill run down her spine, but tries to keep her features arranged in an expression of casual interest.

'Buckteeth refuses to tell her anything, of course.' Chloe rolls her eyes. 'But Carla was walking past the office and overheard them talking and she went and spoke to this woman. And the woman showed her a picture of you apparently. And one of your Liam.'

The blood drains from Keren's face. 'And Carla? Did she—'

'She told her your names, yeah... Is this something to do with why you left in such a hurry?' Chloe asks sharply. 'And why you and Liam suddenly split up.'

Keren nods slowly. 'But, look, I can't talk about it, Chlo, I'm sorry. Not now, anyway. Not until...' She gathers herself. Chloe mustn't see her freaking out. 'So what did this woman look like?'

'I only caught a quick glimpse... middle-aged, fair hair, sort of shoulder length. Pretty-ish, nothing special... d'you know who she is?'

'No,' Keren says quickly. 'Not a clue. You get changed, and I'll go help your mum get supper ready.'

Once she's closed the door of Chloe's bedroom, she tries phoning Liam. It goes to voicemail. She composes a text, relaying what Chloe has just told her. Not so much out of loyalty to him, more as an attempt to safeguard the money from the house. They can't afford for their identities to come out now, not after everything they've been through.

. . .

'You off out somewhere?' Lorraine Dockerill asks Keren when she comes down to the kitchen on Thursday with her bag slung over her shoulder. 'Job interview?'

Keren makes a vague noise of assent, refusing the offer of something to eat first. Her stomach is churning, and the smell of frying bacon is making her intensely queasy. She has barely slept for the past two nights. All of Wednesday was spent trying to contact Liam and simultaneously trying to work out what she should do. And now she's decided.

'It's a waitressing job. Weekend shifts.'

'You'd do well to put a bit of slap on first, babe,' Chloe observes. She's sitting at the breakfast table and waves her piece of toast in the direction of the bruise-like shadows under Keren's eyes. 'And maybe wear something smarter.'

Keren looks down at the denim cut-offs and scruffy trainers. 'Like I said, it's just a waitressing job. Nowhere smart.'

She excuses herself before anyone has a chance to ask more questions and catches the overground to Liverpool Street, then the tube to St Pancras. There's a fast train to Gravesend about to pull out.

'Are you all right, love?' a woman asks as Keren pauses at the open door to the train, leaning on it slightly as she fights the urge to be sick.

'Yes. Thanks,' she replies weakly, forcing herself to climb in and take a seat just as the closing-door sensor pings. She's thought about taking more supplies several times since leaving Sycamore Gardens, and when she reaches Gravesend, she buys a large bottle of water and a packet of crackers. Then she catches the bus to the now familiar housing estate on the edge of the marshes. Muscle memory carries her along the Saxon Shore Way, picking her way over the scrubby, uneven ground. It's a humid, overcast day, with the thick, low cloud muffling the cries of the marsh birdlife.

Please, she repeats over and over in her head, like a mantra. *Please, when I get there, let there still be two people in the fort, and let them both be alive.*

There's no idea or plan in her head beyond that: just making sure both Hamlins are alive.

She descends the steps to the munitions store with exaggerated care, hesitating for a few seconds before pushing on the heavy wooden door. At first, she's not sure what she's seeing and fumbles in her bag for her phone. She switches on the torch function and shines it around the storeroom.

There are two people, and they are both alive. Keren's relief is so primal, so intense, that to start with she doesn't take in what she's actually seeing. She moves the torch beam around slowly with her right hand, her left hand flying to her mouth to suppress her cry of alarm.

Stephanie Hamlin is there – or at least a frail, emaciated version of her. And there is a second person, chained to the wall just as Stephanie is. It's someone Keren knows all too well.

But it's not Richard Hamlin.

PART THREE

LIAM

TWENTY-SEVEN

APRIL

Liam Devenish parallel parks the sleek Mercedes limousine, and brushes an imaginary speck of dust off the leather upholstery.

It's an Uber Executive car hired from a friend of a friend for the cost of the fares he'll be losing, plus a little bit extra. Not that Liam currently has the money with which to pay him, but if all goes according to plan today, he will be able to get his hands on it tomorrow. A few hundred quid is a small outlay for what he stands to gain.

He checks his reflection in the rear-view mirror, adjusts his tie. He's wearing his only suit, the one some well-meaning auntie bought him for his mother's funeral. He's put in many hours in the gym since then, so it's a little snug over the thighs and upper arms, but it still fits. Sort of. His shoes are the lace-ups with narrow toes favoured by estate agents. He's shaved and had his hair trimmed, and sprayed the last dregs of some after-shave Keren bought him last Christmas. He pulls his phone out of his pocket and fires off a text to his brother.

All good your end?

He hasn't brought Lance with him because the two of them are so clearly related, it might look a bit odd. A bit unbusiness-like. And also because this part of the job requires smooth and Lance doesn't do smooth. He's straight thug, even in a suit. He wouldn't give off a reassuring vibe.

His phone beeps with a reply: a simple thumbs-up emoji. Smoothing his hair in the mirror one last time, Liam puts on his shades and climbs out of the car. He walks up the path of the red-brick Edwardian building and rings the bell for the first-floor flat.

'Mrs Hamlin? I'm from Prodomus... can I come up.'

'What is this regarding?' The tone is a little wary.

'It's about your house draw win.'

He's let into the flat by Richard Hamlin, who smiles, but looks distracted. The hall is filled with cardboard packing crates. 'Sorry... we're both working at home today.' He indicates one desk in the corner of the living area and Stephanie, seated at her laptop at the kitchen table. She's wearing cream jeans and a gauzy top printed with butterflies. 'It's even more of a squeeze at the moment.'

A dog lying at her feet gets up and comes over to sniff his shoes. Christ, he hadn't thought that they might have a pet. Another layer of complication to deal with.

'Not for much longer, eh? Now you've got a beautiful new home to move into,' Liam says, smiling cheerfully. He intro-duces himself as Alex Thomas, showing them the business card with the name and the Prodomus logo that Lance arranged to have made up at the print shop where he works. He's bestowed himself with the title 'Client Liaison Director'.

'We've already had the keys handed over to us,' Stephanie Hamlin says doubtfully. 'They did a little presentation ceremo-ny.' She held out her hand when he introduced himself, her handshake cold and limp as a fish, but hasn't bothered standing up.

Liam explains that the conditions of the draw were that the winning ticket didn't only mean being given the house. There are other large prizes involved, including the one he's here to show them today.

'Ah yes, I think I remember reading that.' Richard Hamlin has a lilting Welsh voice. 'To be honest, I was so shocked to win that I haven't given it much thought. Something about a luxury yacht, was it? Or was it a holiday?'

Liam taps the side of his nose, making a mental note to check later and somehow make sure that the Prodomus administration doesn't come bearing gifts once the Hamlins are out of the picture. It could get awkward otherwise, although given his and Keren's resemblance to the true prize-winners, would they even notice? 'I'm afraid the bosses won't let me spoil the surprise,' he says, 'but I've got the car with me, and if you can both come with me now, all will be revealed.'

Stephanie frowns. 'We both have a lot to fit in before we have to collect our daughter from her nursery.'

'And I'm due on a video call in a couple of minutes,' adds Richard. 'Could we make an appointment to do it another time?'

Liam clenches his teeth. *No. No you bloody well couldn't.*

'No problem,' he says smoothly. 'It won't take long, just thirty minutes or so. I'll wait outside in the car, shall I? Until you've finished your call.'

'Shit!' he mutters to himself, sliding back into the driver's seat of the car. He wasn't sure what he was expecting, but it wasn't this. Most people would be only too thrilled to have some lavish prize heaped on them. Why were they being so bloody difficult? Would they even come at all?

But after about half an hour, he hears the front door of the building slam and there they are, Richard in a bomber jacket and Stephanie in a trench coat with a smart designer bag. It's raining slightly and there's a chilly spring breeze, which isn't exactly helping build the excitement. He climbs out of the car and ushers them into the back seat of the Mercedes. Once the Hamlins have fastened their seat belts, he discreetly engages the child locks on the rear doors.

'All aboard the magical mystery tour!' he says cheerfully in a voice that doesn't really belong to him. 'Temperature all right for you? I'll turn the heat up a touch, shall I?'

Avoiding making eye contact in the rear-view mirror, Liam moves the car smoothly through the traffic and onto the South Circular. As they leave central London behind them, Stephanie fidgets, checks her watch frequently, fretting about the time.

'Alex, we do have to be back before six to collect Poppy from nursery,'

'Plenty of time,' Liam reassures her, glancing back at her with a disingenuous smile.

Richard Hamlin is trying to work out where they're going. When he realises that they're headed towards the outer banks of the Thames, there's a glimmer of excitement in his eyes. The car pulls up outside a freight storage facility in Erith; somewhere suitably remote, and where one of Lance's less law-abiding mates happens to have a lockup.

'I think it is, you know,' Richard whispers to Stephanie. 'It's got to be a boat of some sort.'

'Or a car,' she murmurs. 'A car would be better; the Renault's on its last legs.'

'All will be revealed.' Liam's heart is pounding in his chest as he opens the rear door of the Mercedes, adrenaline coursing through him. 'Follow me.'

He leads the Hamlins to the door of the standalone storage unit, which is the size of a double garage. They don't hesitate, but then why would they? They saw the business card, and they genuinely think this is just another facet of their extraordinary fortune. Their recent good luck has left them feeling invincible. He slides open the metal door and herds the Hamlins through it, shutting and locking it behind them before they have digested the fact that there is no yacht inside. Or a boat of any description. Or even a car.

Instead there's just a white transit van and the looming figure of Lance Devenish with a hoodie pulled low over his face.

TWENTY-EIGHT

APRIL

In the couple of seconds that it takes for the Hamlins to understand that something is very, very wrong, Lance already has Richard Hamlin down on the concrete floor, felling him so brutally that he is winded and unable to resist the plastic cable ties that Lance attaches round his wrists and ankles. Stephanie screams and tries to back away, but Liam is behind her and grabs her roughly by the wrists, holding her still while Lance attaches ties to her too.

'Take his phone off him,' Liam barks, rooting through Stephanie's bag to find her mobile and sliding it into his jacket pocket.

'What the hell's going on?' Richard moans. 'Who are you? If it's money you want, we can pay you. We—'

'Shut up!' Lance is on edge, jittery from the adrenaline rush.

'This is something to do with the house, isn't it?' Stephanie's voice is breaking with fear. 'Why else would he say he's from Prodomus?' She squirms on the floor until she's pressed herself up onto her elbows, then screams at the top of her voice. 'Help! Someone please, help!'

'We need to shut them up,' Liam mutters to his brother. 'This is doing my head in.'

Lance finds a couple of oily rags in the van and clumsily gags the Hamlins, but not before Stephanie has shouted, 'We have a baby, for God's sake! If nobody turns up to fetch her, they're going to know something's happened to us!'

Once silenced, their captives stop struggling. The brothers lift them and lie them on the floor of the empty van, having first removed the hoodie, joggers and trainers that have been stowed in there for Liam to change into. He removes the suit and smart shoes, bundling them under the passenger seat, then lights two cigarettes and hands one to Lance. As they smoke them, Lance asks: 'You know you said we can't risk going to the fort till it's dark, right? So what are we going to do for the next couple of hours?'

'We're going to use the time to go back to their flat...' Liam pulls Lance out of earshot of the van and jerks his head in the Hamlins' direction, '...and pick up what we need. The keys to the prize house, for starters. Apart from anything else, we don't even know the address of our new place yet.'

Lance drives the van, retracing the route Liam has just taken. They arrive back in Herne Hill just after five o'clock and park a few streets from the Hamlins' flat. After they've let themselves in using the keys Liam has removed from Stephanie's bag, they start sorting through the piles of correspondence and box files on Richard Hamlin's desk.

'You need to let Kez know what's going on, remember,' Lance says. 'So she knows it's okay to take the kid. Like they said, if no one collects her, it'll be a big red flag.'

All sorted. Over to you

Liam sends the brief text, just as his brother triumphantly holds up a clear plastic folder. Inside are letters from Prodomus, legal contracts and a copy of the title deeds to 12, Sycamore Gardens, London SW8.

'Sweet!' Liam high fives his brother.

'Does this mean we're good to go?'

'One second.'

Liam sends the location to Keren and a text to the owner of the borrowed Mercedes, giving him the address of the storage facility and confirming that the keys are on top of the front near-side tyre. He's tempted to linger and go over the flat in earnest and see what else they can find. The Hamlins' Ultra HD television, in particular, is tempting him. But hanging around any longer is risky. The occupants of the other flats will probably be returning from work soon. Lance puts down food and water for the dog, and then they make a swift exit from the building. They'll need to come back, but it can wait.

'Bruv, have you thought about... you know?' Lance ventures as he drives the van back in the direction of Kent.

'About what?' Liam asks, but he's being deliberately obtuse. He and his twin are so adept at reading each other's minds he knows exactly what Lance is referring to.

'About what we do with them.' Lance jerks his head towards the body of the transit. 'You know, after. After we've taken them there.'

It's not as though Liam hasn't thought about this. But he probably hasn't thought about it enough. In the past, he's been in trouble here and there, but nothing that you'd call big time. He's got a caution on his record, that's all. And Lance did a short stretch in a borstal as a teenager after he got into a fight and the boy he hit ended up with a brain injury. But that was several years ago, and although he hangs around with some unsavoury characters, he's not what you'd call a criminal mastermind. This venture – abduction and false imprisonment – is well out of his league. Out of both their leagues.

'What we're going to do,' Liam tells his brother firmly, 'is we're going to keep them there and take care of them just long enough to get the prize house sold and bank the cash. And get a plan in place to get the hell away, abroad or whatever. Once we've done all that, we can let them go.'

Lance frowns. 'I don't get it. How's that going to work if we're abroad?'

'We'll phone someone anonymously, tell them where we've hidden them. The police, or their family, or whatever.'

'It's going to be difficult, though, keeping them alive.'

'Jesus, bruv, I know!' Liam slaps the flat of his palm against the passenger window. 'We're just going to have to box clever.'

A heavy silence hangs between them, broken only by the beating of rain on the windscreen as they weave their way through traffic on the A2.

'I mean—'

'What?' snaps Liam. From the rear of the van, one of the Hamlins starts kicking rhythmically on one of the side panels. 'Christ!'

'Wouldn't it be easier if we just... took care of things for good.'

Liam turns his head to the right and stares at his brother. 'And how do you propose we do that? Shoot them? Stab them? Strangle them in cold blood? Are you really up for that? If this goes tits up, d'you really want to be looking at life without parole?'

Lance drums his fingers on the steering wheel. 'Yeah, but couldn't we just, you know, not bother to feed them.'

'Leave them there to die, you mean? Get real, Lance. That would still be murder if we got caught.'

They lapse into silence until they reach Gravesend, when Liam tells Lance to pull over at a retail park with a large home goods superstore. He goes into the store and comes out with a plastic bucket, some bottles of water, biscuits and a couple of sleeping bags. When they reach the eastern end of town, Lance switches off the headlights and parks at the far end of a quiet cul-de-sac. Beyond it lies the marshes, dark and empty.

'How the hell are we going to get them out there?' Lance asks, gazing into the blackness of the horizon, just streaked with a fading silver light. 'From what I remember back when we were kids, it's a bit of a trek.'

'We're going to have to untie their legs and they're going to have to walk it,' Liam says after a few seconds. 'It's way too far for us to carry them, and we've got all the other stuff to take too.'

'But then they're going to try and run for it.'

'You bring the chains like I told you to? And the torch?'

Lance nods, holding up a canvas tool bag.

'We're going to have to chain them to the wall. Got a knife?'

A flick knife is produced from Lance's hoodie pocket.

'Good. Make sure you let them see it, okay? And that you intend to use it.' Liam opens the door and jumps out of the cab. 'Shake a fucking leg, we need to get moving! We've got to get to the fort and back, then drive back into town and fetch my pickup with all the stuff in it. Kez will have got the kid by now, so she can't hang around forever.'

Lance is already hauling the gagged Hamlins out of the van and releasing their ankle ties, and removing Richard Hamlin's glasses, which he hands to his brother. After attaching the length of chain round first Richard's wrists, then Stephanie's, he positions himself behind them, knife in hand. Liam walks ahead carrying the supplies he has just bought, and this bizarre group starts moving down the coastal path to Eastmeade Fort.

TWENTY-NINE

APRIL

Liam loves the house. This, he decides on his first morning waking up here, is the home he deserves.

Of course it would be a hell of a lot more fun if for the short time he lived there he had it to himself. But, unfortunately, Keren is an essential part of the plan. The beauty of the whole thing, the essential pivot that made it all possible, is Keren working at the very same nursery where the Hamlins send their child. If there were any question of the kid being abandoned or abducted, then alarm bells would have rung straight away. The fact that they were able to get Poppy away without anything seeming amiss was a stroke of genius and one that Liam is fully prepared to take credit for.

And, for now, it's vital that Keren sticks around, because he needs her to take care of the Hamlins' daughter. From what Liam's seen in the last twelve hours, Poppy is going to be a right pain. Keren doesn't seem any more enamoured with her than he is, but at least with her training she knows what to do. Knows how to look after a baby.

As far as he's concerned, it's been over with Keren for a while now. When he met her, she was super-pretty, shy and easily impressed. But then he made the mistake of agreeing to move in together and, like most women, she turned out to be a closet nag. An armchair critic. But by then they were stuck sharing a roof, and that always makes things complicated. They rubbed along after a fashion, and he had his little flings on the side, but it was hardly wine and roses.

And he has to tell her how to do everything. Like this morning; explaining how they need to use the Hamlins' phones to resign from their jobs and keep their families at bay. Most of the time, she doesn't have a clue. Like letting in the nosy woman from a few doors down just after they'd arrived. He could see the expression on the cow's face as she scoped out their situation, her beady eyes taking in every little detail. Pointing out that they didn't have a highchair, like she's the parenting police. She obviously thought he and Lance were the removal crew too. Keren would never have thought to have just shut the door in her face. But he can't go on at her about it because, for now, he needs to keep her sweet.

For now, he needs her.

That afternoon, Liam and Lance drive back to the flat in Herne Hill, taking Keren and the baby with them. Keren's not exactly thrilled about the dog, but once she's got her hands on the Hamlins' fancy buggy, she's happy to take Poppy and leave them to it.

Liam lets her believe that they are going to store the flat contents, but he has no intention of doing so. Apart from the hassle, a lockup full of the Hamlins' possessions is potential evidence. The bedrooms both have built-in wardrobes and shelving, leaving a double bed, a sofa, kitchen table and chairs, and a desk to dispose of. They deal with this in a couple of trips to the local tip, then pack up the TV and the baby equipment to take back to Sycamore Gardens. Liam takes care to find the

Hamlins' passports, bank details and birth certificates, stowing them in Richard Hamlin's own leather messenger bag. The sale of number 12 will require them to verify their identities as Richard and Stephanie, and there will be money-laundering checks; he knows that much. He also packs up some of Richard's clothes, deciding that his new persona will be more convincing if he can dress the part.

And they have to take Buster with them too. Lance has taken a liking to the dog, and although Liam would personally rather take it to a shelter, it occurs to him that the Hamlins are the sort of people who would have chipped their pet, and that could be yet another potential red flag. Any decision they take has to be thought through with just one question in mind: will this make people wonder what's happened to the Hamlins?

But he can pull this off, Liam tells himself. He's perfectly confident that he's got this.

Jane, the woman from number 5, has clearly not taken the hint.

As he drives back to Sycamore Gardens the following day, he sees her door-stopping Keren and once again trying to engage her in conversation. He's not going to let this pass.

'What the fuck did she want? Bloody busybody.'

Keren gets all defensive, saying she was just offering to help.

'Well, stay away from her, okay? And the other neighbours. We can't afford to let people get too close, or they'll start asking awkward questions.'

He knows he sounds aggressive, but he doesn't really care, just as long as he keeps a lid on things. Keren herself has started asking awkward questions, constantly demanding to know where the Hamlins are 'staying'. But a couple of weeks later she does also come out with something that might prove useful. He finds an invite to a barbecue in the communal gardens pushed through the front door, and while they're debating the ins and outs of attending, Keren lets slip that she's seen Jane Headley's husband with another woman.

Liam makes a mental note to observe the couple's dynamic when he goes to the party. Because he's determined to attend, to feel that while he's here, he just as good as all the other people who live on this street. That he belongs. After all, the hardest part of the plan is now done: time to enjoy the rewards.

So, on the afternoon of the barbecue, he dresses in a pink shirt of Richard Hamlin's, puts Hamlin's glasses in his pocket, and goes to rub shoulders with the other residents of the postcode's most desirable street.

He notices her straightaway.

How could he not? She would have been the first person anyone noticed, at any event. Liam is used to attracting pretty girls, but this woman is way, way beyond pretty. She's exotically beautiful, and so exquisitely groomed and polished that everything about her gleams: her skin, her hair, even her fingernails. The fact that she has two children with her barely registers with Liam, nor does the engagement ring she's wearing. He's hardpressed not to just stand and stare at her like a clueless schoolboy.

His reverie is interrupted by Jane Headley, who – with her floral dress, velvet hairband and sensible shoes – looks exactly as you would expect a primary school teacher to look. The last thing he wants is to talk to her about his work, or rather Richard Hamlin's work, about which he knows less than nothing. He catches sight of her husband, hovering near where the meat is being cooked. Of the two Headleys, he has definitely aged better, and has an air of patrician confidence that Liam envies a little. It's not all that surprising that he's playing away.

Then, just as he's wondering how he can escape from the

woman's unsettling scrutiny, she makes the discomfort worth-while by introducing him to *her*.

'Irina, this is Richard Hamlin. You know; half of the lucky couple who won number twelve.'

'Irina Semenova.'

The feel of her skin against his as she shakes his hand is like an electric current. Nobody else notices it, he's sure, but her fingers linger just a fraction longer than they should.

'You're Russian, right? Or Czech?'

'I am Siberian.' Her eyes bore into his, the irises as silvery and mysterious as a winter sky.

'And... don't tell me... you're a model?'

'Like nobody ever said that before,' she scoffs, but there's a hint of playfulness around her mouth. 'And you?'

'I'm an accountant.'

'I don't believe you.'

Liam takes a second to compose himself, to realise that she's teasing him rather than exposing him. 'You'd be right, actually,' he counters, 'because I've recently given up accounting to go into property development.'

He came up with this lie to Jane Headley a few minutes ago, and to his mind, it has a convincing ring to it.

'How do you find the time?' she asks him now.

'Come again?'

She presses an immaculate shell-pink fingertip against his upper arm. 'You spend a lot of time in the gym. I can see this.'

He grins and shrugs. 'What can I say? Guilty as charged.'

The fingernail traces lightly towards his wrist. 'You are good with your hands too, I think.'

Their eyes meet, lock.

'And I know something else about you too...' Her hand reaches up and fiddles with the diamond clip in her hair, flicking one of the long chestnut locks over her shoulder. 'You are not faithful to your wife.'

THIRTY

JUNE

In the days following the barbecue, Liam thinks constantly, obsessively, about Irina Semenova.

No woman has ever had this effect on him before. If he were able to articulate it, he would describe what he's feeling now as a powerful sort of longing. It's not just for Irina's singular beauty, but for what she represents: a glimpse of a lifestyle that he would once only have witnessed on the television or cinema screen. And now he finds himself loitering in the street near her house in the hope that she'll be coming or going, or that she'll see him through the window. That they'll cross paths again.

But they don't, and eventually he bumps into her nanny in the local convenience store, engaging her in small talk long enough to learn that she's taken the children to visit her mother in Vladivostok. 'For a few days,' is all the nanny reveals, and Liam doesn't want to draw attention to himself by pressing her for an exact date.

He resorts to online stalking and finds modelling shots, which he screenshots and saves to his phone, staring at them at night when Keren is asleep. Most unsettling of all, he finds that she's appeared in high-profile lingerie campaigns, showing off a body that is more perfect, more sexy than any he's ever seen. He zooms in on the curve of her breasts, the gleaming length of her thighs. No one should be allowed to be that hot, he thinks. It's plain disturbing. He almost can't bring himself to look at the lingerie shots: they're too much.

'You're in a horrible mood,' Keren points out to him. 'You should be happy, now you get to live in a place like this. It's what you wanted, after all.'

Ah, but now it's not enough, Liam thinks. He wants more. He wants Irina.

When he and Lance removed the Hamlins from their flat and imprisoned them in the basement of the fort, they agreed that for the foreseeable future it would be safest if it's only Lance who makes the journeys back to Eastmeade to drop food and water.

A few weeks after the barbecue, Lance texts Liam after his latest trip to Kent.

Bruv, I reckon someone else has been going there

Liam feels a quiver of unease in his stomach as he reads the message.

He replies: *Why what's happened?*

We took the one bucket, but I've just realised there are more of them. They have spare ones now. So WTF?

Liam closes his eyes after reading this, shaking his head with frustration. The whole idea of Lance doing the donkey work is because now Liam is supposed to be Richard Hamlin, respectable chartered accountant and family man. This news means he has no choice but to go straight back to Kent himself. He doesn't want to, but can't afford not to.

The next morning, he drives down to Gravesend and makes the long walk out along the shoreline to the fort, taking a couple of bottles of a sports drink, some apples and toilet roll with him, on the grounds that even though Lance has just taken food, going empty-handed makes poor logistical sense.

The smell in the place is revolting, but, to his relief, he sees straight away that the Hamlins are both still there, still chained to the wall. They seize on the sweet-flavoured drink as though he's bought them vintage champagne. Richard doesn't say much, blinking uncertainly in the half-light, his eyes unfocused without his glasses. His skin as pale as paper and he doesn't look well. Stephanie, as usual, is the noisy one, crying and pleading one minute, swearing angrily the next. She has a packet of tampons next to her sleeping bag, Liam notices.

He pokes them with his foot. 'Where did you get these?'

'The girl brought them.'

'What girl?' Liam asks, although he's pretty sure he already knows.

'The girl. I know her: she works at Poppy's nursery. She's called Keren.'

Liam makes no comment, but considers this piece of news as he trudges back along the Saxon Shore Way, lighting up a fresh cigarette as soon as he's reached the end of the last one. It's not that much of a surprise, given Keren's constant questioning, and better her than somebody else. But her knowing where the Hamlins are being kept prisoner definitely raises the stakes. One the one hand, it increases the pressure to keep the couple alive and well, because if anything were to happen to them, there's a risk that she might blab. On the other hand, there's also a distinct risk she might take pity on them and try to let them go.

To his mind, this risk is only increased by Stephanie and Keren already knowing one another.

Back in London, he says nothing immediately, but keeps a close eye on Keren's movements. She can't be dragging a heavy buggy all the way across the marshes, so she must be doing something with the baby that frees her up to make the trip to Kent. Sure enough, about a week later, he catches her picking up Poppy from one of the flats at the far end of Sycamore Gardens.

When he challenges her, she admits that she's been leaving the baby to go to the fort. Not just with the Indian lady at the flats, but with nosy Jane Headley, on several occasions. And with the knowledge of her husband too. He tries to make Keren see that by taking favours from the neighbours, they're putting themselves at risk of discovery. And that now that risk has become real, they need to counter it by getting some dirt on the Headleys.

Keren thinks they're too squeaky clean, but to Liam's mind, nobody is that perfect.

'Didn't you say her old man was playing around?'

They're in the kitchen with the wretched baby shrieking somewhere upstairs. Liam lights a cigarette to try and calm his nerves. 'Well, maybe we can use that to our advantage somehow. Who is she? One of the neighbours?'

'I don't think so. I've never seen her round here apart from that one time.'

'Well, I need to find out who she is, yeah? Get on to it. Let's face it, you're going to have time on your hands now you're not going down to Kent anymore.'

'Who says I'm not?' The sound of crying still permeates the room. Keren stamps over to the kitchen door and slams it.

'I do.' Liam inhales on his cigarette and gives her a hard look. 'Seriously, you'd better not, Kez. No more trips to East-meade, yeah? Or you'll regret it.'

He tells her that she needs to try to find out who Fergus Headley's fancy piece is, and, to give Keren her due, she goes and does some snooping at his place of work and comes back with a name. Predictably, the bit on the side is one of his students: Selina Permeti. Liam makes a note of her name on his phone and saves it. It's collateral, he tells Keren, and he intends to use it.

Liam distracts himself from his obsession with the occupant of number 17 by trying to work out the best way to put pressure on the man who lives at number 5.

The next morning, he pretends to be going for a run, slowing down outside the Headleys' house and looking in through the windows. Their ugly Volvo is parked outside, but since Fergus Headley works in the centre of London, he almost certainly commutes on public transport, so that means nothing. He's just about to ring the doorbell and see if Fergus is in when a large black limousine glides to a halt beside him. There's a uniformed driver in the front, and blacked-out windows in the rear. One of them glides down slowly, revealing Irina in grey Lycra workout gear, her lustrous tresses tied up in a high ponytail.

'Richard.'

She makes the two syllables sound like a dirty word.

Liam's mouth opens, but he can't think of anything to say.

'Come,' she says, with a catlike smile. 'Come to my house, now.'

THIRTY-ONE

JULY

'Where are your kids?' Liam asks as soon as the door of number 17 is opened to him.

'Out with the nanny,' Irina says coolly, walking straight to the foot of the stairs. She didn't seem to be in any doubt that he would come, or that he will follow her up to the bedroom without question. Which he does.

'And your old man?'

'In Zurich, on business.' She pivots on the thickly carpeted landing as though it's a catwalk and gives him a smug little smile. 'And the housekeeper has day off.'

The master suite is the most opulent Liam has ever seen. Instead of a headboard, the entire wall behind the ten-foot-wide bed is padded with palest pink velvet. A huge Art Deco chandelier is flush-mounted at the centre of the ceiling and the heavy drapes are trimmed with crystal beads. The cream carpet is overlaid with a huge sheepskin rug dyed to look like a cloud of pink candy floss. Liam reaches instinctively to remove his trainers, feeling at once thrilled and intimidated. The master bedroom at number 12 is nice enough, but it looks like a page from a John Lewis catalogue. Nothing like this.

'I have been to gym, I need to shower,' Irina tells him matter-of-factly, disappearing into the huge bathroom and reappearing a few minutes later wearing nothing but a white towel.

Liam is still standing there in his shorts and gym socks, exactly where she left him. He's afraid to move in case he somehow breaks the spell and messes something up, but he's also extremely aroused and reaches out for her, his fingers slipping on the smooth, oiled skin of her arms.

'You have been running?'

He nods.

'So you must shower too.'

When he emerges from the bathroom, a bottle of champagne in an ice bucket and two glasses have appeared from somewhere. Irina is dressed in skimpy black underwear and posed coquettishly on the bed. Her body is intimidatingly perfect, and for the first time in his life, Liam wonders whether he will be able to perform. But he does, more than once, and with the help of various sex toys that Irina pulls from a white leather box next to the bed.

'Your old man into all this, then?' Liam murmurs, tracing a line down her tanned back with a red and black leather bullwhip.

'These are mine,' says Irina calmly. 'This is my room. We have separate bedrooms.'

'So you and he...'

'He is not interested now we have children.' She turns down the corners of her mouth as she reaches for her glass of champagne. 'He is only interested in business. Always making calls, twenty-four hours.'

'Okay then...' Liam props himself up on one elbow, looking around the room with lingering awe. 'So why me?'

Irina gives a coquettish little shrug, purses her lips. 'When I see you, I think you are very cute, you know? Very sexy. I decide then, I will have you.'

'So you decided we would do this the night we met?' Liam grins. 'What took you so bloody long?'

She shrugs again. 'I do things when I am ready. Also, you are married and is not often I am alone here. Is not easy.'

'But you want to do this again?'

Irina doesn't answer, reaching for her drink again, but there's the hint of a smile playing around her lips. Imagine being her fiancé, Liam tells himself. Having sex with her like this is already the most amazing thing that's ever happened to him, but imagine being with a woman like this, properly, all the time. It would be the most incredible thing ever.

Irina takes Liam's mobile number, but she doesn't give him her own.

'It's better like this,' she tells him coolly, without elaborating.

So, for the next few days, Liam walks around in a state of torment, unable to text or phone her, waiting for her to contact him. This is not an arrangement he's ever experienced before. Nor has he ever experienced wanting a woman before, not like this. Girls have come and gone, and since he was fifteen he's always had at least one on the go, but they've always been in the background. Any desire he's felt for them has been quickly extinguished with the first sexual encounter, and thereafter they've just been... there. For him to use as and when he's in the mood. Part of the fabric of his life, occasionally fun or at least convenient, but never wanted, deep down in the pit of his being, like he wants Irina Semenova.

Michael Kovacic returns from Switzerland the next day, and Liam can only look on helplessly as members of the household come and go in a series of chauffeur-driven vehicles.

Eventually, he gets a call from a withheld number.

'Tonight,' Irina's voice says, 'Michael is away, in Frankfurt. But leave it until after ten, when nanny has gone up to her flat.'

He does what he is told, and is admitted by Irina, tiptoeing up the stairs to her room and engaging in passionate, if muted, sex. As before, there is no communication between them until she summons him again a few days later and the same scenario plays out: intense, muffled sex in her luxurious pink and cream boudoir while the children and nanny sleep upstairs.

This is his life, Liam thinks in wonderment after this third time. He not only lives in a big house in a smart street, but he gets to sleep with a Russian supermodel. Just as he convinced himself he was entitled to win the prize draw, he now convinces himself that he's entitled to Irina too.

On the third evening, emboldened, he says: 'I'm really into you, you know.'

I love you, is what he wants to say, but is afraid of being cheesy.

'Michael is coming back tomorrow,' is her only response.

He pulls a face as he tugs his shorts back on.

'But don't worry; I have a solution.'

She explains that the family who live next door to the Headleys have gone on holiday and left the key at number 17, so that Irina's housekeeper can go in and look after their house. They can meet there easily, she tells him: all she needs to do is to grab the key and slip out once Michael has headed up to his room. She doesn't ask if he's okay with this plan. She already knows he will be.

'You don't need the glasses.' Irina pulls them out of his pocket during their second tryst at number 6. She twirls the glasses by the arm. 'You always have them with you, but you don't really need them, you know, to see.'

'I'm long-sighted,' Liam says, hoping this explains the fact that he carries Richard Hamlin's glasses like a prop. This house is nowhere near as flash as the one she shares with Michael, but even so, it's smart and stylish, like something out of an interiors magazine. After being locked up for days in a heatwave, the interior is hot and cloying, so once they've helped themselves to cold drinks, Liam takes Irina by the wrist and leads her out into the back garden. They've both kicked off their shoes, and the grass feels pleasantly cool underfoot, the air warm but fragrant with honeysuckle and jasmine. As he leans in to kiss her, he looks up at the house next door and sees a backlit figure in one of the upstairs windows. Jane Headley.

He doesn't mention this to Irina, knowing instinctively that she will want them to stop if he does. Instead he puts on a show, hoicking up her dress and humping her against the wooden picnic table, before pulling her down onto the lawn with him. His roughness thrills her and she arches her back and moans with pleasure.

'You're good,' she moans, 'You're so good at this.'

I'm the king of the bloody world.

Afterwards, when they're lying curled around one another on the grass, he holds up her left hand and turns it this way and that, making the huge diamond catch the light. It must be at least five carats, he thinks, doing a quick mental calculation of its value.

'That's quite some rock,' he observes.

'Yes, I know.'

'So when are you getting married?'

'Who says I'm getting married?' She pulls her hand away and turns onto her back, staring up at the dark purple sky.

'Isn't that what people do when they get engaged?'

'Not necessarily. We already have children. And I have

prenup. It says even if Michael and I do not marry, I will get five million if I walk away.'

Liam lets out a low whistle. 'Five million quid! Bloody hell.'

She smirks. 'I know. Think what we will do with this money.'

He leans up on one elbow, hardly able to believe what he's just heard. 'What "we" will do?'

'Yes. If I leave him, still I will be rich. We could have fun with that money, yes? We could go overseas with it. Monte Carlo perhaps. Or Bermuda. Oh... except you are married.' She pulls a mock sad face.

Except that he's not married, not to Keren or anyone else. But he can't tell her that. Instead, he curls his fingers round her wrist and pulls her round so that she's looking at him. 'Trust me, for five million quid, I can arrange to be single.'

THIRTY-TWO

JULY

After that night in the garden of number 6, Liam thinks about Irina constantly, just as he always does. But now he's also thinking about her five-million-pound exit package. The sale of number 12 promises to net close to three million, probably less if they push for a quick cash sale. He hasn't quite decided how he will split the proceeds with Keren. Certainly not fifty-fifty; in his mind, she deserves no more than thirty per cent, if that. And, of course, he will need to give Lance a share. It's only fair to reward his twin's total loyalty.

But it's apparent that his own share is going to be a fraction of the wealth he could enjoy if Irina left Michael for him. Around a million and a half would be nice, but six and a half million would put him in another league. And she actually said she wants them to go and live abroad with the money. Liam doesn't have much experience of being abroad, having only been to Magaluf once. Left to his own devices, he wouldn't have a clue, but with Irina Semenova dangling off his arm, it would be a completely different matter. He pictures their life together as something from a James Bond movie: all casinos and speed-boats. The thought that Irina has two small children is pushed firmly to the back of his mind. As is the question of where Lance would end up living. He can hardly take Lance along to be the third wheel in his new love nest. Keren tolerated his brother's constant presence, but he can't see Irina doing the same.

He wonders how long it would take her to get her settlement from Michael, how long before he could leave Keren, leave South London and simply disappear? But, in the meantime, he has to deal first with the Headleys, then the Hamlins. That nosy bag Jane Headley already knew too much about their business, but now she also knows he's sleeping with Irina too. He needs to shut her up.

The opportunity presents itself the following evening when he sees her leaving the house on foot, all dressed up as if she's going somewhere. He lets her get to the end of the Gardens before jumping into his pickup and following at a safe distance. She disappears into a bar on South Lambeth Road, where it looks as though a group of people are waiting for her.

Liam parks where he can see the entrance to the bar and waits for an hour and a half until she emerges carrying a balloon and a gift bag. Putting on Richard Hamlin's glasses, he jumps out of his truck and walks in the same direction, until, inevitably, she becomes aware that there's someone directly behind her.

'Can I help you?' Jane asks, when she recognises him.

'Should be the other way round, shouldn't it?'

She looks nervous now. 'I... I'm not sure what you mean.'

'What I mean is... it's you who seems to want something from me.'

'No, I don't.' He can tell from the way her voice rises that she's a bit tipsy. 'What on earth gives you that idea? I did what any good neighbour would do welcoming new people to their street. And I certainly didn't go looking to babysit your daughter!'

'I'm not talking about that. I'm talking about you following me about, spying on me.'

'I don't spy on people.'

'I'm talking about watching through windows. Looking into other people's houses. And gardens.'

'Look.' She goes all schoolmistressy on him now. 'Despite what you might think, I don't care what you get up to behind Stephanie's back. Your private life is your own concern.'

'Good. And it better stay that way. You understand?'

He stares at her, making it clear he expects her to say something.

'Yes. I understand.'

'Your old man needs to keep you under better control, know what I'm saying?'

He leaves her on the pavement, looking suitably shocked, and walks back to his truck. The problem of her husband still needs dealing with, though, and by Liam's calculation, with Jane being on foot, he's got at least a ten-minute jump on her. That means another ten minutes of Fergus Headley being home alone.

He drives recklessly, cutting up other drivers and jumping a couple of red lights, pulling up in Sycamore Gardens a couple of minutes later.

'Can I help you?' Fergus Headley echoes his wife's words as he opens the front door. *Jesus*, thinks Liam, the pair of them are like a middle-class Punch and Judy. 'It's Richard, isn't it? Is this about babysitting little Poppy? Only Jane's out, I'm afraid.'

Liam pushes the glasses up his nose, then inserts his hands deep into his pockets. 'Nah, it's not about the baby. It's about your wife.'

Fergus frowns. 'Jane? What—'

'Or should I say, it's about Selina Permeti.'

The other man stares, his face growing pale.

'You know what I'm talking about, yeah? The student you're messing around with.'

'How do you know about that?' Fergus sounds angry know. 'I mean what the hell—'

'Your missus doesn't know about it, though, right? And I'm guessing you don't want her finding out. So I'm telling you right here, right now: you keep her out of my business, or I let her know you've been playing away.'

'But—'

'Just make sure she keeps her nose out, okay? I don't care how you do it, just make sure you do.'

Jane Headley is not the only one causing problems: far from it. Lance reports that when he's been to check on the Hamlins, Stephanie won't stop mouthing off about Keren, and how she knows exactly who she is.

'I dunno, bruv.' His brother, usually so unconcerned, sounds rattled. 'It just feels like it's making things a whole lot riskier, her making that connection. If they got out somehow, and they were gunning for Kez... well, that would lead them straight to you. To us.'

Lance is right. Keren going to the fort has put the whole abduction enterprise into jeopardy. Letting them go at some point depended on him and Keren maintaining anonymity, but now that's been blown. He pictures himself living in a Mediterranean villa somewhere with Irina, and Interpol turning up there to arrest him. Ruining their idyllic new life. He'll be damned if he lets Keren mess things up for him.

And then Irina and Michael go away on holiday with their children, leaving Liam restless and miserable. He can't even message Irina, because he still doesn't have her number.

He takes advantage of having more time on his hands to

regularly chase the estate agent, reminding them of their promises about a quick sale. One of the agents at the firm he's using, a guy called Alfie, phones him and reports that a woman called at the house while he was there showing prospective buyers around, and introduced herself as Stephanie Hamlin's sister. Keeping the Hamlins' real life at bay has been like trying to dodge an incoming tide. And now the waters have reached the shore.

When they first arrived, the name of the game was to leave as fast as possible. But since meeting Irina, that has changed. Liam now wants to stay at 12, Sycamore Gardens, because it puts him only a few doors away from the object of his desire. But despite the lure of his high-octane love affair, Alfie's news spells out that he and Keren are going to have to move on, and soon.

When Keren gets back on the evening of the viewing, she's alone and announces that she's taken both the baby and the dog to her sister's place in Chelmsford.

'How do we know we can trust her not to blab?' Liam demands, going into the en suite where she's soaking in the tub like the lady of leisure she now is.

'Because she thinks Poppy is ours. She looks like she could be. So what would there be for her to blab about?'

Keren's right, but because she's not Irina, and because he's sore that he hasn't heard from Irina for days, he gives her a hard time anyway. He accuses her of not doing enough to keep Stephanie's relatives happy and thereby putting the whole plan at risk. Their argument could have lasted all night, but it's interrupted by Lance's arrival. Liam has asked his twin to come over for an urgent discussion.

Because, after weighing up the options, he's made a huge decision.

. . .

First, he has to make sure that the two of them are out of Keren's earshot, so he leads Lance into the dining room and closes the door behind him.

'Look, bruv, there's something big we need to talk about, yeah? I've been thinking, and the way things are going, I don't think we've got much choice. I think it's time for us to cut our losses.'

'You mean finish things completely?' Lance mimes holding a gun to his temple.

Liam nods slowly.

'How?'

'Can you get your hands on a weapon?'

'I dunno man... I can try. When?'

Liam fumbles in his shorts pocket for his cigarettes and lights one. 'Not tonight obviously. But as soon as you've got hold of the... equipment. And it needs to be at a time when you can get an alibi. Someone other than me and Kez: we're too closely involved, obviously.'

Liam hears a noise from the hall and holds a finger to his lips, nodding in the direction of the door.

'Thursday there's a game of pool on at the Golden Lion. I can get Derren to say I was there.'

'This Thursday? Can you get hold of what you need by then?'

'I reckon I can, yeah.'

'This Thursday, then, okay,' Liam says. It's his turn to mime holding a gun to his temple.

Lance grins, and gives his brother a silent high five.

THIRTY-THREE

AUGUST

Liam has set up an alert on his phone for new stories concerning the North Kent coast. If anything happens in the vicinity of Eastmeade, he wants to know about it. The next morning he's sent a link to a local news story on the BBC site.

Abandoned local fort slated for development

A disused artillery fort built in the 1780s to guard the entrance to the Thames will soon be the subject of a redevelopment project. The local marsh nature reserve is under the jurisdiction of the Royal Society for the Protection of Birds, and with the help of funding from Gravesham Borough Council, the Society intends to create a visitor centre at Eastmeade Fort...

'Shit!' He swears out loud when he reads it, scanning the text for a date relating to this proposed plan. There is none. Even so, this project changes the landscape. Literally and metaphorically.

He phones Lance, who picks up with, 'Mate, I'm in the van.'

'You got the... you know.'

'Just on my way to pick it up from a mate of Kasher's.'

Taking the sideways step from abduction to murder has been relatively easy, Liam thinks. It's amazing how once you've crossed a certain line, you grow very used to being on that side of it. But, actually, killing a person is not easy. He and Lance have used the private messaging app Moxo to debate the best way to go about it, and there's no method that is unproblematic. Lance suggested poisoning, but Liam dismissed it as complicated and having too many variables. Stabbing, unless it's a hate crime, seems not only messy but unreliable. What happens if you don't stab someone in the right place or the right amount? Then they might survive.

'Do it multiple times,' Lance suggested. Lance, who carries a knife with him to look hard but has never used it in anger.

'No way.' Liam was firm. 'We're not fucking animals.'

So they settled on using a single shot to the brain, assassin-style. Again, they talk about this as though it is simple, when, in reality, it is not simple. Not at all.

'Here's the thing...' Liam walks over to the living-room window and pulls back the curtain, his eyes straying automatically in the direction of number 17. The shutters are closed in the front windows. Irina and Michael and the children are still away, and he hates it, burning with impatience to see her again. 'We can't just off them and leave them there, okay. Not in the fort.'

'Why not? I thought that was what we agreed was best.'

'That was when we thought they would never be found afterwards.' His words are tumbling out in a rush now, 'But thing is, it looks like they're about to go in and develop the place. That means them being identified. DNA, dental records, and the like. And as soon as they know it's the Hamlins, they find out that they won this place. Which is bound to lead them to us, one way or another.'

Outside, the door of number 17 is opening and Liam's heart lurches in his chest. But it's only the housekeeper. She has a duster and a bottle of polish and starts cleaning the heavy brass knocker. He swears under his breath.

'What was that, bruv?' asks Lance.

'Nothing... Look, you're going to have to move them. Or move the bodies at least.'

'Fuck no: listen, I can't carry two of them along that path by myself! You know what it's like underfoot round there. Even supposing no one sees me. And where am I supposed to carry them to, anyway?'

'Okay, so before you, you know... pull the trigger, you're going to have to get them out of there. Like we moved them between the van and the fort, yeah? Make them walk, only use the gun this time. Get to the water's edge, then fire the gun and make sure they end up in the water. Somewhere they'll decompose before they're found.'

There's a long pause. Liam can hear his brother drumming his fingers on the steering wheel. 'I dunno, mate, I don't think it's going to be that straightforward.'

'Well, whatever you do, you can't leave the bodies behind, okay? It's just too bloody risky.'

On Thursday morning, Liam watches through the window as the convoy of cars brings back Irina, Michael, the children and nanny. A few hours later another limo appears and whisks Michael away.

He's already like a cat on hot bricks, messaging Lance constantly on Moxo to find out how things are going. And now he has to tie himself in knots waiting to hear from Irina too.

At seven o'clock she phones him, withholding her number as usual.

'Michael is not here, so... would you like come here?'

'Do you need to ask, babe?' Despite his stress about what's happening in Kent, he feels a little bubble of joy rise and burst in his chest at the question, posed in her heavily accented English. She still wants him.

'Come after eight, then kids and nanny will be out of the way.'

He emerges from the shower, slaps on the Tom Ford after-shave that Irina claims to love and jogs downstairs, trying Lance's number yet again. His brother does not pick up, but Keren appears in the doorway of the kitchen, giving him a questioning glare.

'Just popping out for a bit.'

She exhales noisily, but says nothing.

'Does your wife know you're here?' Irina asks, after they've had more of the intense but quiet sex in her bedroom.

He stares up at the ceiling. He wishes he could light up, but Irina won't let him smoke inside. 'I think so, yeah.'

She runs a finger over his right pec. 'So what does she think about it?'

'Not much. I mean, we're not actually...' He's about to say 'we're not married' but remembers just in time that he is still supposed to be Richard Hamlin, ex-accountant, and Keren is supposed to be his legal spouse, Stephanie. 'She knows the score, okay? So when are you going to tell your old man? About us?'

She ignores the question. This is what Irina usually does if she doesn't want to discuss something. Even so, a defensive flicker crosses her face.

'I was thinking when we were on Amalfi Coast, that this

would be a good place for us to buy a house.' She puts on a seductive, dreamy voice, and runs her fingers over his chest again, teasing his right nipple this time. 'Or maybe you'd prefer the Cote d'Azur?'

Liam doesn't know where either place is. 'Yeah,' he says, 'sweet. Either would be sweet.' He reaches over the side of the vast bed and grabs his phone, checking for messages or calls from Lance. There are none. 'Shit!' he mutters, snapping upright and starting to type frantically.

WTF is going on bro? Update me!

'What are you doing?' Irina asks, her voice cool and hard. She's sitting up in bed too now, and her expression has completely lost its post-coital mellowness.

'Just business,' Liam mumbles. 'Nothing you need to worry about.' His heart is hammering against his ribs, but he forces a smile as he turns to face her. What would she think, he wonders, if she knew he were checking on the commission of a double murder?

'Well, do not do it, please,' she snaps. 'I do not allow Michael to bring business into the bedroom, so why should it be okay for you to do this?'

It's the first time things have been less than harmonious between them. 'I thought you and he didn't sleep together anymore.' His own tone is petulant now.

Irina simply shrugs, watching silently as he pulls on his clothes.

'The Salters are away for the weekend,' she says eventually.

'The Salters?'

'The people at number six. I still have their key.'

Liam knows that she prefers meeting outside her own home, where they can be louder and more abandoned. 'Will you come there tomorrow?'

She's softening a little now, and Liam leans in and kisses her on the lips. 'I'll be there.'

There's still no word from Lance, but Keren intercepts Liam on his way to bed and has a go about him getting involved with Irina. It's hardly a surprise; in fact, he's surprised she's said nothing sooner.

'I mean, look at her. She's well out of your league. She's never going to be serious about someone like you.'

'Actually, Kez, that's where you're wrong. It is serious. Very serious. Me and Irina are planning to be together.'

She stares at him in disbelief for a second before going back into the master bedroom and slamming the door.

Liam sleeps fitfully, waking every half an hour to check his phone for the news that never arrives. When Lance's truck pulls up outside the following day, he already knows that this is not a good sign.

His brother stands on the front doorstep, his arms hanging limp at his sides, his face white as milk.

'I bottled it, bro,' he says in little more than a whisper. 'When it came down to it, I'm sorry, but I just couldn't do it.'

THIRTY-FOUR

AUGUST

'Jesus!' Liam yells, sinking forward and clutching his knees. 'What the... what the fuck are you telling me?'

'I didn't do it. I couldn't. It was too hard, bruv.' Lance is shaking, not meeting his eye.

'Christ!'

He drags out the single syllable, and follows it with a loud roar of rage. Then, realising that the commotion will draw attention from the neighbours, he grabs Lance by the collar of his shirt and drags him over the threshold and into the living room, snapping at Keren to mind her own business before slamming the door.

'So you're saying they're still alive? Both of them?'

Lance drops his head, shaking it slowly from side to side.

'So, go on then: what happened?' Liam rakes his hand through his hair. 'Please for the love of God don't tell me you let them talk you out of it?'

'No, man!' Lance is agitated now. 'I unchained them from the wall, took them up the steps, tried to make them walk, like you said. But they're so weak, they could barely manage more than a few steps. And when I...'

Keren's footsteps grow louder as she comes down the stairs and into the hall.

Lance lowers his voice. '...I threatened them with the gun, to make them move, they didn't care. They just said go ahead and kill them because nothing could be worse than their existence in that cellar. And then...' Lance's voice cracks, and his eyes film over with tears.

'Go on,' Liam spits.

'There were people out there on the shore path. They had birdwatching gear. Apparently, night-time birding is a thing. When they – the Hamlins – saw them, they started yelling. So I had to get them back down the steps as quick as I could, before anyone saw us. Even then, the only way I could get them to go down was by threatening to make something happen to their baby if they didn't do what I told them.'

'So what... you just chained them up again and left them?'

Lance nods again.

'Jesus. So...' Liam starts to pace, trying to force his whirling brain into some sort of coherent thought pattern. 'You've still got the gun, right?'

'It's in the Jeep.'

'Right. Well, there's only one option, isn't there? You're going to have to give it to me and I'm going to have to go down to sodding Eastmeade and do the job myself.'

'I'll come with you, it'll be better if we both—'

'No!' Liam shouts, then lowers his voice slightly. 'How can I trust you not to cock things up again? I'll go down there and I'll put the bullets in them, there in the cellar.' Liam paces, swivelling on his heel and changing direction every few feet. 'Then you and me, we'll go and dispose of the evidence together later, when we've figured out the best way to do it, and when we know what's happening with this stupid birdwatching crap. I reckon we can probably afford to leave it a few days.'

'You sure, bruv?'

'No, I'm not!' Liam snaps. 'But for now, it's all I've got.'

It's only when he's about to get into his pickup and drive to Gravesend that he remembers he's supposed to be meeting Irina at number 6. Cursing her under his breath for refusing to share her phone number, he scrawls her a note. If he simply pushes it through the letterbox, it might be Michael who finds it, so he rings the doorbell of number 17 and hands it to the house-keeper, Bernila, with instructions to hand it straight to Irina.

During the hour's drive to Gravesend, he reaches out every few minutes and touches the Russian Baikal pistol, converted by some hardcore criminal to fire the 9mm rounds that are now loaded in it. The smooth, cool feel of it gives him confidence. Okay, so he's never fired one before, but he's been around guns a few times. Mostly idiots showing off on the streets at night. It needs to be quick, he tells himself. No hesitation. No overthinking. That had clearly been Lance's problem: he got too in his own head. Lance has assured him over and over that the thing is loaded; Liam just needs to release the safety catch.

Once he's parked at the edge of the marshes, he tucks the Baikal into his waistband and sets off. It's a sultry evening, with pale, heavy cloud creating a stifling blanket of heat, and Liam's back is drenched with sweat by the time he reaches Eastmeade. After he's opened the heavy wooden door, he takes in a deep breath and slowly exhales. Then he descends the steps to the munitions store.

His hands fumble around for the torch, but it's not where they left it on the night they first brought the Hamlins here. Instead he reaches for his phone, intending to use his phone torch instead, but before he can find the icon on the screen, there's a rattling sound and shuffling footsteps and he's knocked sideways onto the bare earth floor. A length of chain is pressed against his neck.

'Get the key!' a disembodied voice urges. 'He usually keeps one in his pocket!'

They think I'm Lance, Liam realises, although at this point their mistake makes little difference. He's being pinned to the ground by Richard Hamlin, who's using the chain in a choke-hold, while Stephanie's fingers probe his pocket in search of the padlock key. They must have planned this last night after Lance's failed attempt to kill them. Realising that they were no longer to be kept alive, they must have plotted to jump whoever returned next, taking advantage of the fact that their own eyes were well accustomed to the dark while their jailers' were not. Lance had chained them up again, but there's just enough play in the chain for a length of it to be used as a makeshift garotte.

Stephanie has found the key, which was indeed in Liam's pocket, and is fumbling in the dark to unfasten their chains and release them from the iron loop in the wall. 'Go, Steph!' Richard urges her. 'Don't wait for me!'

'Shouldn't we chain him up so he can't follow?' she whispers, her voice weak and cracking from underuse.

'All right, let's try.'

There's an awkward tugging and fumbling while Stephanie attempts to loop the chains round Liam's wrists, with her husband still restraining him by the neck. But they are both weak and Liam is healthy and honed from hours in the gym, and he manages to pull his arms free and struggle to his feet, knocking Richard Hamlin to the ground as he does so.

'Go!' Richard groans desperately. 'For God's sake, run!'

Stephanie wastes no time in doing as her husband tells her, darting past Liam and tearing up the steps. Swearing under his breath, Liam lunges for Richard, but he's still unable to see very well and Richard somehow sidesteps him and makes for the foot of the steps. Liam is right behind him, pulling the gun and aiming it. The catch sticks and nothing happens.

'Christ's sake!' he roars at the top of his voice, tugging at the slide lock to release it.

He tries firing again and this time there's a loud crack, jarring his shoulder and making his wrist burn. Richard Hamlin screams in agony as he's hit on his left flank, but somehow he reaches the top of the steps and keeps going, disappearing into the darkness.

Liam looks around wildly, the pistol warm and heavy in his right hand. Up ahead, he can make out a figure on the path. Stephanie is running, or attempting to, but after weeks of imprisonment, her legs are too weak to generate any sort of pace and she's weaving from side to side as though she's drunk.

It doesn't take long for Liam to catch up with her. He grabs her by the sleeve of the same flimsy top that she was wearing when he arrived at the flat in Herne Hill and he pretended to be from Prodomus. It's now ripped, and so engrained with dirt that the pattern of butterflies is barely visible.

'Get down!' He pushes her onto her knees on the path and holds the Baikal to her left temple.

'No!' she whimpers, 'Please, no! I've got a little girl! Think of my little girl!'

The face looking up at him is like Keren's; hollow and angular, but still so similar. The dark eyes, the wavy hair, the light brown skin are all the same. He exerts pressure with his finger on the trigger, but still he can't bring himself to do it. He just can't. Not in cold blood with her looking right at him, eyes wide and terrified, knowing his is the last face she'll ever see.

What was it Lance said... *'It was too hard.'*

'Get up!' he orders, growling to hide the break in his voice. 'Move!'

He marches her back along the path, pressing the muzzle of the gun against her back. Making sure he switches on his phone torch this time, he directs her back down the steps and into the munitions store. Only as he pushes Stephanie to the ground and reaches to loop the chain around her wrists does he notice a five-litre bottle of water, a half-eaten box of crackers and a bag of apples. Lance must have brought them, Liam thinks in disbelief, as he secures Stephanie to the wall again. What an idiot, bringing supplies for the Hamlins when he's planning to kill them. Or does the purchase mean he already knew that he wasn't going to go through with it?

Once Stephanie's restrained, he pushes the supplies to within her reach, then returns the pistol to his waistband. This time he puts the key back up on a high ledge near the doorway, out of reach of his captive. He doesn't want to risk being jumped again, like he was today.

'Try any more stunts like that, and you'll never see Poppy again, d'you get me?'

'Richard's got away,' she croaks. 'He'll get help. He'll come for me.'

'Sorry: not gunna happen,' Liam says darkly.

He heads up the steps, then flicks off the torch, standing still in the dark and looking around, listening. Hamlin can't have got far, he tells himself. Not without the glasses he needs to correct his vision. And with a bullet in him.

He sets off at a run in the direction Richard took. It only takes a couple of minutes to find him, slumped in a grassy hollow to the side of the path. He's clutching the top of his leg and although it's too dark to see properly, Liam can smell the dark, ferrous ooze of blood. There's a lot of blood, gushing out in pulses.

'Help me,' Richard's voice is so faint, it's almost inaudible. 'I've got a wife and child: for the love of God, help me.'

Liam hesitates for a second, then turns and jogs back in the direction of his pickup.

THIRTY-FIVE

AUGUST

Liam sits in the driver's seat for a full minute, his hands braced on the steering wheel in an attempt to control his shaking.

Only now does it occur to him that driving away from the scene of a crime with a firearm on the front seat of his truck is a bad idea. If he's stopped by the cops, even for a petty reason, that would not look good. He vaguely remembers some forensic test that can prove how recently a gun was fired. But Liam also realises he wants to keep it. Okay, so he'd chickened out of using it at point blank range on Stephanie, but he had actually managed to shoot Richard. And – he forces himself to acknowledge this truth – left without medical help and bleeding at that rate, Richard is likely to die. So, in a way, he has actually succeeded in shooting someone dead. With a bit of time, he reckons it would get easier, more familiar. He just needs to get a bit more used to handling the thing.

There's still the problem of Stephanie surviving, though. In an attempt to rationalise himself failing in just the same way that made him rage at his twin, he hits on a theory. From where he stands now, it's obvious: this needs the two of them. That's why they have firing squads; so no one person has the responsibility for delivering the death blow. He and Lance need to get their hands on a second weapon and come here and finish the job together. That way, neither of them will be able to back down. They've always done everything together, and that's how it needs to stay.

Pulling off his T-shirt, he uses it to wipe down the Baikal, paying particular attention to the magazine and the trigger. Then he wraps it in a plastic bag that he finds loose in the footwell. The spare tyre on his pickup is stowed underneath the flatbed, so he lies on his back on the tarmac, inches his body under the wheels and tucks the gun inside the rim of the spare. Only then does he drive away slowly and carefully, switching on his headlights once he joins the main road.

His truck's number plate will be picked up multiple times on the road back into London: there's nothing he can do about that now. Even so, it's all the more important that he gets Irina to vouch for his whereabouts this evening. They've fucked up. Lance fucked up and now he's fucked up, leaving the Hamlin problem more precarious than ever. They should never have gone about it like this; acting like big-time gangsters when they've never been more than petty crooks. They should have paid professionals to finish the job: that's the real truth.

He spends most of that night awake, picking up his phone constantly and staring at the screen to see if there's a message from Irina.

When his mind strays to what happened at Eastmeade, he yanks it back, pushing those thoughts roughly from his mind. He has to stay focused on the here and now. A trip to the gym would help sort him out, but he's too physically drained after his sleepless night to pump iron, so he turns his attention to the mass assassination of Deathloop instead. Games like that, played constantly since his teenage years, make killing seem so simple. He realises this with a rush of resentment. Because it's not.

Then the Old Bill arrive. Keren hasn't done enough to keep Stephanie's family under control, with the result that her mother has requested a welfare check. With a stroke of luck Keren manages to spot the uniform through the window first and they hide in the kitchen until the officer has gone. But it prompts a row, of course. Liam's attitude is that their arrival could turn out to be a good thing, assuming they make enquiries in the street and are reassured that everything is fine at number 12: that the Hamlin family are indeed living there.

'Except that we haven't got the baby anymore!' Keren shrieks. 'Someone's bound to notice that eventually, and tell social services or something. Are you really prepared to risk it, after everything we've been through? Or are you just wanting to hang around so you can see your Russian hooker again?'

She's right, Liam knows she is, but even as she's packing up to leave, still he wants to hang on to Sycamore Gardens. He can't bear the thought of leaving without seeing Irina again, and making sure their plan still stands.

Lance comes round to the house, and Liam tells Keren it's to help with the packing, while really he wants to return the Baikal to its owner.

'Kasher's mate's getting heavy,' Lance mutters to his brother under his breath. 'He wants it back, so what am I supposed to tell him?'

'Tell him I had to get rid of it,' Liam insists. 'Tell him I used it to shoot someone, so no way was I going to risk having that in my possession.'

They decide that Lance will find out how much the gun was worth and Liam will pay cash to replace it, and at the same time he can source a second firearm for himself. 'Kind of two birds with one gun,' Liam quips. Then they'll have their own two-man firing squad to deal with Hamlin's wife, and they can get the job done once and for all.

Lance is unsure. 'You mean we both fire at once? What's the point of that?'

'Because even if one person bottles it, the... problem still gets dealt with. It doubles the chances of success, yeah?'

'Yeah.' Lance chews his lip. 'What if Hamlin survives, though? What if he manages to get help, or someone finds him?'

'You'd better start bloody praying that doesn't happen.'

Lance still seems uncertain, but helps his brother carry some of his stuff out to the pickup, to make it look as though that is indeed why he's there. By the time they've acted out this charade, Keren's ready to leave. She starts creating about the money from the sale again, a sum of money which once would have been beyond his wildest dreams, but now pales in comparison with the sum that comes with Irina once she breaks her engagement. He tells Keren he'll get the money to her, but, oh no, that's not good enough for her. She needs to know where he's going too. He doesn't tell her, because right now he doesn't have a bloody clue.

'I'm going to go now, but if I don't get my share, then I'll be straight round to the police.'

After making this threat, she stands staring at him, as though waiting for some big declaration. He says nothing, because the fact is, he feels nothing. Keren used to be his woman, true, but she's not now; she's nothing to him.

Irina is his woman now.

She eventually phones him at nine o'clock that evening.

'You must come to number six right now. I have a few minutes,' is all she says, before hanging up.

Liam dutifully jogs over to the Salters' house. It's a swelteringly hot night, but he doesn't want to risk being spotted in the garden by the Headleys, so they confine themselves to the kitchen. He tells her about his need for an alibi and Irina seems unimpressed.

'You change our arrangement last minute,' she complains, 'when I have the children and Michael to think of. And my staff. And now you ask me this? This is simply not fair.'

'You're fucking joking!' Liam sneers. 'Your "staff"? You expect me to worry about them?' He has been wanting a romantic reunion, more fantasy house-hunting, but Irina is standing there in her immaculate yellow linen dress, Chanel bag still over her shoulder, arms tightly crossed.

Somewhere in the house, a floorboard creaks. 'Did you hear something?' he asks her.

'What? No, I hear nothing. You are imagining.'

'Look, babe.' He reaches for her, but she pulls back, arms still crossed. 'All I need is if anyone asks where I was last night, to say I was with you. It's not that deep, you know?'

'You say is not deep, but it's a problem for me. You were supposed to be with me *last* night and you don't show up last minute. You don't tell me where you're going. Tonight I am supposed to be going to dinner with Michael, so I have to pretend to him to be ill. What is he going to say if he finds out?'

'Sort it, okay? Lie to him! Fucking drug him if you have to, so he loses his memory: I don't give a shit. Only for the time being, you've got to say that we were together, here. Last night. Okay?'

'Here... in this house?'

'Well, I could hardly be tucked up in bed with you and your old fella, could I?'

'I don't know, what if Michael—'

'You're going to have to tell him sometime, babe, you know? If we're going to be together like we planned. You've got to get the ball rolling sometime anyway, if you're going to get the money you're owed.'

'Look, it's not's that easy, you know?' She's got that snappy, defensive look back. 'These things, they take time to organise.'

'Fuckin' 'ell, Rina, you're doing my fucking nut!' Liam pushes back the kitchen chair he's sitting on and jumps up. 'We don't have fucking time, don't you get it? Not if we're to get away free and clear. You're going to have to find a way to hurry things up, for fuck's sake! And for the time being, you've got to say that we were together, here. Last night. Okay?'

To his surprise, she bursts into tears.

'Come 'ere...' He reaches out for her, and this time she lets him put his arms round her. 'Sorry, okay. Didn't mean to heavy you.'

'I'm scared. I don't know how I will explain to Michael, deal with the lawyers, quickly like you want. And what about your wife? It's complicated, you know?'

Her arms are crossed again and she has taken a step backwards. Clearly, they are not about to have sex, and anyway Liam needs to get the hell out of number 12 before the cops or Stephanie's family come calling again. Not that he's about to tell Irina that, naturally.

'It'll be all right, babe, I promise. Sweet as a nut. Now, I'm going to have to get going, but I'll be back as soon as I can, I promise.'

Liam still has the messenger bag that he took with him from the flat in Herne Hill.

Inside it are the passports and birth certificates, Richard Hamlin's glasses (now with one arm broken and held together with sticking plaster) and the contents of Hamlin's wallet. There's an American Express card in his name, and unlike the debit card and Mastercard, Liam has never used it. He's been saving it for when he really needs it, and that time is now.

If he's going to have to stay in a hotel, then to take the sting out of leaving the house in Sycamore Gardens, it's not going to be a Travelodge or some other budget dive. He books a room at the Savoy, which is the only smart London hotel he's ever heard of. He's tempted by the photos of the suites, but they're £1,400 a night and he's not sure of the credit limit on the card, so chooses a room with a river view instead, for a mere £800 a night.

As luck would have it, the girl on the reception desk is young and attractive, and after making intense eye contact with her for a couple of minutes, she smiles prettily as she holds out the key and says, 'I've given you a complimentary upgrade, Mr Hamlin. Enjoy your stay with us.' So he gets a suite anyway, the thrill of pleasure dampened somewhat by not being able to phone Irina and extend an immediate invitation. He's going to have to change that if they're going to be a couple. He can't have her calling the shots like this.

His buoyant mood is punctured further when he flicks on the TV in the sitting room of the suite and it's tuned to a news channel.

'Police in Kent are appealing for help in identifying a body found in an area of uninhabited marshland near Gravesend. They are asking witnesses or anyone with information to come forward. DS Kevin Carpenter told reporters "The body is of a young male and appears to have suffered a gunshot wound, an injury which unfortunately has led to his death..."'

Liam flicks angrily at the remote until he manages to switch off the TV. As he fully expected, Richard Hamlin bled out from the bullet wound. It's better than him having made it to safety, or being rescued, but Liam feels no pleasure in his assumption being confirmed. If he hadn't been panicking, he would have taken some steps to hide Hamlin and prevent his body being discovered. And there's still the problem of Stephanie, after all. He can't face going back there, and there might now be cops in the area alerted to the fact Richard's wife is missing. He's pretty sure Lance won't be up to finishing the job either, but one of the mates his brother made in the prison system might do it for a sum. Or know someone who will. He messages Lance to this effect; instructing him to try to find someone, and quickly.

He's now the most physically comfortable he's ever been in his life, with his gilded lamps, moss-green velvet furnishings and black and white Art Deco bathroom, and yet he's also the most restless and miserable.

After twenty-four hours, when he's heard nothing from Irina, he decides to take matters into his own hands. She made it clear she didn't want him phoning, but never said anything about contacting her on social media. She has an Instagram that's only for commercial shots, so he opens an account of his own and uses it to send her a direct message.

I've decided to spoil you... meet me at the Savoy? R x

Then he stretches out on his sumptuous mahogany bed, and waits.

THIRTY-SIX

AUGUST

There's no response to the message, but Liam decides he's going to be prepared anyway.

He phones down to the concierge and asks them to bring up champagne, fresh flowers and chocolates.

'And rose petals,' he tells the man on the other end of the phone. 'I want rose petals – the kind you scatter, yeah?' He's seen people do that on the reality dating shows that Keren watches: scatter rose petals over the bed covers as a romantic gesture. Keren's already in his head, because she keeps messaging him about the money from the house sale. Contracts are due to be exchanged by the end of next week, but he's not going to tell her that. In fact, he's not sure he's going to give her any of the money anyway. Why the hell should he? He's the one who's taken the risks, made everything happen. She's mostly sat around on her arse and whinged.

A white-gloved butler knocks at the door and pushes in a trolley covered with a spotless white linen cloth bearing an ice bucket with a bottle of Pol Roger, two crystal glasses and a plate of chocolate truffles and small fancy cakes in delicate pastel colours. Then a uniformed housekeeper arrives with two arrangements of cream and white flowers and a white silk pouch which she hands over solemnly, saying, 'I believe you requested these, Mr Hamlin?'

Liam peers inside. It's filled with pink and red rose petals. Once the staff have left, he tosses them self-consciously over the bedspread, but they don't look right.

The room phone rings.

'It's Janek at reception, Mr Hamlin, I have a visitor for you. May I send them straight up to the suite?'

'Go for it.'

Liam hurries into the black and white bathroom and grooms his hair in the mirror, slapping a generous palmful of Tom Ford 'Noir' over his jaw and neck and rubbing the excess over his bicep muscles. There's a tentative tap on the door and he flings it open to find Lance standing there in his hoodie and trainers.

'Jesus!' Lance exclaims, clapping his brother on the shoulder and pushing past him to admire the elegant Edwardian canopy bed and the ornate brocade window drapes framing the Thames beyond. 'Nice place, bruv? How long you here for?'

Liam shrugs.

'Why's there all these dead bloody flowers on the bed?' Lance sees the two champagne flutes and the chocolates. 'Oh, I get it! You've got a bird coming.'

'Yeah, so be quick, okay.'

'Is it that Russian bird from the new place?' He hesitates a beat. 'Well, I guess it's the old place now, right?'

'Yeah, yeah, it is her. And we're planning to get together properly. You know: get a place together.'

Lance's eyes widen. 'Wow!' Then his expression clouds. 'Hang on a minute though... she thinks you're Richard Hamlin.'

'Yep.'

'And you're not planning on telling her that you're really a South London wide boy called Liam Devenish? Not ever?'

'Of course not!' Liam snorts.

'But, bruv, that means you're stuck living as Richard Hamlin for the rest of your life. Is that really what you want?'

'If it means I can have Irina, then yeah, I'd do it for a thousand years.' Liam turns away, straightens the glasses on the white cloth, twists the champagne bottle in the bucket so that the ice cubes rattle. His hand is shaking slightly. Only now Lance has raised it does it occur to him that Richard Hamlin's body being identified is going to create a massive problem where Irina is concerned. He'll have to make sure they head abroad before that happens. 'Anyway, what's the deal? You found anyone yet?'

'Bruv, it's not that simple. It takes time to find someone with the right... skills. And it's going to cost too. Fifteen or twenty Gs. And they'll want it up front and all. Cash, obviously.'

Liam runs his fingers through his waxed quiff. 'I can't lay my hands on that kind of coin. Not till the after the house sale, at any rate.'

'How long's that going to be?'

'About five more days, maybe four if we're lucky. Reckon you can get someone lined up by the end of the week?'

'I can try.'

'Okay, sweet. Now piss off out of here.'

Lance holds eye contact with his twin for a few seconds, before turning on his heel and leaving the room. Liam watches out of the window, and, sure enough, a few minutes later he sees the hooded figure of his brother loping along the Embankment below. It's dusk, and the clustered buildings of the Southbank Centre look like a toytown cityscape in the dusk. He checks his phone every few minutes for the next few hours, but apart from a couple of missed calls from Keren, there's nothing.

At eight forty-five, just as he's decided to take a shower, the room phone rings again. 'A visitor for you, Mr Hamlin, shall I send them up?'

This time, it is indeed Irina.

'I only see your message an hour ago,' she says sternly. 'And I have to be sure Michael is asleep before I can go out.' She's wearing jeans with a silk camisole and a linen blazer slung round her shoulders, her scarlet painted toenails visible through strappy sandals.

'You're here now, babe, that's all that matters.' Liam, dressed only in a plush white towelling robe, reaches out to embrace her. 'Have a glass of bubbly. And one of these.'

He thrusts the plate with the patisserie and the chocolates in her direction, but she scrunches her perfect nose in disdain. 'Sugar. I cannot eat sugar.' Reluctantly, she accepts a champagne flute and takes one sip before putting it down and ignoring it. 'Why are you here?' she demands.

'I thought it would make a nice change from hiding out in the neighbours' house... Come 'ere, you gorgeous thing!' Determined to be romantic, Liam takes hold of her wrist and leads her into the bedroom. He's been lying on the bed to watch the television, rumpling the sheets, so the effect of the rose petals is lost. They just look messy now, as if someone's spilled them by mistake and failed to clean up properly.

Irina curls her lip. 'What is this?'

'Petals. They're a surprise for you.' He tries to tug the blazer off her, but she resists, steps back. 'Richard, we need to talk.'

She turns on her heel and heads back into the sitting room, flicking imaginary specks of dust off one of the velvet sofas before sitting on it.

'I have decided we need to end.'

Liam, hands thrust into the pockets of the robe, remains standing, staring at her. 'What d'you mean? End what?'

'End this. Us. We must stop seeing each other.'

'But... stop for how long?'

'Stop completely.' She gives him a pitying look, as though he's a simpleton. 'Stop forever.'

'But, Irina, you can't mean that!' He starts towards her, but she holds up a hand like a traffic policeman. 'We're going to live together, that's what we agreed.'

Irina shakes her head. 'No. I don't think so. Michael has decided we should have another baby together, and I have agreed. We want to have a boy,' she adds, as though this justifies everything.

'*We* can have a boy together. You and me, Rina! Why do you want to have a kid with Michael, you don't even love him.'

She shrugs. 'If I give Michael a son, he will give me five million pounds. In my own account, no questions asked.'

'So it just comes down to money?'

She shrugs again, tosses back a lock of shiny chestnut hair. 'Look, it was just a bit of fun, okay? Michael is away a lot, you know this, and I get bored sometimes. It's the same for you, yes? You like a little bit of a break from your wife.'

'Except I'm prepared to leave her for you! In fact, I have done; we've split up: that's what all this is about.' He waves a hand at the cake stand and the clumps of petals. 'You said you'd do the same, otherwise why talk about buying houses together? In Monte Carlo or wherever.'

Irina repeats the hair flick. 'Pillow talk, darling.'

'No,' says Liam through clenched teeth. 'No, I'm not having this.'

'It's over,' she says simply, standing up from the sofa.

Liam blocks her path, but she pushes him aside and strides to the door.

'No,' he calls after her as she heads into the hotel corridor. 'No, Rina. It's not over. It's not over until I say it is.'

PART FOUR

JANE

THIRTY-SEVEN

AUGUST – TWO DAYS EARLIER

After she has managed to escape Danielle Salter, Jane slams the door of number 5 and leans against the cool wall of the hallway, her legs shaking.

The man who lives at number 12 and who passes himself off as Richard Hamlin is not Richard Hamlin. He's someone else, someone who definitely isn't Welsh. So what is Stephanie Hamlin's part in this deception? Or is that person even Stephanie? She looks like the woman in the news piece about the house win, but that clearly means nothing, because the man in the picture looks like Richard Hamlin too. Tom Chen initially thought the man in the pink shirt at the barbecue was Richard Hamlin, because the resemblance was good enough to fool him in a photo.

These thoughts and revelations are so huge and disturbing that Jane's head is pounding, unable to compute them. She stumbles down the steps to the kitchen and pours a large tumbler of water, drinking all of it to try and dispel the thumping in her temples. Tony Waddesdon. She needs to talk to Tony. He'll be able to help her make sense of this extraordinary turn of events, and tell her what she should do next.

She grabs her keys and heads out of the front door, only to meet Trish walking in the opposite direction towards number 5. She waves when she spots Jane.

'I was just coming over to yours,' Jane tells her. 'I wanted a word with Tony. Is he in?'

'And I was just coming to see you,' Trish says with a laugh. 'Great minds think alike and all that. I was about to text, but since I need to pop to the shops anyway, I thought I may as well come in person.' She waves a large canvas shopper to illustrate her point. 'Tony and I are having a bit of a barbecue in the garden for my birthday.'

Jane's hand flies up to her mouth. 'Oh God, Trish I'm so sorry! I completely forgot.'

'Don't worry.' Trish rolls her eyes. 'At my advanced age, you don't go around advertising the fact you're another year older... Anyway, we wondered if you and Fergus would like to join us. It won't be anything fancy, just some grilled lamb and salad, and possibly some birthday cake. About seven thirty?'

'Lovely,' Jane says faintly. 'Fergus shouldn't be back too late. Is Tony there now?' She points in the direction of number 15.

'Golf,' Trish rolls her eyes. 'So much for him being retired: he may as well still be with the Met for all I get to see him. He should be back by this evening, though, so you'll see him then... Was it anything important?'

Jane hesitates. There's no real reason why she can't tell Trish about what she's just discovered, only not here and now, on the pavement, with Trish on her way to fetch groceries, it seems simply too momentous.

'Nothing that can't wait,' she tells her friend with a smile. 'See you at seven thirty.'

. . .

Jane is hoping that tonight of all nights Fergus will be back late and she can go to Trish's house alone. Or that he will plead having too much work to do, as he so often does.

Instead, he seems buoyed at the idea of supper in a neighbour's garden and wastes no time in showering and changing into clean jeans and his favourite green linen shirt, while Jane hunts in her desk drawer for a suitable birthday card.

'Top stuff,' he says cheerfully. 'I just fancy some charred meat...' He brandishes a bottle of vintage champagne given to him by a grateful student and never opened. 'Will this do as a birthday present?'

And then, of course, once they're at Trish's, he insists on doing the macho meat-prodding routine, comparing notes with Tony about the merits of various barbecue fuels so that it's impossible for Jane to get Trish's boyfriend alone. Eventually, just after they've sat down on the patio to eat, there's a distraction in the form of Trish's sister, Miriam, dropping round with some flowers and a gift. Trish insists she stays to eat, and while Tony's in the kitchen fetching a fifth plate and cutlery, Jane gets up from the table.

'Just need the loo...'

Having cornered Tony in the kitchen, she tells him as briefly as she can about the disappearance of first Poppy and then her parents, followed by Tom Chen's revelation that the voice recorded on her phone is definitely not that of Richard Hamlin.

'Hold on... slow down,' Tony pauses with the cutlery drawer open. 'How did you come to be in possession of this recording?'

Jane, already slightly flushed from the combination of wine and sun, turns an even deeper pink. 'He – the man claiming to be Hamlin – was in the Salters' house, having a tryst with Irina Semenova. Who has a key. The Salters were away, obviously. And I also have a spare key.'

Tony does an exaggerated double take.

'I know, it's a bit complicated,' Jane says apologetically. 'I saw a light on while I was out for a run, and I let myself in. But the point is, this man, the one who won number twelve in the house draw, is not Richard Hamlin the accountant who used to work at Stevenson Hunter Paine. Because that man is Welsh.'

Tony sets a knife, fork and spoon out in a row on the countertop, his movements slow and deliberate as though helping refine his thought process. 'Maybe there was some legal reason this guy... whoever he is... couldn't enter the house draw. It's probably a condition that you can't enter if you have a criminal record for example. Maybe he just borrowed Hamlin's identity for the sole purpose of entering the draw.'

'And happened to win? Amongst all the thousands of entries?'

Tony rubs his chin. 'I know it seems unlikely, but what else makes sense?'

'So where's the real Richard Hamlin?'

'And the real Stephanie, come to that.' Tony turns to the fridge to retrieve another bottle of wine. 'I mean, are we assuming the woman who's been living at number twelve isn't her either? Possibly still going about their lives with no idea that they even entered the draw. This couple must have put false address details on their entry.'

Jane reaches into the cupboard for a spare wine glass and puts it on the counter. 'But with the publicity... you'd think the real Hamlins would have heard about it by now. And now number twelve has been sold, this other couple will be getting the money.'

'Ah yes,' Tony grins. 'That old crime-solving mantra: follow the money. And if they have made off with the funds, we're now talking about a pretty serious fraud. Does anyone know where the identity thieves are now? You said they'd moved out?'

'Yes... they left at some point over the past few days. And

separately, apparently, although that could just have been a smokescreen. No one I've spoken to knows where they went.'

Tony hands Jane the bottle of wine, then gathers up the spare glass cutlery wrapped in a paper napkin 'You know, as a copper, my first concern would be to make sure the real Hamlins are all right.' He walks back to the patio door and indicates with a nod that Jane should go out into the garden first. 'But listen, Jane, I know you've had your suspicions for a while, and now this is all getting a bit serious. You need to go to the police with what you know, and sooner rather than later.'

'What on earth were you and Tony talking about for so long?' Fergus asks as they walk back to number 5, uncomfortably full after generous portions of roast lamb and large slices of raspberry and vanilla birthday cake.

'We weren't talking for long,' Jane protests.

'Yes, you were. I saw you through the window. You said you needed the loo, then you went into the kitchen and had what looked like a very intense discussion with Tony, before coming back to the garden without visiting the bathroom.'

'Did I?' Jane adopts a tone of studied vagueness. 'I'd had quite a bit of wine by then, so, to be honest, I don't really remember.'

'Liar!' Fergus snaps. They've reached their own front door, and he spins on his heel, the key already in the lock. There's a look on his face that Jane has never seen before, one of pure fury.

She opens her mouth to protest, but no sound comes out. It's true, after all. She was lying.

'So, what were you talking about? Are the two of you messing around behind your best friend's back?' He stomps into the hall and Jane follows him, closing the front door behind them.

'Don't be ridiculous!' It's her turn to raise her voice now. 'I'm not interested in Tony.'

Fergus swings round to face her. 'Ah, but he's an ex-cop, isn't he? So that makes me think this must be something to do with your ridiculous Miss Marple act.'

'What are you talking about? What act?'

'Running around keeping tabs on the neighbours like you're some kind of amateur PI. I thought we'd been over this that time I caught you peering through the windows of number twelve, convincing yourself something had happened to Poppy Hamlin. And accusing me of having an affair with her mother. I thought you'd seen sense and were going to keep out of it.'

'The Hamlins have left,' Jane says calmly. 'All three of them. And yes, I did mention it to Tony. That's all.'

She decides not to tell him any more than that, and especially not Tony's advice that she involve the police.

'So you were lying.'

Jane stares at her husband. They're standing in the hallway in half darkness, and she can't quite make out the expression on his face. But even if she could see properly, she knows she would still be confused, uncomprehending. How have they come to this? she wonders. They used to have such a solid marriage. A good marriage.

She pushes past him and heads up the stairs without a word.

THIRTY-EIGHT

AUGUST

Fergus sleeps in the spare room following their row, and Jane expects to wake to the sound of him heading out to work without saying goodbye. She's slightly surprised when she eventually comes down to the kitchen and finds him sitting at the table in his bathrobe, drinking a cup of coffee and eating toast.

'I thought I'd work from home today,' he says with a forced casualness.

Jane walks over to the kettle and switches it on without meeting his eyes. *He's doing this deliberately*, she thinks. It's his way of keeping an eye on her, monitoring her movements. Not that she has any concrete plan of action as yet. What she badly needs is time to think. Tony was right; she should really go straight to the police. And she definitely plans to tell them what she knows when the time is right. But not just yet. She's not sure why – although it's probably because of what Fergus would cite as a lack of intellectual stimulus in her life – but she's not ready to let go of her own initiative just yet.

Ideally, she would go straight back to Stevenson Hunter Paine and get some more information on the real Richard Hamlin. That seems the logical starting point given she has no idea where the fake Richard and Stephanie are. Or the baby passed off as Poppy Hamlin. She experiences a sharp pang of anxiety, wondering what has happened to the little girl, hoping she's safe wherever she is. With Fergus sitting guard downstairs in front of his laptop, Jane decides that the obvious course of action is to phone the accountancy firm.

After her encounter with the officious Yvette McGraw, she suspects that the HR department will not be willing to help her. But Tom Chen might. He'd seemed quite sympathetic and genuinely curious about the mystery surrounding his former colleague. Once she has showered and dressed, Jane googles the number for Stevenson Hunter Paine and phones their switchboard, asking to be put through to Tom in the Recovery and Insolvency department.

'People usually phone him directly on his mobile,' the bored woman on the other end says.

'I realise that, but I don't have it. Or I would have used it.' Jane just about manages to quell her exasperation.

'Would you like me to give it to you?'

Even better. 'Yes; yes please.' She scrabbles in her bag for a pen and scribbles down the number she's given on a till receipt.

It would probably be easiest to send him a message, especially as she can hear footsteps on the stairs. Sitting on the edge of the bed, she stares at her phone screen for a couple of minutes, then starts typing.

> *Hi Tom, this is Jane. Headley. I hope you don't mind me contacting you like this, but I have a follow-up query after playing you that voice recording. Do you think it would be possible to find out Richard Hamlin's latest known address? Obviously, the fact that the man in the neighbouring house is claiming to be him is concerning, and I think someone should check that the real Richard is okay. I'd be very grateful. J*

A text pops up on her screen fifteen minutes later.

I can't access his HR file myself, but I know Monique, one of the team, sent them flowers after their baby was born, so she will have a note of the address. However, as you say, this is all a bit concerning, and I'm wondering if you shouldn't just take what you know to the police and let them check on Richard. T

Jane re-reads the message a couple of times. Tom is right, of course, but it's time to employ a small white lie.

Of course, I agree, and I will be sharing the address with my neighbour who is a police officer. I've already raised my suspicions with him and he has advised me about the best course of action with regards checking the Hamlins' welfare.

It's not the whole truth, Jane thinks as she presses 'Send', just a slight manipulation of it. Tony is a retired police officer and she has discussed the issue with him.

A one-line text arrives ten minutes later.

Flat B, 33, Holmdene Avenue, SE26

Her pulse quickening, Jane checks the address on a map, then starts checking bus routes to Herne Hill.

'Where are you going?'

She thought she'd selected a moment when Fergus was on a video call before walking quietly down to the hall and heading for the front door. But suddenly there is his tall figure, looming over her. She's clearly judged it wrong.

'Just out.'

'Where?'

Jane attempts a little laugh. 'This house may have been built in the 1800's, but things have moved on since then. I don't need permission from my husband to leave the house.'

'I need to know where you're going.'

She looks up at him only to find a strange expression on his face, one she's never seen before, poised oddly between anger and fear. She shakes her head in disbelief and reaches for the latch, only to have Fergus grab her roughly by the elbow and yank her backwards, inserting himself between her and the way out to the street.

'Ferg! What the hell's come over you?'

He's never laid a finger on her before in twenty-three years of marriage, or at least only once: that night when he caught her staring through the windows of number 12 and dragged her away. The night when she accused him of having an affair with Stephanie Hamlin, only to be told she had lost her grip on reality.

'You're not going anywhere,' he shouts, and before she has chance to gather her scattered thoughts, he's pushed her into the sitting room and slammed the door behind them. Alarmed, she rummages in her bag for her phone, but he snatches it from her and removes her mobile, thrusting it into his jeans pocket with an, 'Oh no you don't!'

Jane makes for the door, but he blocks her path. She can only stare at him, appalled.

Then, to her horror, he bursts into tears. She's only ever seen him cry once before, at his mother's funeral. And even then, it was a decorous, silent welling of tears. Not these hoarse, guttural sobs. He sinks down onto the sofa and she squats down beside him on the Turkish rug, a hand resting on his knee.

Eventually, he gathers himself and looks up at her. 'Jane, I'm so sorry. This isn't me.'

'I know it's not,' she says, forcing herself to speak calmly even though her thoughts are whirling.

'Listen, I need to tell you something. You're not going to like it, but I can't see any other way out of this.'

Jane recoils slightly, alarmed. 'Out of what?'

Fergus takes a long, slow inhalation of breath. 'I've been seeing someone. Having an affair, I suppose you'd call it.'

Her heart rate speeds up, and there's a ringing noise in her ears. *No, this can't be happening.* 'Steph Hamlin?'

He shakes his head vigorously. 'No. No, of course not. Her name's Selina. She's one of my graduate students.'

'I see.'

So this was the 'S' who had called him when they were in Suffolk. Not Seb as he claimed. Her overriding emotion is relief. She wasn't losing her grip on reality. There had been something going on, something that was making Fergus distant, unengaged.

'I've decided I'm going to end it, which is why I'm coming clean now. I know you won't necessarily believe me after what I've done... how I've been behaving. But it is true. It's a horrible academic cliché, but there it is: a young attractive woman was impressed by me and I was flattered. I let my ego and my vanity get in the way and I ended up in bed with her. And almost immediately realised it was a mistake.'

Jane has straightened up from her kneeling position and now she pulls herself to her feet and steps backwards, needing some physical distance to absorb this shocking truth. His words don't feel real. It's as though she's watching herself in a play.

'So was it...' She sinks down onto a chair. 'I mean, why, Fergus? Was it me? Did you just stop fancying me? Were you bored? I mean...' She realises her words are going to sound pathetic. 'I thought we were fine.'

'We were fine... we are fine, I hope...'

'But we're not, though, are we?' Jane says angrily. 'If we were fine, you wouldn't have been sleeping with someone else.'

Fergus tips his head back and stares at the ceiling. 'I'm trying to say that I wasn't actively unhappy. Not unhappy at all, in fact. But after more than twenty years, you're not immune to feeling an attraction to someone else. And the fact that it was mutual... I was tempted. And I gave in to that temptation. What else can I say: I'm sorry.' He looks over at her, his expression pleading. 'Please don't say this is the end of us.'

She shakes her head slowly. 'I don't know, Fergus. I don't know how I feel, except that I'm bloody hurt. And I need time to process this.'

'Of course. But look, Jane, there's more I need to explain... That guy, Richard Hamlin, he must have found out about Selina. I honestly have no idea how. But he spoke to me about it. It was just before we went to Thorpeness, the night of your leaving do. Just before you got home, I found him on our doorstep. There was a lot of veiled threat and innuendo, but, basically, he said that if I didn't stop you from looking into his affairs, he would tell you about Selina and me. At the time, I didn't want that to happen, so I tried to... discourage you.'

Jane pulls a face at Fergus's choice of words. 'I believe the word is gaslighting. You were gaslighting me.'

He closes his eyes briefly, then nods. 'You're right. That's exactly what it amounted to, and I'm so sorry. I've realised that's no way for a grown man to carry on, someone who's always prided himself on having some sort of moral compass. I know I can't expect you to forgive me, but the least you're owed is the truth. And if your pain and disappointment are the price for getting Hamlin off my back, then please accept that I'm also very, very sorry about that. But at least it's all out in the open, and that's better for both of us in the long run, whatever we decide to do.'

That was quite a speech. Jane is almost tempted to start

clapping. But then Fergus has always been good at constructing an argument. It's a big part of his job, after all. She takes a deep breath to steady herself before speaking.

'Two things,' she says, with more composure than she feels, pushing down her massive sense of personal betrayal. That will have to wait until later. 'Firstly; he threatened me too. Told me to stay out of his business. Again, vague threats, nothing specific.'

She suddenly remembers him miming slitting his throat when he caught her watching him through the window and shudders. That had been specific enough.

'And the second thing?'

'He's not actually Richard Hamlin. That man who's been living at number twelve stole his identity to get his hands on the house in the prize draw. I made a recording of his voice and played it to one of Richard Hamlin's colleagues, who said it definitely wasn't him because Richard is Welsh.'

'Bloody hell, Jane!' Fergus is staring with his mouth open, his fingers raised to his temples. 'That's really disturbing.'

Jane nods. 'There were just lots of little things that didn't add up, and I've proved my suspicion right.'

'And what about Steph? What about baby Poppy? Are they really Hamlin's wife and child, or not?'

Jane shakes her head. 'I've absolutely no idea. Anything is possible at this point.'

Fergus wipes his face with the hem of his T-shirt and stands up, 'Jane, you need to go straight to the police with this information. We're talking about a serious crime here.'

She hesitates.

'What?' he asks sharply.

'I've got the address of the Hamlins' flat, and I thought I'd just go over there and check before telling the police. Just to make sure there isn't an innocent explanation, or it's all some big hoax.'

'An innocent explanation?' Fergus scoffs, running his hand through his dark curls. 'How could there be?'

'Suppose the man living at number twelve is doing so with the real Richard Hamlin's permission. Suppose it's all above board in some way.'

Fergus is shaking his head. 'No. That has to be the least likely explanation.'

'Maybe, but I just wanted to go and double-check.' She reaches for the bag that he took from her and heads to the sitting-room door. Surely after his confession he's not going to try and stop her leaving this time?

'No,' Fergus repeats. 'This... situation has gone on long enough: we need to go to the police, that's non-negotiable. But we can stop off in Herne Hill and take a look on the way there.'

'*We* can?'

'I may not be in a position to stop you, but I'm sure as hell not letting you go alone.' He's already reaching for his jacket and the car keys. 'I'm coming with you.'

THIRTY-NINE

AUGUST

There's silence in the car for most of the ten-minute drive to Herne Hill.

'Do you want to talk about it?' Fergus says eventually. 'I mean, are there things you want to ask me about it? About what happened with... me and Selina?'

Jane keeps her eyes focused on the windscreen. She has so many questions. *Why was I not enough? Was it because she was younger? Am I supposed to just forget about this? To forgive it?* She feels not just hurt and humiliated, but foolish too. There she was, silently judging Irina and the man pretending to be Richard Hamlin for getting together behind their partners' backs. And her own husband was doing the exact same thing.

'No,' she says flatly. 'No, I don't want to ask you anything.'

When they reach Herne Hill Road, she makes a conscious effort to quash her thoughts about Fergus and to concentrate on the reason they're here. For now, that's all that matters. They pull up and park opposite number 33, Holmdene Avenue, one of a row of red-brick Edwardian semis with white rendered architraves and mullions, now divided into flats.

'Right,' Jane says, unclipping her seat belt. 'Wait here, okay? Hopefully I'll only be a couple of minutes.'

But Fergus is releasing his own belt. 'I'm coming with you. What if that guy is in there? The fake Hamlin? God knows what he might do to you.'

He follows Jane up the path and stands beside her as they wait for the doorbell to be answered. Anyone who sees them would think they're just a regular married couple, she thinks bitterly.

'Hello?' A female voice comes over the intercom.

'Hi... we're looking for the Hamlins,' Fergus says.

There's a brief silence, then the door is buzzed open. The door to Flat B is opened by a smiling young woman with a strong Italian accent, who introduces herself as Giovanna. She's a student, and she and her boyfriend moved into the flat in May. As far as she's aware, the previous tenants moved out a few weeks earlier. She apologises profusely about not being able to help, but she knows nothing more about them, and there's no forwarding address.

'Ah, wait,' Giovanna says as they head for the stairs. 'There's a lady next door who says hello to us. She offered to have the spare keys for us, and she said she kept the keys for your friends, the...?'

'The Hamlins,' supplies Jane.

'Yes. She might know something about them. Number thirty-one, the ground-floor flat.'

'Thank you.' Fergus flashes his most charming smile, and Jane feels a surge of irritation.

'I'll go,' she tells him. 'You wait in the car. I'm sure this woman won't turn out to be an axe murderer. She may not even be in, anyway.'

She is in, and her name is Michelle. A toddler peeps out from between her legs when she answers the door, and races off to fetch a truck to show Jane when she's invited in to the colourful but very untidy flat.

'Yes, I knew Stephanie a bit, just to say hello to,' she tells Jane, now perched on the edge of a bright pink sofa covered with toys. 'But they moved away suddenly, and she didn't say goodbye. Which I did think was odd, if I'm honest.' Michelle takes the tie out of her hair and fans it with her fingers before twisting it up and securing it in a ponytail again.

'Did they say anything about where they were going?'

'No, but I saw online that they won a house in one of those prize draws. I guess they were meant to keep it all under wraps, or something. I messaged Steph and she said it had all been very sudden.'

'You've been in touch with her since she left?'

'Yes, just to check that she was okay.'

Jane leans forward. 'And what did she say?'

'Just that the house was great, but that she was super busy now she had Poppy with her full-time...' Michelle reaches forward and grabs the TV remote from her son, who's now loudly demanding to watch Peppa Pig. 'Poppy used to be at nursery while Steph was working, but it sounded like she'd jacked in her job. Which surprised me, because she was the career type rather than the stay-at-home type.'

'I see...' Jane tries to process this information. 'Do you know which nursery?'

'Yeah, it's only about five minutes away. It's called Stepping Stones.'

Ruth Buckby, the manager of Stepping Stones nursery, is not a good advertisement for an establishment aiming to provide a healthy environment for young children. She has stringy hair, watery eyes and an unwelcoming energy. Although she leads Jane into her office, there is a distinct lack of enthusiasm in her manner and she leaves the door open to indicate that she expects this interview to be brief. Jane wonders whether she should have brought Fergus with her, rather than leaving him in the car again. He could probably charm even this charmless member of the opposite sex.

'I understand that you had a child here called Poppy Hamlin?'

'Who wants to know?' Ruth Buckby demands.

'I do. I'm a friend of the family.'

'Sorry, but I'm sure you appreciate that information on our clients is confidential,' the woman says sourly. 'There are data protection rules.'

'But if you could just—'

'I'm sorry, Mrs Headley, but if you are a friend of the Hamlins, then I suggest you speak to them. Now, if you don't mind, I have staff rotas to attend to.' She indicates the open door, and realising she's going to get nowhere, Jane leaves the office.

'Hi, hang on a minute!' As she is heading out of the single-storey building and back to the car park, she's stopped by a short woman of about forty wearing a blue tabard. 'Did I hear you say you wanted to know about Poppy Hamlin?'

'Yes, that's right.'

'You're wasting your time with Buckby: she'll never tell you anything. But we all thought it was odd that Poppy was removed so suddenly. One day she was here, and the next she was gone. No notice or anything.'

Jane looks at her. 'And you are?'

'Sorry, I'm Carla.' The woman extends a hand. 'I worked in the baby room when Poppy was here.'

'Great. Would you mind holding on just a second, Carla?' Jane fumbles in her bag and pulls out her phone, opening her photos app. She selects a photo of Poppy taken when she was at number 5, sitting on the rug playing with Joss and Evie's old toys.

'This is Poppy Hamlin, yes?'

Carla takes the phone. 'Yes, that's her. Gorgeous little thing.'

Jane scrolls to another picture, taken in her garden when Steph came over to collect her. 'And this is her mother, yes? This is Stephanie Hamlin.'

Carla squints at the image, confused. She uses her fingers on the screen to enlarge the face. 'No, that's Poppy with Keren.'

'Keren?'

'Keren Stockley. She used to work here. She left suddenly and all. About the same time.'

Jane's heart starts to pound. 'Are you absolutely sure?'

Carla nods.

'Okay, how about this?'

Jane flicks through her photos until she comes to the ones of the Sycamore Gardens barbecue that Danielle forwarded to her. There's one image of 'Richard Hamlin' where he's not wearing glasses. 'Do you know who this is?'

Carla takes the phone and peers closer. 'Yeah, I think so. That looks like Keren's boyfriend. I've heard her talking about him with Chloe, who still works here. She was always showing pictures of him working out at the gym.' She straightens up and hands Jane her phone back. 'Liam, he's called. Liam Devenish.'

FORTY

AUGUST

'Okay, next stop really does need to be the police.'

Jane has re-joined Fergus in the car and told him what she's found out from Carla, the nursery nurse.

'I mean, this is starting to look very dodgy indeed. Bad enough that this pair – Keren and Liam – are impersonating the Hamlins, but this woman says the baby they were pretending to parent is actually Poppy Hamlin. Have I got that right?'

Jane nods mutely.

'Well, that has to be the most worrying thing, surely? Because if the Hamlins were alive and well, the abduction of their baby would have made front-page news.'

There's silence for a few seconds.

'Jane? Don't tell me you don't agree?'

'Of course I agree,' she says eventually. 'It's just a lot to take in. And I can't see how it's going to end well.'

'All the more reason to act as quickly as we can.' Fergus starts the engine and pulls away from the kerb. 'We'll call in at Brixton Police Station on the way home and tell them everything we know. Then it's over to the authorities.'

. . .

But once Jane is inside the police station, things are not that straightforward.

Firstly, there's a queue of people waiting to speak to the desk sergeant and she has to wait forty minutes before she's even called forward. And then her jumbled account is met by a blank expression and incomprehension. It's only when she mentions the possible abduction of a baby that she's taken back to an interview room to speak to a DC Lester Boateng.

'So let me get this straight...' He's a serious young man who seems reluctant to smile or make eye contact. Even so, he has an attractive face, with pointed incisors like little fangs that Jane can't help staring at. 'These people: Richard and...' He looks down at his copious notes. '...Stephanie Hamlin won a house in your road in a competition run by a lottery charity company called Prodomus? The address being twelve Sycamore Gardens, SW8?'

'Yes... well, no.' Jane is tired and tense, and struggling to remain patient. 'A couple moved in to number twelve, but it turns out that they're not really the Hamlins. They're actually called Keren Stockley and Liam Devenish.'

'And you became aware of this because?'

'I was suspicious, so I recorded him – Liam – talking to another neighbour and played the recording to one of the people at Richard Hamlin's workplace. And he confirmed that the person speaking wasn't Richard.'

'Mrs Headley, you are aware that recording someone without their consent is illegal in some circumstances?'

DC Boateng looks at her directly now, and she flushes.

'Okay, moving on... this colleague is called Tom Chen?'

'Yes. The firm is Stevenson Hunter Paine.'

More scribbling.

'I used to babysit the baby they said was their daughter, and when I showed a photo of her to someone at the nursery the

Hamlins used, they confirmed it was actually the Hamlins' daughter. Not a child of Liam and Keren.'

'I see.' Boateng chews his lower lip. 'Okay, here's what's going to happen. I'll run a PNC check on Devenish and Stockley, and we'll make some enquiries. And then, if need be, someone will be in touch with you to take a formal statement.' He gathers his notes and stands up.

'So that's it?'

'Yes, that's it. For now, at least.'

When they get back to Sycamore Gardens, Fergus throws the car keys onto the hall table, but hovers there, his jacket still on.

'I think I ought to go and do it now,' he says awkwardly, looking down at his shoes.

'Do what?' Jane asks, although she has a feeling she knows.

'I ought to go and speak to Selina. Tell her you and I have talked, and that it's all out in the open.'

He makes it sound very collegial, very chummy. And that's far from what Jane feels. She feels as though her marriage is a land mass and she a tiny boat, being swept away from it, far out to sea. All she can do is shrug and head in the direction of the stairs. She's longing to soak in the bath, preferably with a very strong drink. To hell with the fact that it's not even three in the afternoon.

'There's no point putting it off: better to meet the situation head on, don't you think?' Fergus calls up the stairs.

'I suppose so.'

Jane's head is pounding, and her ability to form an argument, or even a rational thought, seems to have deserted her. On the first-floor landing, she leans against the wall for a few seconds, resting her burning cheeks against the cool plaster. Then she stumbles into the bathroom and turns on the bath taps. Downstairs, she hears the front door slamming as Fergus leaves. She walks barefoot down to the kitchen and fetches a glass of ice-cold Sauvignon Blanc, sipping it as she leans back in the bathwater. Is Fergus really going to tell this girl, this Selina, that it's over? Or will it be a question of persuading her to lie low until the dust has settled and they can resume their relationship? She has no way of knowing, and until she's sure, she intends to protect her own heart.

She's in the sitting room watching a documentary about American politics when Fergus comes home. Or at least, she's sitting on the sofa staring at the TV screen, without really taking in what the talking heads are saying. When her husband comes into the room, she points the remote at the screen and switches it off.

'So...' Fergus positions himself between her and the TV. 'I've done it. It's over.'

Jane nods, but says nothing.

'What I need to know now is, where do we go from here?'

'What do you mean?' she asks, aware that her voice sounds cold.

'Well, you and I. Moving forward. Are we going to be able to get things back on track?' He sits down next to her on the sofa and takes her left hand in his. 'I really want to, if you do.'

Jane sighs heavily. 'I don't know, Fergus.'

'What do you mean?'

'I mean just that. That I don't know. I don't know if I want us to continue. I don't know if I can forgive you. I don't know if we... work, any longer.'

It's Fergus's turn to sigh. 'Are you at least prepared to try?'

'I suppose so. But for now, I want you to stay in the spare room.'

. . .

The following morning, Jane goes upstairs to make her bed, lifting the dozing Oreo from his nest in the bedclothes and putting him down carefully on the chair. As she turns back to the bed, she spots a police car.

Putting the duvet down again, she moves closer to the window and watches. A marked patrol car has pulled up outside number 12, and two uniformed officers get out, strolling up to the front door with a distinct lack of urgency. They ring the bell and knock, and then since there's no answer, they press their faces against the glass of a ground-floor window, just as Jane did herself a week ago. They then knock on the door again, harder this time, and since even Buster the dog isn't there to bark now, they give up and stroll back to the patrol car, one of them speaking into an airwave set.

Is that it? Jane thinks. Surely now they'll go house to house, making enquiries? But after sitting inside the patrol car for a few minutes and talking over the car radio, the police officers drive away. Only then, when she's wondering if they plan to return to speak to the neighbours does the thought of Irina surface in Jane's mind. How much does she realise, if anything, of what's been happening? Does she think the man she's been sleeping with is really Richard Hamlin, or does she know he's a criminal conman called Liam Devenish? The idea of Irina being party to such a lowlife scam seems unlikely; Irina with her stellar modelling career and fabulously wealthy fiancé. Why would she sink to his level? Or perhaps she does know and likes a walk on the wild side. Either way, he's clearly dangerous.

Jane sits down on the edge of her unmade bed and reaches for her phone. Despite Liam's threats, it had never been her intention to interfere between him and Irina. Her surveillance had simply been to discover more about him. But now she needs to be more proactive. She needs to warn Irina.

She pulls up Irina's number and composes a brief message.

I need to talk to you about something. It's really urgent.
Are you around? Jane x

It's very late in the evening before she receives a reply.

Come over to mine. Now.

Jane stares at her phone screen. The message seems a little abrupt, but perhaps the tone of Jane's own message has made Irina anxious. Fergus has texted to say he'll be working late to make up the time he lost the day before. Jane considers letting him know where she's going, then thinks better of it. After his recent revelation, she doesn't feel like filling her husband in on her every move at the moment. Besides, she'll only be gone a matter of minutes so will probably be back before he gets home from LSE. Taking only her phone and her keys, she walks the fifty yards to number 17 and rings the doorbell.

The door swings open, but the sardonic grin of welcome is not Irina's.

'Well, well, well, if it isn't our amateur detective.'

It's Liam Devenish.

FORTY-ONE

AUGUST

'Look, darlin', it's our neighbour,' Liam drawls in his South London twang.

He stands back and ushers Jane into the grand hallway with a mock-obsequious bow. He's dressed in branded jogging bottoms and hoodie like the ones he was wearing when he and Keren first arrived in Sycamore Gardens. Jane's initial assumption is that she has interrupted one of their lovers' trysts, because clearly Michael can't be at home. But as soon as she goes into the kitchen and sees Irina's face, she knows this is something very different. Irina's usually golden, glowing complexion is pale and waxy. She looks terrified.

'Where's Michael?' Jane demands.

'He took the children to Serbia to see his family,' Irina's voice comes out as a croak. As if anticipating the next question, she adds, 'He took the nanny.'

'And Bernila?'

Irina shakes her head, and Jane sees tears starting in her eyes. 'She has the day off.'

Jane has already started backing towards the kitchen door. 'Don't worry, Irina, it's going to be okay. I'm going to call the police, okay?' She fumbles in her pocket for her phone, but before her fingers have gripped it properly, Liam has reached past her and pulled it from her jeans.

'Oh no you don't. I'll have that,' he says smoothly. 'Another one for my collection.' He holds up another phone and waggles it in Jane's face. It's the latest smartphone in a crystal-studded case, and she recognises it immediately as Irina's. So it was him who sent the reply to her text, asking her to come over. Ordering her to come, in fact. And she walked straight into his trap.

Her lips are numb and her tongue is sticking to the roof of her mouth. For some reason, her gaze lands on a jeroboam of champagne on the countertop – probably a gift from one of Michael's clients – and she focuses on that, taking a few slow, deep breaths to slow the thudding of her heart.

Irina is shaking her head, urging her to stay silent, but Jane ignores her.

'What's going on?' She faces Liam now. 'Are you going to tell me?'

'Me and Rina have some things to sort out. That's what's going on.'

'No,' Irina says, her voice pleading. 'No. There is nothing to sort out. I told you: it's over between us.'

'It's over when I say it is!' Liam snarls, making Irina shrink back. He turns to Jane. 'And it seems you just won't take the hint; still sticking your fucking nose in. So I'm going to have to deal with you, once and for all, aren't I?'

He's pulled something out of his pocket, and Jane sees with a cold stab of horror that it's a gun. She knows virtually nothing about firearms, but this one looks real. Behind her, Irina makes a little whimpering sound.

'Right, I'm going to tell you what's about to happen. We're going to go outside – you and me – and we're going to get into my truck, nice and casual, like there's nothing wrong. You make a sound, try to attract anyone's attention, remember I've got this' – he waves the pistol carelessly – 'pointed at you.'

Would he really fire it, here in the bourgeois, self-satisfied enclave of Sycamore Gardens, with the neighbours all at home and tucked up in their beds? It all seems so bizarre. She locks eyes with Irina as Liam marches her out of the kitchen and towards the front door.

'Irina!' she gasps, but before she can complete the sentence, the muzzle of the gun is jabbed into her side.

'And you – you stay put and don't move. I haven't finished with you yet,' he shouts over his shoulder at his former lover. 'No funny business, like calling the cops, or your mate here' – he prods Jane again – 'will be the one who pays for it.'

He hesitates then. Keeping the gun trained on Jane with one hand, he starts rummaging through drawers and cupboards with the other, swearing as he tries to find something he can use as a restraint. Eventually, he finds some plastic twine that looks like washing line and pushes Irina onto a kitchen chair and ties her hands behind her back.

'Sorry, babe, but I just can't risk leaving you to your own devices,' he tells her, adding with a sardonic smile, 'And I know you like a little bit of bondage.'

Once they're out on the street, Jane looks around wildly, for someone coming back from a party or taking a dog for a late walk, but there's no one. It's completely dark now, and with the end of summer approaching there's a faint, musty chill in the air. Irina probably won't dare call for help, she thinks with rising panic. Even if she does, she probably still believes this man is Richard Hamlin. Nor would she be able to tell the police what vehicle he drives – Irina would never notice a mundane detail like that – or where they're going.

She climbs stiffly into the pickup's passenger seat, her limbs so rigid with terror that she almost feels paralysed.

'Seat belt on, right?' Liam says with a grin. 'Don't want to get stopped by the Old Bill, do we?' He has the gun on his lap, the barrel resting on his left thigh and pointed at Jane.

They drive along the Old Kent Road and out of London heading east, the blur of city lights gradually giving way to pockets of dark cloudy sky.

'Just as well Keren warned me, eh?' Liam's tone is casual, conversational. 'So I knew you were on my case.' He turns and looks at her. 'You know who Keren is, right? My ex-girlfriend.'

Jane manages to nod her head, teeth tightly clenched.

'She's got a good mate who works at the nursery. Chloe, she's called. And when she heard that someone matching your description was there yesterday, asking questions about us, she told Kez. And Kez had the good sense to text me and let me know. We may not always see eye to eye, me and her, but when it comes down to it, she's a good girl. She's got my back.'

Even after the shocking way you treated her? Jane wants to ask, but her mouth is too dry to speak.

'So, I say to myself why not kill two birds with one stone?' He grins at the irony of this metaphor. 'Pay a visit to my current squeeze and sort you out at the same time. And lo and behold, you can't help yourself, can you? You have to try to get to Rina too. Trouble is, I was too quick for you; I already had her phone. And you came running, just like I knew you would.'

Jane can't tell how long they've been driving. She's tipped sideways against the passenger door, her terror so intense that she's unable to keep her body upright. It's an effort just to get air in and out of her lungs. It's warm inside the truck, because Liam has kept the windows closed and the air-conditioning off, but she's freezing cold and shivering violently. She catches glimpses of scenery and road signs, but they might as well be written in a foreign language. Eventually, they flash past a sign that registers: 'Welcome to Gravesend. Twinned with Cambrai, France'.

So they're in North Kent. A few miles from Ebbsfleet, where she followed Keren that time. There must be some connection. Surely Liam isn't about to take her through the Channel Tunnel and on to France? Not if he intends to get back to Irina before anyone else can.

They drive through the town and out to a quiet residential development which consists mostly of bungalows set back from the road. Liam brings the pickup to a stop at the far end of a cul-de-sac and waggles the gun to indicate that Jane should get out of the truck.

He pushes her in front of him, onto a cut-through, which in turn opens out onto a gravelled track. It curves away into an unlit distance, and Jane can hear the lap of water and the call of seabirds.

'Keep walking!' Liam barks and Jane obeys, stumbling across the marshes over the uneven, swampy ground.

Where are all the people? she thinks desperately, then remembers how late it is. Of course there won't be anyone around. They walk through this emptiness for what feels like an eternity, until up ahead there's some sort of low-rise, semi-derelict structure. When they reach the walls, Liam indicates that she should go down the flight of stone steps. There's a rotting wooden door at the bottom of them.

Her knees buckle. 'No!' she gasps. 'No, please, you've got to let me go! You can't do this.'

The barrel of the gun is jammed against her spine. 'Don't worry,' Liam says with a strange little laugh. 'You're not going to be down there long.'

Jane stumbles forward, groping with her fingers against the side of the staircase since she can't see where she's placing her feet. Her destination – whatever it is – remains completely dark until, behind her, Liam switches on his phone's torch. Even now, there's not much to see, some sort of a corridor with square spaces leading off it. The smell is terrible, decay and human waste. Pointing with the gun, Liam indicates that she should sit on the ground. He twists a loop of chain around her wrists, fastening it to a heavy padlock. For a few seconds, he stands over her, the gun pointed directly at her. Jane closes her eyes, unable to think of anything but her children; their faces when they were little. Then she hears him turn and leave without a word. She opens her eyes again, but the light has gone with him.

As her eyes become accustomed to the dark, she can make out a shape a few feet away. Bile surges in her throat. It's a dead body.

But then there's a sound, a croak that's not quite human. Then a word. 'Hello?'

The sound is faint and echoey, and at first Jane thinks she must be delirious with shock. But it comes again, still croaky but a little louder this time.

'Hello?'

'Hello.' Jane's own voice sounds cracked and guttural. 'Who is that?'

'I'm Stephanie. Stephanie Hamlin.'

FORTY-TWO

AUGUST

Jane's stomach lurches with the contradictory pull of horror and relief.

Horror at the realisation that Stephanie has probably been here for months, relief that she's not here in this hellhole alone.

'Who are you?' Stephanie whispers, her voice hoarse from lack of use. 'Why's he brought you here?'

'I'm Jane Headley. I'm here because...' She falters, unsure how to begin to explain. 'I live in Sycamore Gardens. A few doors from the house that you and your husband won.'

Stephanie starts making strange choking noises, which settle into a rhythmic sobbing.

'Do you know where your husband is? Richard, isn't it? Isn't he here too?'

The crying continues for a while, a thin, exhausted sound. 'He shot him – that man shot him. I don't know who he is. One of the two who brought us here.'

Jane flinches. 'He shot him? You mean—'

'Only at the top of his leg, as he was trying to escape. He got away. But that was ages ago. And he hasn't fetched help. When

I heard people coming down the steps just now, I thought... But it was him. And you.'

With a flash of realisation, Jane remembers a recent news story about the body of an unidentified male being found on the Kent marshes. She also realises that she absolutely shouldn't mention this.

'Stephanie, when did he bring you here?' she asks gently. 'It must have been before they moved into the house, and that was back at the end of April.'

'They moved into the house? Who did?'

'The man who just brought me here. Liam Devenish, and his girlfriend.'

'Keren,' Stephanie supplies. 'Keren Stockley. Yes, she's been here too. She's one of the people who brought us food.'

So that's why she was coming to Kent.

'And she used to work at your daughter's nursery?'

At the mention of her daughter, Stephanie weeps again. 'Poppy? You know about my baby? What's happened to her?'

Jane hesitates, which prompts fresh wailing. She's unwilling to lie, but nor does she want to inflame the poor woman's despair. 'As far as I know, Poppy is fine,' she says eventually.

She goes on to explain how she helped look after the baby, and that Keren was caring for her well. She does not mention Poppy disappearing shortly before Keren and Liam abandoned number 12. 'When I last saw her, she was absolutely fine,' she finishes.

Now that her eyes are growing accustomed to the darkness, she can make out her surroundings a little. They're in some sort of storage chamber, with a passageway outside it letting in a pale haze of moonlight. The chains that have been secured around her wrists are secured to the structure of the wall through a large iron loop. From the little she can see, Stephanie is secured in the same way.

Be practical, she urges her spinning mind. *Don't think about what ifs, focus on the here and now.*

'What have you been eating and drinking?' she asks, because the Hamlins couldn't have survived down here without access to food and drink. 'You said Keren brought stuff?'

'They bring food and water. Not the man... the one who just came...' Stephanie's voice is cracked and husky, and she seems disorientated.

'Liam,' Jane supplies.

'It was his brother. Think he must be a brother; he looks just the same. And Keren came a few times.' She gives what passes as a laugh and adds, 'She brought tampons with her.'

'But Liam didn't leave anything this time,' Jane adds with alarm. 'That might mean they're planning to come back soon, or...' She daren't articulate the alternative. That they're just going to be abandoned down here to starve.

'There's only a tiny bit of water left,' Stephanie whispers, 'and a few crackers. That's all.' Then she repeats her earlier question: 'So why did he bring you here?'

'Because I worked out what he's done. What he and Keren have done. And he wanted to shut me up.'

'So they were in the house that we won? They actually moved in?'

'Yes,' Jane says heavily. 'They pretended to be you and Richard. And for a while they got away with it.'

'Keren looks just like me; that must have given them the idea.' Stephanie shifts her position, rattling her chain. 'We've both got white mums, and my dad's from Trinidad. I think hers is West African? It used to be commented on at Stepping Stones. People used to think we were sisters. And I suppose that man' – she seems to have difficulty recalling or repeating Liam's name – 'looks a bit like Richard. Or he would if he was wearing glasses.'

'Tell me what happened,' Jane urges her. 'If we're going to have a hope of getting out of here, we may as well share what we know.'

Stephanie gives a bitter little laugh. 'How the hell are we going to get out of here? We're chained to a solid stone wall, and nobody ever comes to this place. We can scream all we like, but no one will hear us. Believe me, I've tried.'

'Tell me anyway.'

Stephanie groans again, and starts rocking back and forth, shaking her head.

'Take your time,' Jane says gently, adding wryly, 'It's not like we've got anything else to do.'

There's silence for a minute or so, then Stephanie takes in a deep gulp of air. 'We were really happy, you know, when we found out we'd won the house. We'd been hoping to buy somewhere, but we'd never have been able to afford somewhere like that...' The tearfulness starts to return, but she takes a long, deep breath to steady herself. 'We'd just signed all the paperwork and been given the keys to the house, when someone – that man – called at the flat saying that he was from Prodomus, and that we'd won an additional prize. We were hoping it was going to be a new car, because ours was on the way out...' She gives a dry little laugh.

Jane swallows hard. Knowing what she does now, this is painful to hear.

'He drove us away in a nice limo. Poppy was at nursery that day... Looking back, I suppose Keren must have known we would be at home without her. We were driven to this sort of warehouse place on the coast. And by the time we'd twigged that something wasn't right, they – the man and his brother – had tied us up and bundled us into a van and brought us here. They waited until it was dark, then walked us both out here at knifepoint and chained us up. Then they must have gone back to the flat and got the keys for the house, and collected Poppy from nursery. Oh God... and our dog was in the flat!' She sounds anguished all over again. 'Do you know what happened to Buster?'

'It's all right,' Jane assures her, 'They took your dog with them too.'

'And you said you looked after Poppy? Was she all right?'

'She was doing just fine,' Jane tries to sound upbeat. 'Almost walking when I last saw her.'

Stephanie drops her face into her hands and whimpers as though she's in pain.

'Don't worry; you'll see her again very soon, I'm sure of it.' Jane is far from sure of this, but can't think what else to say.

Stephanie raises her head again. 'Do you have children yourself? A partner.'

'Two grown-up children.' At the mention of Evie and Joss, it's Jane's turn to swallow the urge to break down into sobbing. 'And a husband. For now, at least,' she adds quietly.

'Why, where is he? Will he come looking for you?'

Because the pain is still fresh, and because she needs to tell someone, Jane relays the story of Fergus's infidelity, and the part it played in the events of the last few months. 'If I hadn't been unhappy at home, maybe I wouldn't have paid so much attention to what Liam and Keren were doing. And then I wouldn't have wound up here.'

'I'm glad you did,' Stephanie whispers. 'I know that's selfish. Sorry.'

'It's okay...' Jane crawls forward, groping through the darkness until she's close enough to pat Stephanie on the arm. This prompts another bout of eery sobs.

'What I don't understand is why he didn't shoot me,' she gasps eventually. 'He tried to kill Richard, and he could have killed me too. We talked about it when we were first left here...'

Stephanie's voice cracks again, but she gathers herself. 'We speculated endlessly about why they'd left us here rather than just killing us and getting rid of our bodies somehow. Or even just leaving us to starve to death. I know that sounds morbid, but it didn't make any sense to us. Finding this place and then keeping us alive... it made the fraud so much more complicated. Richard said he thought they were just small-time crooks who were out of their depth. They either hadn't thought it through, or they didn't have it in them.'

'He could have shot both of us just now,' Jane agrees. 'He had the gun with him.'

'He'll come back,' Stephanie moans. 'He'll come back and he'll do it then because he has to now, doesn't he?'

'Listen,' Jane urges, 'I've already spoken to the police: they know what he and Keren have done. They'll work everything out now: it's only a matter of time.'

She thinks back to the lacklustre reconnoitre of 12, Sycamore Gardens earlier that day. Surely they won't just leave it there? Will Fergus have realised she's missing yet? It occurs to Jane now that he'll just think she's gone off somewhere in a fit of pique because of his cheating. Irina could raise the alarm. But will she get the chance?

They halve a cracker and share a few sips from the one remaining water bottle, and Stephanie explains the primitive bucket toilet system, and how she'll have to inch down her clothing bit by bit with her chained hands, before squatting. Then, eventually, after crawling into the sleeping bag that used to be Richard's, Jane falls into a light, uneasy sleep.

When she opens her eyes again, there's murky daylight coming into the chamber from the passage outside, revealing the grim reality of their living quarters. Her mouth is tight with thirst, her stomach roiling with hunger. Then, with a jolt, she realises why she's been woken.

There are footsteps on the stone steps, and the sudden flash of a torch. Stephanie sits up, blinking in confusion, and they both stare at the familiar figure. But before either of them can speak, this person has turned and retreated as abruptly as they came and they are alone again.

FORTY-THREE

AUGUST

'It was her!' Stephanie points in the direction of the stone staircase. 'That was Keren!'

Jane buries her face in her hands, trying to suppress the despair that threatens to overwhelm her.

'Why would she leave like that?' Stephanie gasps. 'I don't understand.'

Jane reaches for the water bottle and takes a gulp before handing it to Stephanie. There are only a couple of inches left, and it's all they have. 'She's probably gone to fetch food and water for us,' she offers, although she doesn't really believe it.

They take it in turns to use the bucket, then sit hunched on their respective sleeping bags, no longer having the will or the energy to talk. It's impossible to know how much time passes.

'Wait,' Stephanie breaks the silence eventually. She raises an arm, and now that there's a little more light in the chamber, Jane sees for the first time how painfully thin she is, her skin ashy and mottled and her hair filthy, matted into dreadlocks. She's wearing a trench coat over a thin top and jeans that must have once been white. 'Did you hear that?'

'No... what?'

Stephanie holds a finger to her lips to shush her. And there it is; growing gradually louder. The sound of footsteps. Jane braces herself to face Liam Devenish down the muzzle of a gun, but it's Keren. She has come back.

'I'm sorry,' she whispers. 'I'm so sorry.' The words tumble out of her. 'I was going to run away and leave you and then I realised that Liam's not going to give me any of the money. He probably never was. He just used me.'

There are tears running down her cheeks and Jane is struck by how very young she is. Much younger than Stephanie, despite the resemblance. She hesitates, turns back towards the entrance.

'For God's sake!' In her desperation, Jane manages to raise her voice to a shout. 'The police already know what you and Liam have done. They know all of it. But if you help us now, it's going to look much, much better for you. I mean, that's obvious, surely?'

'What shall I do?' Keren clutches at her neck. 'I don't know what I'm supposed to do.'

'The padlock key,' Stephanie instructs her. Her voice has gained a new energy too. 'You need to find it. I saw him put it high up on that ledge somewhere.'

Keren starts to search, her fingers groping the stone walls.

'I think it's over there, somewhere near where he keeps the torch.'

But Keren is a lot shorter than Liam, and she can't quite reach. She shrugs helplessly, at the equally helpless Jane and Stephanie, their chains too short to allow them near.

'Use that!' Jane points at an empty litre water bottle on the ground.

With the cap end used as a primitive tool, Keren scrapes the bottle along the stone shelf, and a second later there's a bright flash of metal as the key drops to the ground.

Stephanie whimpers with relief as the chains are released, but then stands stock-still: too dazed or too weak to move.

'Come on!' Jane urges her, pulling her by the sleeve of her coat. 'Let's move!' She snaps her fingers to break Stephanie out of her trance, then pulls her by the wrist. Through the wooden door, up the stone steps, and into the light.

Jane bends double, filling her lungs with air. Stephanie gasps and screws up her eyes at the first daylight she's seen in nearly four months.

'Poppy!' she gasps, as though being in the fresh air has reignited her concern for her daughter. 'Where's Poppy?'

'She's fine!' Keren shouts, already marching along the shore path ahead of them, without waiting for them to follow. 'My sister's looking after her. She's absolutely fine, you don't need to worry about her.'

Jane is acutely aware of the need for them to hurry, but Stephanie is so weak, she can barely walk at all, let alone walk fast. 'Wait!' Jane calls to Keren. 'You need to wait; she needs help.' She's also aware that of the three of them Keren is the only one with a phone. 'You need to call 999, Keren! Get an ambulance!'

Ahead of them, Keren stops in her tracks and points. There are two figures coming towards them along the track. They're moving at a semi-jog, gaining ground rapidly.

'Oh no, it's them,' Stephanie whispers. 'They've come back.'

As Liam and his brother approach, Keren looks round her wildly, frozen to the spot.

Jane's first instinct is to turn and run back to the fort, to try to hide. But that would be pointless. They'll just be trapped, like cornered prey. Because it's obvious as Liam and his brother get nearer that they each have a gun this time. They're both wearing dark jeans and black hoodies, and Jane is struck forcibly by how alike they are. *They're twins*, she thinks, wondering why this never occurred to her before.

'What's *she* fucking doing here? Take out one each, you said! Now what do we do?' It's the brother who speaks, the one introduced to her as Elliott Hamlin. He points angrily at Keren.

'Lance!' Keren screams at him. 'Don't be an idiot! The police know what you've done.'

Liam points his gun at her, and jerks his head at Lance, who trains his own weapon on Jane. Stephanie, too weak to escape anyway, sinks to the ground, moaning.

Then, out of nowhere, there's a faint pulse of beating air, growing gradually louder until it becomes a rhythmic hum, and a police helicopter appears overhead. Further down the coastal track, there's a blur of dark blue. A helmeted SWAT team is moving in formation towards them, semi-automatic rifles raised.

'Drop your weapons!' a disembodied voice shouts from above them, but the brothers ignore the instruction, muttering inaudibly to each other.

'For Christ's sake, Liam! Don't you get it? It's over!'

With a roar of rage, Keren launches herself at her former boyfriend. There's a sharp crack, not quite obscured by the noise of the helicopter blades, and Keren's body is propelled backwards as she falls to the ground. There's a bright red dot on her white shirt that blooms into the shape of a large red flower.

Jane lurches forward, her instinct to try and help, but hands are on her, pulling her back, the hands of the armed police officers who are suddenly on them in a swarm.

'It's over,' the disembodied voice is saying as she closes her eyes and allows herself to be half dragged, half carried away. 'It's all over.'

EPILOGUE

FEBRUARY

In her cell in HMP Bronzefield, Keren Stockley is writing a letter.

Not to Liam: she never wants to speak to him or hear from him again. Or any other man for that matter. She'll never get burned like that again, and intends to stay clear of the opposite sex when she's finally let free from this place. She thinks back to the look on Liam's face when he was arrested; that look of pure rage. He even turned his head and spat in her direction as he was led away. As if it was all her fault. But it wasn't her fault. Her only fault was to believe him, to let herself get swept away in his mad plan.

Even so, she's going to write to Jane Headley. Tell her that she's sorry for dragging her into all this by asking her to take care of Poppy. To try to explain that she's not really a bad person, but that without a stable family life it was only too easy for Liam Devenish to lead her astray. And a similar letter to Siobhan; to tell her sister she's sorry to have dragged her into the mess by dumping Poppy on her.

She's going to try to write to Stephanie Hamlin too, but that letter will be harder. What can she say to the woman? That

Keren's resentment and envy of her were a big part of what led to her agreeing to be Liam's accomplice, to a chain of events that resulted in her husband's murder? No, she can't say that. But she must find some way to apologise for her own part in Richard Hamlin's death, and to assure her that she did her best to take care of Poppy.

About thirty miles away, in Belmarsh Prison, Liam Devenish has no intention of writing any letters to atone for what he's done. He came close to getting away with his grand plan. In his head, the only reason he didn't was because others fucked up. Keren. Lance. Irina. That bitch Jane. At least Lance and Keren are paying the price too, even if Keren did get off with a stupidly light sentence. For now, Lance is in HMP Wandsworth, but Liam already has plans to request that one of them is transferred, so they're in the same place. Okay, so Lance messed up but he's still his twin. They've always been together, and it feels like a double punishment being separated from him.

Jane Headley has a black mark against her name, but there's not a lot he can do about that now. Unless he can get somehow organise something on the outside. Plenty of time to figure out what, and how.

And Irina... well, Irina is in a different category. He would contact her if he could, but he has no idea where she is. He's pretty certain she'll no longer be in Sycamore Gardens. He'll find out where she's gone eventually, though, once he gets internet privileges. He'll be able to watch her from a distance, monitor her life digitally. And when he's finally out of prison? Well, even if things go badly at trial and he ends up doing the maximum time, he'll still only be forty-something. Not old. In his prime, in fact, given he can keep up his gym work on the inside. In his prime and raring to go and find Irina Semenova.

And he will; he's promised that to himself. He will find her.

. . .

Jane Headley is in the sitting room of number 5, Sycamore Gardens, taking books from the fitted shelves that line the walls and stacking them into cardboard packing boxes. Oreo the cat is crouched under a Nordic leather lounge chair looking unsettled and miserable.

Before sealing the box with tape, Jane pauses and looks past the delicate outline of the black walnut trees in the communal garden to the houses opposite. The new year has brought three more estate agents' boards to Sycamore Gardens. The stately number 17 currently has a For Sale sign outside. Irina Semenova and Michael Kovacic are selling up and moving to New York, where Michael is heading up a new investment capital venture.

The last time Jane saw Irina was just before Christmas, emerging from her house wrapped in a huge white fake fur coat. In answer to Jane's enquiry about how she was, she replied simply, 'Pregnant.'

'Congratulations!' Jane had enthused.

'We went to clinic in Italy. Gender selection of embryo is legal there,' Irina said baldly. 'We only wanted to have boy.'

'A son... lovely,' Jane said, waiting for some sort of acknowledgement of what happened on that day in August. It did not come. Irina has been away so much since it happened that that was the first time they'd spoken to each other. Still there was no mention of Liam, or any reference to the upcoming trial, but there was a haunted look behind Irina's pale grey eyes. She hurried off without prolonging the encounter, and Jane has not seen her in Sycamore Gardens since.

Yet it was Irina who – despite the threats from Liam – raised the alarm that led the police to Eastmeade Fort. She did not cower in number 17 to wait for Liam's return, but fought herself free from the amateurish restraint on her wrists and went first to find Trish and then Fergus. Irina, the self-absorbed, disdainful Siberian beauty who, it seemed, rarely thought past the next cosmetic appointment, had risked her own safety to go and find help. Jane knows she will almost certainly never set eyes on Irina again, but nor will she ever forget the surprising courage she showed. And that, because of that courage, she probably owes Irina her life.

There's also a For Sale sign outside number 12 once again. The previous sale was voided and the funds traced and returned to the unfortunate Canadian couple who unwittingly found themselves at the centre of a massive fraud. The news headlines and criminal case were enough to make them seek a purchase north of the river. And this time, the proceeds of the sale, when it happens, will go directly to Stephanie Hamlin. The blow of her husband's death was only slightly mitigated by being reunited with her daughter; the baby being returned safe and healthy after being cared for by Keren's sister, Siobhan. The two of them and Buster the dog have moved back to Yorkshire to start a new life. Jane can't help wondering who will live at the house next, and whether they will be anything like the young couple who moved in the previous spring and – for a while at least – fooled them all.

Liam and Lance Devenish are about to go on trial at Southwark Crown Court, indicted with multiple counts that include murder, child abduction, kidnapping, false imprisonment, theft and fraud. Keren Stockley's gunshot wound proved to be superficial, and once she recovered, she pleaded guilty to some of the lesser charges. Her barrister successfully argued a defence of coercion, and with her attempt to rescue Stephanie and Jane also taken into account, she was given eight months, and will soon be out on licence. The Devenish twins are expected to spend at least twenty years behind bars if found guilty. Jane and Fergus, who will be giving evidence, are confident that they will.

The third board is a 'SOLD' sign, and is outside their own house. The Headleys will also be starting a new life; in the West Country. Fergus has accepted a head of department position at the University of Bath, and Jane has applied to take a full law degree. Eventually, if she goes on to take a legal practice course too, she will be not just a paralegal but a fully-fledged lawyer. There will be no more accusations of her being unambitious, or wasting her potential when she reaches her goal. Her recent, shocking brush with the criminal justice system has only inspired her further.

In a few weeks, the graceful lime and chestnut trees will be coming into leaf and the communal lawn will be bright with daffodils. Someone – probably Trish – will be thinking about planning a summer party there for the residents. There will be new neighbours; a sense of renewal. And someone else to gossip about.

As she turns back to putting the contents of the room into cardboard boxes, Jane wonders if the spring will also mark a new start for her marriage. Fergus says that nearly losing her has brought him to his senses and that he will never stray again. Does Jane believe him? The truth is that she's not sure. But she's willing to try and find out, and she's ready to leave Sycamore Gardens behind her.

It's time to go.

A LETTER FROM ALISON

I really hope you've enjoyed reading *The New Couple*. If you'd like to keep up to date with my new releases, please sign up by clicking the following link. Your email address will never be shared and you can unsubscribe at any time.

www.bookouture.com/alison-james

When a house near where I live in South West London was won in a house lottery by a young couple with a child, I was instantly intrigued by the potential for drama in that situation, with the neighbours providing a ready-made cast of characters.

I would be so grateful if you could write a review of *The New Couple*. I'd love to hear what you think, and it makes such a difference helping new readers to discover one of my books for the first time.

I love hearing from my readers – you can get in touch on my Facebook page, Twitter or Goodreads.

Thanks,

Alison James

facebook.com/Alison-James-books
twitter.com/AlisonJbooks

ACKNOWLEDGEMENTS

With huge thanks to all my team at Bookouture, especially Natasha. I couldn't do it without you.

FIVE GO TO SMUGGLER'S TOP

FIVE GO TO SMUGGLER'S TOP

ENID BLYTON

Illustrated by
Eileen A. Soper

Hodder
Children's
Books

a division of Hodder Headline Limited

Text copyright © Enid Blyton Ltd
Illustrations copyright © Hodder & Stoughton Ltd

Enid Blyton's signature is a Registered Trade Mark of Enid Blyton Ltd.

First published in Great Britain in 1945
by Hodder and Stoughton

This edition 1997

22

A Catalogue record for this book is available from the
British Library.

ISBN-10: 0-340-68109-8
ISBN-13: 9780340681091

Typeset by Hewer Text Ltd, Edinburgh
Printed and bound in Great Britain
by Clays Ltd, St Ives plc

The paper and board used in this paperback by Hodder
Children's Books are natural recyclable products made from
wood grown in sustainable forests. The manufacturing processes
conform to the environmental regulations of the country of origin.

Hodder Children's Books
a division of Hodder Headline Limited
338 Euston Road
London NW1 3BH